To Bruce

Gold Fever

Don G. Porter

8-24 2013

D1662395

Treble Heart Books Publishing

Gold Fever
Copyright © 2011 by Don Porter
All rights reserved.

Cover Art and Layout
Copyright © 2011 by Lee Emory
All rights reserved

Published by Treble Heart Books
http://www.trebleheartbooks.com

ISBN: 978-1-936127-53-5
1-936127-53-9
LCCN: 2011929589

Bible References used by permission from
the King James Version,

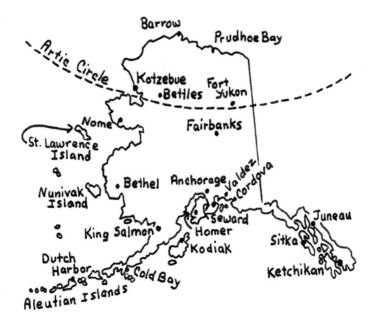

Alaska

Endicott Mountains · Brooks Range

John R. · Wild R. · North Fork · Coldfoot

Malamute Fork · Middle Fork

Inset → · Bettles · South Fork

Arctic — — — Circle

Koyukuk R. · Allakaket · Tanana Trail

Hughes

Malamute Fork · John R.

K.J.'s Mine → · ← rock slide · Wild River · North Fork

new river route →

Waterloo Lake · John R. · Koyukuk R. · Bettles Village

Bettles Field

Introduction

Get ready for a wild ride when you crack open Gold Fever. Don Porter, master storyteller of the arctic northwest, will keep you glued to the pages of his latest novel of life in Alaska in the exciting 70s. You'll find yourself on a revved-up snow machine blasting into a journey filled with mystery and adventure, riding along with Ben Stewart as he tests his mettle against the deadly arctic wilderness in search for gold.

I've known Don Porter as a mentor, instructor, and friend. He's much like the heroes of his books, a first-class pilot and a true gentleman, one who will pull you right into the middle of the action with his skill in the written word and his knowledge of the Alaska bush country.

As a fan of Don's other Alaskan novels, I found Gold Fever to be his best to date. It's filled with breath-holding excitement, eccentric characters, and the laugh-out-loud humor he's known for, as well as the authenticity of someone who has actually lived the life he writes about. I couldn't put it down, and I suspect, neither will you.

Joanne Taylor Moore
Author
Blood Mountain series

Acknowledgements

Authors need help and most books list the names of helpers, but my cadre deserves a lot more and meeting these remarkable people will surely be of interest to readers.

All of the folks we'll list scour the documents for typos, spelling errors and such, but they also suggest and add.

Let's start with Joann Condit. She grew up in cowboy and Indian country but has covered the globe as a missionary, held various university posts, and earns pin money editing doctoral theses. A couple of examples from Jo will illustrate editor additions.

In *Humpy Cove* Renaldo reads the label on a garment: "Couture by Celeste." That's from Jo, I'd never heard of couture. In *The Dealership*, Maggie stamps her foot and complains, "It's not fair. Mother and three sisters could do fine in a contest with Jersey cows and I get the figure of Peter Pan." Pure Jo Condit. And many more.

Ivan Pierce also escaped from the Idaho farm for a career in the military, in law enforcement, and a stint as a long haul truck driver. His own books are set in Vietnam and Alaska and he generously shares experiences. In *Yukon Murders* an entire chapter takes place in Vietnam and the details and jargon are from Ivan. In *Jailbird's Daughter* they hitchhike in an eighteen wheeler, again details from Ivan. He has gone over this book with a computer program that produced fifty suggestions for improvement.

While most of us were growing up in the wild and wooly west, Gale Gill was a debutante, straw hats and white gloves in the big cities of the east. She writes a great book herself and many a chapbook and short story, and she brings experience and a point of view that we westerners can't even imagine.

If you read the dedication of this book then you know who Bill Marsik is. He's a literary type, but he knows Alaska, bush flying, and gold mining. His own book is Sci Fi but he wrote the introductions to *Humpy Cove* and *Murder Pro Bono.*

Joanne Taylor Moore has been writing since grade school. She's written a wonderful series set on Blood Mountain which is now in process of publication by Poisoned Pen Press. She took time off from her own writing to go over this book line by line and taught me a lot, especially about point of view and character descriptions.

C.J. Seidlitz, (Carol Jane, but her family has two) has been over every one of my books, editing, punctuating, suggesting. She's the youngster of our group, still has two beautiful and brilliant fledglings in the nest. She's invaluable because her generation is comfortable with computers in a way we oldsters will never manage. She's usually in the mode of trying to teach old dogs new tricks. She edits out of love for words, and I think pity for us has-beens.

Dedication

This book is dedicated to William, (Bill) Marsik because I owe the character Stew to him. Bill is a free spirit, bargaining with life for all it has to offer. His search for adventure has led him from Mexico to Alaska and many occupations.

Bill is an author and newspaper reporter, but equally at home with construction trades and truck driving. It was his willingness to drop them all and venture into the Alaska mountains to prospect for gold that fomented our partnership many years ago.

The impending birth of his first daughter dragged him away from a placer mining operation in the middle of the Kilbuck Mountains in western Alaska and back to Great Falls, Montana. He did the fatherhood chapter in his life, raising two daughters, but that was a twenty-year intermission in his zest for whatever life has to offer.

In this book you'll read reference to two men leaving a crippled helicopter in the Akhlun Mountains and surviving the Arolik River torrents in a canvas fold boat to Quinhagak Village on the coast. Bill was the other guy, and to the extent those days are not reported accurately it's because I've tamed them down to keep them believable.

When he's not working on his own science fiction books he's running riverboat tours of the Missouri Breaks and the adventures continue at The Missouri Breaks River Company. Check him out at: www.missouribreaksriverco.com.

Chapter 1

Let me live in a house by the side of the road
where the race of men go by.
—Sam Walter Foss

Spring of 1970 was struggling to assert itself. I leaned the creaky wooden chair back on its hind legs and rested my head against the rough bark of the spruce logs. Theoretically, I was watching the world go by from the sagging front porch of the tiny one-room cabin, but in actuality, I was nursing a glass of Wild Turkey. Precious little world goes by on the Steese Highway at the end of April. The Alaska Highway Department keeps the Steese plowed all winter for the fifteen miles from Fox to Fairbanks, and between snowstorms they try for the next twenty miles to Chatanika.

There's another crew at the other end of the highway, struggling to keep it plowed from the banks of the Yukon

at Circle City to Circle Hot Springs at the northern edge
of the mountains. They keep that stretch open most of the
winter, and by now they'll be attacking the mountains from
the north side. With a little luck and no more blizzards, the
crews will meet at Eagle Summit by the middle of May, and
the Steese Highway might be open from end to end, all one
hundred sixty-two miles of it, from Fairbanks to Circle City
on the Yukon River.

Another highway, the Elliot, branches off to the west
toward Livengood and that one is open most of the time. The
last storm put the kibosh on Chatanika. The snowplows are
using my front yard for a turnaround, so no one has passed
and the only people who use the highway are traveling
between Fairbanks and the sad remains of the gold dredge
at Fox. By June, people will be driving up to Eagle Summit
to gawk at the midnight sun, or going over the mountains
for a dip and a party at the Circle Hot Springs Lodge. I have
no intention of being on my porch to see that because in
May construction outfits from Seattle will be arriving and
cranking up. I'll go to work in Fairbanks as a carpenter or a
painter, and hit the bars every Saturday night with a thousand
dollars in my pocket instead of a hundred and eighty.

I'd been attending the University of Alaska with an
academic career in mind until one picnic with friends when
I worked a gold pan full of gravel and found a flake of gold
in the bottom. That ruined everything. When I'm working
construction in the spring, I'll be earning two or three times a
college professor's salary, but when a few bucks stack up in
the bank I can't help seeing them as a grubstake. Before fall
sets in, I've invariably quit my job and headed for a likely
looking creek to pan buckets of gold.

Just as invariably, I won't find the gold, end up broke

and scrambling for moose meat, bourbon, and beans for the winter. The gold isn't all of it, of course. What happens to a man by himself on a creek can only be understood by reading The Spell of the Yukon by Robert Service, but condensed to two sentences, it's "The freshness, the freedom, the farness. Oh, God how I'm stuck on it all."

So, I'll undoubtedly repeat the cycle. When construction starts I'll be there, hat and union card in hand. By that time, my little cabin will be on a busy tourist route, cars and even buses rushing by. People will probably be pointing at my cabin and saying, "How quaint," but for now, the one pedestrian I could see, walking up the middle of the road from the direction of Fairbanks, was so unusual that I wasn't sure my eyes weren't playing tricks on me.

At first, he was just a black dot on the white road. Birch trees on the low hills along the highway had shed their winter load of snow, so the shadows they cast in the late afternoon sun were like lace. The solid black speck in the middle of the road stood out, and seemed to be moving.

It could have been a moose, but it wasn't fast enough. When a moose is ambling along, he takes six-foot strides, and moose usually cross the road, not walk down the middle of it. The spot was still half a mile away, so I went into the cabin and poured another glass of Wild Turkey. I noticed the bottle, my last, was only half full, but if I had counted right, it was Thursday evening and I'd get a new bottle, or two, on Sunday. If the Wild Turkey didn't hold me until Saturday night, there was the emergency bottle of Old Granddad on the shelf, just in case. I didn't have any ice, but it was cold enough outside that I really didn't need any. I sat down and went back to watching the black spot get bigger.

My winter job isn't much by most standards, but in winter, in Fairbanks, anything that pays for beans and Wild Turkey is a good job. This particular job was jack-of-all-trades, converting the old Goldstream dredge to a historical attraction for tourists. It was better than my old winter job back in the days when the dredge was operating. That job was driving steam points for the Fairbanks Exploration Company, or FE as they're affectionately known in these parts. For many years, FE ran the gold dredge all summer, but the process of thawing the permafrost went on year around.

In those days a twenty-man crew drove steam points into the ground with sledgehammers. We drove the points in a four-foot grid, six feet into the permafrost, the steam from the hoses thawing the way as they went down. In midwinter, it might be forty-five degrees below zero, but that only freezes a few inches on the surface. The permafrost we were thawing had been frozen for so long that there are mammoth tusks and teeth in it and fossils of giant tropical ferns. Once the ground had been thawed by the steam, the dredge could work it in the summer.

A workweek, then and now, consists of six ten-hour days, and the FE Company has a very simple, very effective incentive program. Every morning they hire one new man from the endless queue looking for work. At the end of the day, they fire one man, the one who has driven the fewest points in the old days, now the one they deem least productive. They pay three dollars per hour, but in cash, no nonsense about withholding taxes, or even writing down names. Every Saturday night I hitch into town with $180 in my pocket, and if some bar girl doesn't get it all, I come back Sunday night with a week's supply of beans and Wild Turkey. I wasn't living entirely on beans; I still had a quarter of moose hanging, but that goes without saying, and we don't talk about it because there was no connection between my shooting that moose and any hunting season.

The spot on the road was definitely a man, taller than most, a little ragged around the edges, but striding along like a marathoner, intent on covering ground, and with a purpose. His hair was long and wild, merging with a matching beard, and his mustache was just part of the mat, growing the way Mother Nature had planted it so it covered his mouth. Most of the hair was dark brown, but there was a streak of gray two inches wide on his right side, just above his ear. He had a bedroll slung over his back with a piece of clothesline rope that cut into his old mackinaw, and that was all of the gear I could see.

I stood up, waved my glass, and hailed him. "Howdy. Care to sit for a spell and sample a glass of God's bounty?" He turned and tromped across the snow ridges the plows had left. I got the impression of a mechanical man, a robot like a comic book character. He walked straight to the edge of my steps and did a military halt. I couldn't read his expression through the hair, but I got the uncanny feeling that he wasn't wearing any expression, except for his eyes. They were wild enough to match the hair, and the emotion I was reading in them was the one you see on a fox or a badger that's caught in a trap. The animal knows it's all over, understands very well what's going to happen next, but is prepared to fight to the last breath.

Those eyes made me wonder if it had been a mistake to hail him, but I noticed that part of the fierceness came from the way his eyes didn't quite match. His left eye was staring at me, and I decided the expression in that one was neutral.

His right eye was looking over my shoulder, and that was the wild one.

I made a sweeping bow and welcome gesture, like a headwaiter with a twenty-dollar tip, and pointed him toward my chair. I went inside, fetched another chair and another glass of amber ambrosia. When I came back, he was sitting in my chair. I handed over the glass, he took it, and thanked me with a dip of his head. He found his mouth through the thicket, tilted the glass, and slugged down half of the bourbon.

Too late, I realized he had been thirsty, and bourbon is the dangerous way to slake a thirst. I should have offered him a glass of water first, but prescience has never been my long suit. He gasped a couple of times, then tilted the glass again and drained another fourth of it before he turned to look at me with his left eye. This time the expression was skeptical; he was trying to figure out my angle, wondering what I wanted from him.

"Hi," I said. "Name's Ben Stewart, but most folks call me Stew. I work over there in the ice-to-gold factory." The top of the dredge, boom and buckets, was visible over the scrub alder trees. The mechanical monster was hibernating in winter mode, but still looked ready to chew up the earth the moment the dredge pond thawed. Behind it we could see the tailing pile, a ribbon of rock that lay in rows and wound away into the valley.

When the dredge was working, it floated in its pond, swung back and forth by electric motors and cables. The buckets on the boom went around like steps on an escalator, biting into the earth ahead, one yard of dirt per bucket, and tilting down to cut sixty feet deep. The dirt disappeared into the maw, and a stream of rocks that had been washed clean spewed out the back to make the tailing pile. What didn't come out was the gold. That was routed into a maze of processing, and when it did emerge, it was in white bags surrounded by armed guards.

Occasionally, tourists come to work the tailing piles. They pick up mammoth ivory, sometimes chunks four feet long and eight inches in diameter, and teeth the size of footballs. There's always the rumor of nuggets too large to fit through the sluice screens, but I'm afraid those are rural legends.

My guest glanced over at the dredge, and gave another nod. He understood how it worked, so he wasn't a stranger to gold mining. He extended a hand.

"Name's Johnson." I shook the hand, and it was surprisingly soft. I'd been expecting a steel grip and calluses to match his appearance, but the hand was almost feminine. "Gold mining is my game, too." He let it go at that and finished his drink. I took the empty glass and went to pour him another.

I saluted him with my glass. "Which mine are you with?" I asked.

"Got my own digs. That's where I'm headed now."

"Hard rock mining?" I asked. I was trying to think which mine farther up the Steese Highway might be about to open for the season. Gold City is up there, or, I thought, maybe he was squatting on the abandoned Gilmore Creek mine. Alaska is dotted with mines that closed in the 1940s. In those days, the price of gold was fixed at thirty-two dollars per ounce, so those miners who weren't drafted into WWII could make more money in the defense industries. Now, the price of gold is flipping around from four hundred to over six hundred dollars per ounce and the gold is still there, but most mines haven't reopened.

"Nope, placer, just a shovel and a sluice. I want to get there before freeze-up."

That crack got my attention. It was springtime, the next season on the agenda is summer, even in Alaska, and we were optimistically hoping for seven months before freeze-up came around again. I admit that insanity was one of the possibilities I was considering to explain this guy. Maybe he had just escaped from a loony bin somewhere and had his seasons mixed. He was big enough that, in spite of the feminine hands, I was inclined to humor him. There was something strange about this guy. He looked scruffy enough to be a prospector, but something about his diction reminded me of a professor from Harvard.

We sipped in silence for a while. The sun had passed west, and was scooting along the horizon toward the north. It would drop below the hills that separate us from Fairbanks, but not for a couple of hours. In the meantime, the warmth had gone out of it, and the light seemed to have a bluish cast. If you ignored the ruts in my front yard, the scene, low hills south and west, serious mountains still in sunshine to the north, was pristine with a Christmas card ambience. The internal heat from the Wild Turkey was neutralizing the chill in the air.

"Where are your digs located?" I asked. That question was okay in general terms. An exact location would be a secret, guarded to the death, but I wasn't asking for specifics.

"I'm on the John River." He finished his drink, which was also the end of the bottle. The next step was the emergency bottle of Old Granddad and I had a feeling that was going to go, too.

"You mean John Creek, up by Eagle Summit?"

"No, I mean the John River, twenty miles above Bettles."

"Good grief, man, you're walking to Bettles?"

"Yep, that's why I'm in a hurry. I want to cross the Yukon while it's still frozen, about another month, I figure."

I took his empty glass and went inside to open Granddad. I needed to think for a moment. There was no longer any doubt; this guy was as nutty as a Planter's peanut factory. Bettles is two hundred miles northwest, well above the Arctic Circle. The White Mountains, Yukon River, and the Ray Mountains are in the way. There are no villages for a hundred miles after Livengood. If he was really going to walk it, he'd be lucky to get there before freeze-up, and very probably he wasn't going to get there at all. Lewis and Clark made a longer trip, but it wasn't across the Arctic wasteland. Compared to what Johnson was proposing, the Lewis and Clark expedition was a walk in the park.

I unscrewed the cap from Granddad and chugged the glasses full, but glanced at my rifle to be sure it was leaning in the corner because I was starting to think I might need it in a hurry. If the oversized loony tune on my porch got violent, I could reach in the door and grab the rifle without getting out of my chair. I keep it ready to fire, because when a moose appears in the brush you need to be fast, and the occasional moose is a welcome addition to the beans.

"Well," I said, "you may as well bunk here tonight. I just have one cot, but you're welcome to roll out your bag on the floor next to the stove. I've got a couple of moose hides for a mattress. I was just about to boil up some beans and fry me a moose steak, plenty for two."

"No, but thank you kindly. I'm not planning to stop or sleep tonight. I'm on a tight schedule and I need to pass Livengood by day after tomorrow." He pronounced Livengood correctly, so he did know the territory. Livengood is pronounced with a long i. It was named for an early gold miner, Jay Livengood. People who have just read the map invariably pronounce it with a short i.

"Okay, then let me fry you a moose sandwich for the road, won't take a minute." He nodded, so I tromped around behind the cabin and used my hunting knife to whack two steaks off the quarter that was hanging. The truth is I was relieved that he didn't want to stay. Making the offer wasn't optional, that's just what you do in the Arctic, and dealing with a little insanity is part of the Arctic too, but it can be a dangerous part.

When I crossed the porch I grabbed my chair and nodded for him to follow. He brought his chair inside and leaned against the wall by the door. Too late, I realized that he was between me and the rifle. I pumped up the Coleman lamp, lit it, got it to hissing a good healthy glow, and hung it on the wire hook between the table and the stove.

I trimmed the black crust off the outside of one steak and dug the iron frying pan off the warming shelf. The iron skillet weighs six pounds, so if I needed a weapon that would be it. I could see that he wasn't turned off by the crust on the meat. More proof that he was a woods-wise miner. These days, people think meat has to stay frozen, but if it's hanging in fresh air and sunshine, it's reliably healthy for several weeks.

I took the stove lid off, poked up the fire, and put the pan to heating. I was equating the crust on the meat to the old days when Eskimos preserved fish heads by burying them. When salmon were running and plentiful, Eskimos were smoking strips, even making kippers, and getting fat on fresh fish, but if food ran short before spring, and it usually did, they'd dig up the heads. They called that feast "stinky heads" and they were, but healthy. When civilization introduced Saran wrap and they wrapped the heads to keep the dirt out, it also kept out the oxygen and allowed botulism to grow.

The lard was melted. I sprinkled on lemon pepper and garlic salt, the extent of my culinary arts, and set the steak to sizzling.

"How far have you walked?" I asked, wanting to keep the conversation going, but neutral.

"I hitched from Seattle, but seems like I walked half the way. Most people are afraid to pick me up."

"How long have you been on the road?"

"Since December. I couldn't walk too well at first, because I'd just got out of the hospital, but I'm getting the hang of it now."

"You were in the hospital in Seattle?" I was afraid that he was going to name Steilacoom, the Washington State mental hospital, and I slipped on a hot mitt in case he took the question wrong and I needed to grab the skillet.

"Yep, two years, VA hospital. Had a nasty concussion and some broken bones. Maybe you noticed the plate in my head?" He leaned forward and parted his hair. Sure enough, there was a shiny metal plate making up for some missing skull just behind his temple.

The steak was smoking. I speared it with a fork and used the tip of my knife to make several cuts in it before I flipped it over. Moose is a little tough if you shoot it in the early spring, and the cuts make it easier to chew.

"Mining accident?" I asdked.

Johnson let the hair fly back into place, and I noticed that his glass was empty so I filled it again.

"Thank you kindly. Nope, we were bushwhacked, my partner and me. Like I said, we hit this really rich lode on the banks of the John, and we cleaned up about thirty pounds of gold that summer. We were expecting the pilot to pick us up the next day. We were just putting things away for winter when we were jumped. Next thing I knew, it was summer and I was in the VA hospital in Seattle."

I checked my loaf of bread. It was a little stiff, but not moldy. I slathered on lard, salted it down to make the bush version of margarine, and tossed it into the pan beside the steak so it would toast a little and melt the lard. "What happened to your partner?"

"He was DOA, I reckon. The pilot lugged the body back to Bettles and they buried him there... neither of us having next of kin nor heirs apparent."

"Too bad about the gold." I ventured. If Johnson had said thirty ounces, I might have been excited. Thirty pounds of gold is outrageous. I expected he would offer to sell me a map to the mine. He did the next best thing.

"Well, I've been figuring that the bushwhackers never found the gold. See, we had buried it, for safe keeping like. Hey, that steak smells mighty good…so maybe if I get there before freeze-up, I can fly back to Seattle in my own jet. If the stash is gone, I can still sluice out a few ounces to get me over the winter."

I forked the steak onto one slice of bread and covered it with the other. Lettuce and stuff like that are not part of my menu. The sandwich was too hot to handle, so I wrapped it in paper towels.

Johnson dropped the other shoe. "Either way, I been thinking I could use a partner. You wouldn't be interested, would you?" He grabbed the sandwich, still way too hot, and gnawed off a hunk.

"Oh, gee, I wish I could, but I've got this really good job here, under contract you know, so if I left I'd be breaking my word, and I couldn't do that."

"Yep," he said, "when the chips are down, a man's integrity is all he really has. Well, I best be on the road, and much obliged for the vittles."

"What will you eat on the road?" I asked. "You know, there are no stores for hundreds of miles the way you're heading."

"Don't need stores, I don't have money anyhow. I've got this .22 revolver and two boxes of shells, so I eat a rabbit or a squirrel almost every day." He pulled a High Standard target pistol out of his jacket pocket.

"You shouldn't be walking around without some money," I said. I dug in my pocket. "Here's ten dollars. That's every cent I've got until payday, but I'd be obliged if you would take it as a gesture of northern hospitality."

"Nope," he said, putting the pistol back in his pocket. "Can't take your money, although I know you mean it well and I appreciate it. Food and booze are one thing, that's hospitality, but money is a handout, and a man ought to earn his own way in this world. I'll be going now." There it was again, he just didn't fit the mold I'd imagined for him. He took another bite of the sandwich while he strode out the door.

Chapter 2

There is a sucker born every minute.
Attributed to Phineas Taylor Barnum

S hakespeare had it right: "Come what come may, time and the hour run through the roughest day." Also the roughest week. Saturday night did come. My bottle of Old Granddad was drier than a James Bond martini, and I had skipped the beans Friday night and Saturday morning for social reasons. I heated a pan of water, washed and shaved. The Ben Stewart in the mirror looked pretty good. Thirty-four years old, all of his hair left and none gray. Actually a handsome Scot, in my opinion. I put on my going-to-town shirt and jeans, thirty-two inch waist, probably thanks to slinging hammers and shovels all day. Since I wear them only on weekends, they stay clean for a month, and they were only on their second week.

I had to hustle to be out on the road before the white collars headed to Fairbanks. The caste system in India has nothing on a gold mine. The guys in the office are rajahs, the guys in the mud are untouchables. Never shall an untouchable set foot in the cab of a pickup, but twenty of us packed into the beds of three pickups. We blasted over the hills just as the lights were coming on in Fairbanks.

The first outpost of civilization is the Rendezvous Club. The pickup slowed to a walk and several of us clambered out. There's a speaker outside. Noise is not a problem because the next neighbor is half a mile away. We could hear "Satch" Bianchi blowing his tenor saxophone and Brenda singing. We couldn't get inside fast enough.

Inside the club there's only enough light to drink by, except that the stage is spotlighted. The room is the size of a basketball court with furtive couples occupying fifty dark tables, and the stag line, a mixture of stevedores, outlaws, and bankers, clustered around the stage. I had stopped just inside the door, letting my eyes adjust to the darkness and my natural inclinations adjust to Brenda.

She was wearing a black evening gown, but it was split up the sides to the waist and mostly off the top, meant for accent, not to hide anything. She's half Cherokee Indian and half Italian, the best halves of both. She's five-foot-ten, even without the stiletto heels, with the same dimensions as a Barbie doll. The song she was belting out was from a musical, and I think the original words were, "Whatever Lola wants, Lola gets..." She was singing, "Whatever Brenda wants," and she was convincing.

My nightclub vision was almost good enough to let me walk between tables when a familiar figure jumped up from the first row. He'd been sitting next to the stage, using the edge of the stage for a table. He shouted, "Hey, Stew, over here," loud enough to be heard over the saxophone. He was waving a bottle of champagne, and he must have been really glad to see me, because Joanne had been trying to climb onto his lap, and he very nearly dumped her on the floor.

No problem, as long as he had the bottle, she'd be right back. Joanne is an attractive girl, but she plies her trade with the bulldog tenacity of an IRS agent. Face and figure by Vargas, temperament and biography by Edgar Alan Poe. She has a degree in geology and is a certified mining engineer, but after college she found an easier way to make money. Maybe someday she'll get into mining. In the meantime, do not call her a gold digger because that causes bloody riots.

Alex shoved people aside and grabbed an extra chair for me. The bottle he was waving is known as a "thirty-dollar-bottle" in nightclub parlance. In the grocery store it might cost six bucks, but in the club Joanne had wheedled it out of him, and her cut was fifteen dollars.

I made it to the edge of the stage. Alex pumped my hand and pulled me into the chair, three feet from Brenda's gyrating charms. He shoved his champagne glass over in front of Joanne, took a swig from the bottle and handed it to me. I took a healthy belt, let the bubbles tickle my nose and worked the sour-apple taste around my tongue. Alex took another pull from the bottle, then turned and topped off both of Joanne's glasses. Joanne, of course, was more than happy to share, because the sooner we finished that bottle, the sooner she could pester Alex to buy another and the sooner she could stash another fifteen-dollar cut in her garter.

Speaking of garters, Brenda was doing dips that made

her garters available and guys all along the stage were stuffing bills into those. A couple of favored individuals with larger bills stood up and stuffed them into her bodice. It was altogether a pleasant, friendly scene, but running into Alex Price was the best part of it.

Alex and I are Elooks. That's a Yup'ik Eskimo word, and hard to translate. It means partner, sidekick, maybe inseparable friends, but it's more than that. In the Eskimo world life can be tenuous, and your life may well depend on your partner, so maybe Elook means the guy your life depends on. We earned that title in the Bethel area, which is the heart of the Yup'ik Eskimo nation. Meeting Alex in Fairbanks, which is Athabaskan Indian country, was a fluke, but a very welcome one.

Bethel, where Alex holds sway, is on the Yukon/ Kuskokwim Delta, surrounded by flat, treeless tundra, and four hundred miles south of the Arctic Circle. It's located at the northern most point on the Kuskokwim River deep enough to accommodate the ocean-going barges from Seattle. The name is biblically derived, bestowed by Moravian missionaries, and the population is ninety-eight percent Yup'ik Eskimo.

Bettles, Johnson's fantasy destination, is a hundred miles north of the Arctic Circle at the edge of the Endicott Mountains. The Endicotts are part of the Brooks Range, the last terra firma before the North Pole. Five tributaries boil down out of the mountains to form the Koyukuk River, and Bettles is on the first level spot large enough for an airport. Don't call those natives Eskimo, they prefer to be called Inuit.

We finished that thirty-dollar bottle in a hurry, and

Joanne ran to fetch another. Brenda finished her number, the spotlights dimmed and Satch took over the stage with his tenor sax. Jack Temeyer joined him, rhapsodizing on a piano. We moved to a quieter and darker table, and Brenda joined us. Alex was buying two or three thirty-dollar bottles to my one, but my hundred and eighty bucks was endangered specie.

The hostesses, or "B-girls," at the Rendezvous play fair. That is, they drink their share of the champagne, so the four of us were getting gloriously drunk. Brenda left us to do another number, but she was all over the stage, grabbing onto the fire pole to keep herself upright, and at one exciting juncture she fell flat on her kiester. The crowd loved it and stuffed the green all over her before Satch helped her back to our table and pointedly plunked her down in her chair.

I didn't worry about Satch getting angry. He probably gets a five out of every bottle, and likely half of what gets stuffed into Brenda's garters. Joanne had made it into Alex's lap and had stopped going for bottles; she was doing well to wave for the bartender to bring them over, and Brenda seemed to have discovered my manly charms. In a funny kind of a way, Alex and I being together made the whole thing safe, although by closing time neither of us could have fought our way out of a hostile kindergarten.

Alex and I go back several years together, and have faced many a situation more overtly threatening than a couple of B-girls, although in fact none may have been more dangerous. Alex is a partner in a charter air service based in Bethel, so he usually had a few bucks, and has access to several company aircraft. I had been bitten by the gold bug, even worse in those days, and Alex wasn't hard to sway in that direction.

When we heard a rumor, or just had a hunch, Alex would drop me off with a floatplane, or a helicopter, or whatever was appropriate. I'd pan the creek or hillside that had caught our interest. He'd come back, usually in a week, with supplies, but if I hadn't found gold, we'd move to the next fantasy. That was usually the case. People all around us seemed to find gold, some of them lots of it, but our take was always a film canister with black sand, rubies--worthless, too small and not gem grade--and not enough gold to fill a tooth.

That may not sound dangerous, but it had its moments. On my end there were grizzly bears, flash floods, unfriendly rifle-toting neighbors, and landslides. And, of course, when it was time for Alex to pick me up, he'd be there, even if it was raining so hard that I couldn't see the river, or blowing so hard that gravel was flying.

A few instances stand out, like the time he dropped me on a gravel bar on Kowkow Creek in the middle of the Ahklun Mountains. He had just lifted off in the helicopter, was checking it out in a three-foot-hover, when a crack like a gunshot came from the tail boom. The boom whipped toward me like a scythe, I hit the dirt, and Alex slammed the chopper back onto the gravel bar.

The tail rotor was gone, along with a chunk of the gear case, and we never did find it. Technically, that rotor is called the anti-torque rotor, and it's there because of one of Newton's laws, the one about equal and opposite reactions. When the engine spins the main rotor one way, there's an equal force trying to spin the helicopter the other way. The tail rotor is there to counteract that force.

Fortunately, I'd been planning to explore up the creek and had a canvas and aluminum foldboat with me. We dumped the mining gear, loaded up groceries, and spent the next three days paddling down Kowkow Creek and the Arolik River to Quinhagak on the coast. Sometimes the river was running so fast that all we could do was hang on and try to steer. Dead trees hung over us like the last stage in a limbo contest. We were flashing past snags that could have ripped the boat in two and us along with it. At times like that, you get to know the other guy very well, and yes, your life depends on his doing his part.

When Satch turned on the lights and booted us out the door at four in the morning the taxi was already waiting. It took us to the Polaris building and the four of us held each other up in the elevator on the way to Joanne's apartment. I really don't know what might, or might not have happened in that apartment, and in any case I'm sure none of us remember. I woke up in a bed that had other bodies in it, but I didn't notice which bodies. When I stumbled out of the bathroom, Alex was standing by the outside door with my clothes in his hand. I struggled into the clothes, although the socks he handed me were one green, one blue. I was thinking that I came in with two brown ones, but couldn't think why it should matter.

The world came back into focus in the Model Café where Alex and I were drinking coffee and orange juice, and trying to face scrambled eggs. I've learned from painful experience that at times like that, you have to be careful not to drink too much, even though you're thirsty, and water is a no-no. Drink a couple glasses of water and you'll be drunk again, I guess on the dregs of the champagne. I was telling him the story of Johnson, my traveling guest. At first we were laughing, but the laughter tapered off.

"You know, Stew, some of the richest gold strikes that have ever been made were around Bettles. DC-3 loads of gold came out of Gold Bench on the Middle Fork. Erling Nesland is on Tramway Bar right now, cleaning up half a pound a day. Then there was the Coldfoot Mine, and Crevice Creek; you've heard those legends."

"Alex, you're not suggesting that Johnson's story might be true?"

"Of course not...but what if?" We finished our breakfasts in silence. The toast went down just fine.

Chapter 3

Hope springs eternal within the human breast.
—Alexander Pope

Alex had brought a load of educator types from the Kuskokwim Community College for a conference at the University of Alaska in Fairbanks. They'd be meeting for a few more days, so Sunday was free, and one of Bushmaster's Cessna 185s was parked at the airport.

We made up a survival pack for Johnson: Hershey bars, two cans of beer, little pop-top cans of Vienna sausages and custard pudding, and some dry wool socks. I wrote a note to Johnson, telling him to meet us at the Livengood airport. We rigged a parachute with the large orange napkin we had stolen from the Model Café, just four strings connecting the corners of the napkin to the package. It would drop slowly and would be easy to find in the snow.

By the time we were ready, it was afternoon and Alex appeared sober enough to fly. Of course, I was making that judgment relative to myself. The Cessna 185 is on the big, heavy side for Bush work, but it is considered STOL. That's aviation shorthand for short take off and landing, and it's the three-hundred-horse engine that puts it in that category. The only drawback to that particular airplane was that it was on wheels for landing at plowed airports, and we were headed the wrong direction for those.

The sky was a perfect blue dome, the hills appearing golden brown from the bare trees that covered them, but the carpet of snow always showed through. We followed the Steese and made the turn over my cabin. It did look quaint. We wanted to cover the entire road, just in case Johnson had come to his senses and turned back. Apparently he hadn't.

We expected to overtake him near Livengood, and I was keeping a close watch on the road and the edges that were half hidden by trees, but no Johnson. There were car tracks, four-wheel drive, and snow machine tracks, but no pedestrians.

You have to know where to look to find Livengood because it consists of a few log cabins hidden under forty-foot spruce trees, but there is an airport, by Bush standards. It's a rectangular gash through the trees, fifty feet wide and two thousand feet long, and it had not been plowed. Several snow machines had crossed it, and some of the tracks looked pretty deep. I assumed there was no possibility of landing there on wheels.

We continued flying over the highway. Various tracks, mostly snow machines followed the road for a few miles, but when they tapered off, there were no more tracks. Moose and woodland caribou had crossed the road here and there, leaving tracks a foot or more deep, but we had to concede that no pedestrian had traversed that snow ribbon. Alex banked us around and flew back to circle Livengood.

"We must have missed him under the trees somewhere." I suggested.

"I don't think so, but there is one way to be sure." Alex was flying low and slow, circling the airport.

"Remember, we're on wheels. No chance of landing in that snow pile."

Alex was nodding in agreement. "You are sure Johnson said thirty pounds of gold?"

"Yep, thirty pounds. That's how I knew the whole thing was a lie."

"Has to be a lie," Alex agreed. "See there in the middle of the strip? There's a place where the trees have blocked the wind and the snow doesn't look too deep."

"Yeah, I see it. Good place to try a helicopter landing. Shall we go back and rent one?"

"For three hundred dollars an hour? Maybe Joanne would like to lend us the money." Alex climbed us up to eight hundred feet and pulled the mixture control lean. We were too slow to keep the prop wind milling, so it stopped. He touched the starter a couple of times to line the prop up crosswise and pulled us around toward the airport.

If Alex says he's going to land somewhere, then he is, and it's not up to me to worry about it. He's picked me off of sandbars so short that our wheels left a wake in the water for thirty yards, and parked helicopters where you couldn't fit a sheet of paper between the main rotor and the rocks. I just cinched up my harness until I felt my ribs bend, got a grip on my seat with both hands, and didn't worry.

We came around way too high, and almost above the spot Alex was looking at. He jerked us into a hard left bank and stomped the right rudder to the floor. That maneuver is called a sideslip, the bank trying to turn us left, the rudder trying to turn us right. It's a legitimate way to lose altitude without gaining speed. He had pointed our left wing at the postage stamp he was concentrating on, and we were falling sideways, right down the path the wing was pointing.

I had lunch with Trooper Tom in Bethel one time. Tom had just come back from a trip to the coast with Alex and he was still shaking his head over it. "You know, Stew, Alex could land a plane on this table and not muss the cloth." I hoped Tom was right.

The stall warning had been screaming since Alex killed the engine, but he didn't seem to mind. Except for the stall warning, the silence was deafening, just a hint of wind, and groans from the metal airplane in the unusual attitude.

We fell right on down, below the trees, the wing still pointing at the ground. Obviously the thought of gold had driven Alex crazier than Johnson, and he planned to stick the wing right into the snow. At the last second, he jerked us level and we fell in a pancake stall.

Pancake stalls are usually fatal. They happen when a pilot is trying to stretch a glide, trying to make a runway that is out of reach, and is flying too slow. The plane falls down flat, and if you're more than thirty feet up, the landing gear jams right through the cabin and through whoever is in the cabin. In this case, we dropped six inches, with a whoof of flying snow, and we were stopped.

The windshield was covered with snow, but I could see out the side window, and we were right side up. A WW

II-vintage jeep came plowing through the snow from the trees and stopped beside us. We opened our doors, and the guy climbed out of the jeep. He was the solid specimen you expect to see in the bush, bearded, but neatly trimmed. He was wearing a beaver parka over a snow machine suit, shoepacks, and a beaver hat that matched the color of his beard.

"Boy, lucky thing you were right over the airstrip when your engine quit. Amazing that you didn't nose over."

I was a little hesitant to step down off the tire because the snow was a foot deep and I was wearing sneakers, but Alex had already climbed out and waded around.

"Yeah, lucky," Alex said. "We're looking for a guy named Johnson who was walking up the highway."

"Oh, good. You must be state troopers. Good idea not to wear uniforms, because Johnson is crazier than a fox with his tail on fire. My name's Mack."

"Alex, and Stew. Johnson is here, then?" Alex shook hands with Mack. I waved from my perch on the tire.

"Yeah, he's over in the clinic. Hop in and I'll take you over there. You gonna call a helicopter to lift the airplane out?"

"No, I think we might fly it out. Can we get you to drag it back to the end of the strip?"

"Sure, no problem." Alex waded around to the passenger side of the jeep; I made it to the near side and climbed in back. Mack set the four-cylinder engine to chuckling like a Model A, and all four wheels spun while he turned us around. Mack continued our enlightenment.

"Johnson came walking in here last night, babbling that he was walking to Bettles. Certifiably nuts, clear danger to himself and others."

Mack backed the jeep around behind the airplane. Alex and I climbed out into the snow and held the tail up while Mack lashed the tail wheel to his trailer hitch. The jeep did some more wheel spinning, but we dragged the plane backward to the end of the strip making tire tracks a foot or more deep all the way. We untied the plane, dropped the tail wheel into the snow again and left it sitting under the trees at the village end of the strip.

We drove right between the trees, or maybe in summer it was the road from the village to the airport. Mack skidded onto the one-lane track that the jeep had made through the village. We were under tall spruce, passing log cabins and caches, just the way one pictures bush Alaska. The air smelled equally of spruce and wood smoke. Mack continued his spiel.

"Cissey lured him into her cabin with a bowl of chili, and when he sat down she noticed blood oozing out of his shoes. She called me. I'm the nearest thing to police we have, and I called the health aide. The three of us got his shoes off, him fighting us all the way. The blood was coming from blisters, but his toes was frozen black."

Mack parked the jeep and led the way into a log cabin, no different from the others, except this one had a hand-lettered sign, CLINIC. "We dragged him over to the clinic and Millie is trying to hold him down. She hid his pants, so that's helping some, but he's raving that he's got to get going. Planning to walk to the Yukon before it thaws. Ever hear such nonsense?"

Mack led us up three wooden steps into the clinic. "Just to show you how crazy he is, he claims to have thirty pounds of gold stashed in Bettles, and he offered me a partnership in his mine. He actually thought I might believe that. Seemed to think I could drive to Bettles in the jeep."

It was almost dark inside the clinic. Light bulbs hung from the ceiling, but they were dim and pulsing brighter and dimmer with a regular rhythm. That meant the village generator was overloaded to twice its capacity and was putting out eighty volts instead of the usual hundred and ten. Mack pulled aside a curtain that was covering a doorway. Johnson was sitting up in a bed, covered with a quilt from waist to feet, and his feet were bandaged so they looked like plaster casts.

"Hi, Millie," Mack boomed, "these are a couple of..." He caught himself, but the word troopers hung in the air for a moment before it evaporated... "friends of Mr. Johnson's. They're here to take him...to his mine in Bettles." He gave Alex and me a broad wink. Millie was fifty-ish, at least half Indian, with thick black braids wound around her head. She was wearing a gray sweatshirt over jeans, and the expression of long-suffering competence.

Johnson inspected us with his good eye, and he perked right up. He was smiling, if beards can smile. "Hey, my partner, Stan."

"Stew," I corrected.

"Yeah, Stew, we've got to get going if we plan to make it across the Yukon, and this harridan has hidden my pants." He pointed an accusing finger at Millie. There was the enigma again. How many miners know the word harridan?

"No problem," I said. "We came by airplane. We'll have you in Bettles in a couple of hours." I turned to Mack and gave him back his wink.

Alex conferred with Millie. "Can he walk?"

"He's in better shape now than he was when he walked in here, but don't get those bandages wet or his toes will freeze off." Millie disappeared through the curtain and came back with two plastic bags. She slipped the bags over Johnson's bandages and taped them around his ankles. Then she reached under the bed, pulled out his pants, and tossed them to him. She demurely stepped outside the curtain.

Johnson threw back the quilt and started wriggling into his pants. He wasn't naked. He was wearing at least one layer of long johns, probably two. He was a lot more covered than Brenda had been by her evening gown, but I guess underwear is underwear, and maybe it's the semantics that count. He swung his legs down to the floor and stood. His mouth and eyes shot wide open, and he swayed like he might faint, so there must have been considerable pain, but he caught himself and extended his arms. Alex and I jumped to become crutches and we followed Mack back outside. We let Johnson pretend to be walking, but his full weight was on our shoulders and we lifted him into the front seat of the jeep.

Millie came running out, carrying Johnson's shoes at arm's length with her head turned away so she wasn't smelling them. I grabbed the shoes and caught a whiff. That was a mistake. Mack bumped us back through the trees to the airplane and the three of us hefted Johnson into the back seat. I tossed his shoes into the baggage compartment. Mack motioned me aside with a jerk of his head.

"Maybe you should handcuff him now," Mack suggested. "He's apt to get violent when he realizes you're not heading toward Bettles." I nodded wisely and patted my pocket as though it contained handcuffs. Mack nodded, Alex and I shook his hand and thanked him. He backed the jeep away and we climbed into the plane.

Alex held the brakes and wound up the engine until the tail wheel came up. When he dropped the brakes, we gained speed fast. He kept the wheels in the ruts they had made when we dragged the plane backward. If he'd missed those ruts by six inches, we'd have slewed away into a snowball, but of course he didn't. We came to our original splash down, he racked down flaps and hauled back the yoke. We ballooned into the air. He pointed us down again, skimming the snow, bleeding off flaps, and watching the airspeed indicator climb. When it passed seventy, we soared away, missing the spruce trees at the end of the strip by several inches, and climbed into the wild blue yonder.

We were flying through a bowl with serious, snow-covered mountains all around us, too bright to look at in the sunshine. Ground below was getting higher, spruce trees thinning out. We had angled away from the highway, so there was no sign that the planet was inhabited. As often happens in the bush, our itinerary hadn't been anticipated, so we had no flight plan. At such times, the deep drone of the engine takes on a special significance. If it stopped, the next several days would be an inconvenient camping trip, if we survived them.

Chapter 4

How like a prodigal doth she return, with over-weathered
ribs and ragged sails.
The Merchant of Venice—Shakespeare

Johnson was doing a lot of squirming around and
grimacing. I opened the survival pack that we had meant
to drop and handed him a beer. He guzzled it down,
leaned back, and maybe went to sleep. The 185 augured the
rest of the White Mountains under us in twenty minutes and
the snow-covered ribbon of the Yukon appeared.

From Circle City, past Fort Yukon and Stevens Village,
the Yukon had been meandering through the flats, twenty
miles wide with islands and sloughs. We crossed it at the
head of the funnel where the White Mountains and the Ray
Mountains squeeze it down to a half-mile-wide millrace.
The ice was a pristine white strip, showing no sign of the
raging torrent going on under the surface.

There's a bit of the honeybee in Alex. He rarely looks at maps, just points the airplane toward where we're going and we never turn until we get there. The Ray Mountains tapered off. The South Fork, Middle Fork, and North Fork came together, joined the Wild River and the John to make the Koyukuk, and Bettles Field was below us, looking like a city after the mountains. In actuality, it has a two-story log lodge and some outbuildings and garages lining a runway that can handle jets.

In the early days, Wien Airline built some emergency fields in strategic locations, places where a plane in trouble, either mechanical or from weather, could set down. During the cold war, the military got involved. They flew daily sorties to harass Russia, and the result is some well-equipped airports along the western coast where the only people are the maintenance crews. Bettles Field is just a couple of miles downstream from Bettles Village, but the village has nothing to do with the location of the airport.

Johnson was awake, doing his vacant stare at the airport. Maybe he didn't realize we were over Bettles. Alex turned around in his seat to talk to Johnson.

"Reckon you can spot your digs from the air?"

"Yeah, I reckon. Big bend to the west, just below Caribou Creek."

Alex nodded, and we followed the John into the edge of the Endicott Mountains. The bend to the west was clear enough, but it was in a canyon. Johnson was watching, but we came to the Caribou Creek and he hadn't said anything. Alex ballooned up out of the gorge, turned us around, and flew back down the John, cliffs grazing the wingtips on either side.

"There, there," Johnson was bouncing and pointing. I saw a cut bank go by, bare ground so steep that no snow was on it, but I didn't see anything that didn't look natural to me. In these mountains there were several feet of snow, and I was glad Alex didn't appear tempted to land. He climbed out of the gorge again. I handed another pain-killing beer to Johnson, and we flew back to Bettles Field.

Andy and Stella have been running the lodge for many years. I think Andy is a retired Wien pilot, but now he's the Wien station manager. That entails keeping the runway maintained, manning the bank of radios, reporting weather, and running the lodge. The epicurean cuisine in the big communal dining hall is Stella's doing. It is amazing what a superb chef with a battery of marinades can do with moose meat.

Alex parked right in front of the lodge door. We helped Johnson climb down and did our crutch routine up the steps and into the lodge. I get a special feeling in the Arctic, maybe because the air is crisper and cleaner even than my pristine ambiance in Fox. It might be because there are no man-made pollutants, or anything else, within hundreds of miles, and it seems like I can feel the isolation.

The front room of the lodge is large and dark with wood paneling, wooden floors with throw rugs, an oversized stone fireplace across the room, and a light bulb hanging from the ceiling. On the right is the chest-high customer counter and behind that a solid wall of radios. On the left, a twenty-foot-long dining table is surrounded by thirty chairs. In summer, with miners, fishermen, and maintenance crews coming and going, that table would be crowded. At the end of April, ours was the only plane out front, and I thought probably we were the only guests.

Andy jumped up from his radios and bounded around the counter, hand extended to greet us. If he were to change his twill work pants and suspenders over a denim shirt for a red suit, he could be Santa Claus. Come to think of it, considering how close we were to the North Pole, maybe someone should keep an eye on him Christmas Eve, but for now he was the epitome of the glad-handing innkeeper. He held his hand out until he realized that none of us was free to shake it. Then he saw who we were holding up. His mouth dropped open and he did the seeing-ghost stare.

"Hi, Andy," Johnson said.

"Well, I'll be switched. K.J., I never expected to see you in this world again. Perry used a spatula to toss your brains out of the airplane after he brought you in." Andy sort of sagged backward and leaned against the desk.

"Got me a patch," Johnson explained. He lifted his arm off of Alex's shoulder and parted his hair to exhibit the plate in his head.

Andy came out of his daze, ran around the counter and came back pushing a swivel chair on wheels. We eased Johnson down into it. With our hands free, Alex and I shook hands with Andy.

"Hi, Alex. Hi...Stew." Just a moment's hesitation there. "You guys are a little out of your usual territory, aren't you?"

"Stew's my new partner," Johnson piped up.

Andy shook his head, either in disbelief or sympathy. "Does he know what happened to your last partner? We didn't even try to lay him out, just tossed all the pieces Perry could find into the coffin and buried it. You'll be staying here until breakup? Only two other guests in the lodge at the moment and they eat like birds. Stella will be glad to have some appetites on board."

Johnson spoke up. "I'd be powerful grateful if you could find some painkiller before dinner. Froze off a couple of toes on the way, and they do throb something awful."

"Sure, sure. Got a couple of cases of Jack Daniels." Andy grabbed the back of the chair and wheeled Johnson over to the dining table, detouring around the throw rugs. He glanced out the window at the airplane. "You froze your toes?"

"He walked the first three thousand miles." Alex explained.

Andy accepted that as probable. He bustled into the kitchen and came back with four glasses and a bottle. He poured an inch into each glass and dealt them out. Johnson reached over, grabbed the bottle, and filled his glass.

"Here's to gold." Andy proposed. We each sipped and grimaced, except Johnson. He drank the bourbon down like water and reached for the bottle again.

"Hey, easy does it, K.J. You're welcome to the painkiller, but I want you to die on your claim with your boots on, not at the table from alcoholic shock."

"K.J.?" I asked.

"Klondike Johnson," Andy explained. "He's been skunked in every gold rush since the Russians dumped Alaska on the unsuspecting USA."

"Until this time." K.J. was down to half a glass and he topped it off again, just in case Andy should grab the bottle.

"Right," Andy said. "This time you got your brains beat out, and you didn't have any extra to begin with. I don't suppose you stopped by to settle your grubstake?"

"All in good time, my man. I'll pay for last time and this one with a basket of nuggets."

"Right; and I'm Santa Claus." Andy didn't flinch when he said it. "How many of you guys are staying?"

"Not me," Alex said. "Stew?"

"I think you and I had better take a walk." We finished our painkiller and wandered out onto the runway.

"Well, what do you think?" Alex stuck his hands in his pockets and turned to stroll along the edge of the snow berm.

"Damned if I know. You tell me if K.J. is real, or the craziest coot we've ever met. He sure is awful free with offering partnerships."

"Yeah, but that's not so crazy. Remember the foldboat trip down Kowkow Creek? Neither one of us could have made it alone, but together no problem. Besides, two guys workin' a hand sluice can work four times as fast as one guy. One just keeps shoveling, the other pours water. If two guys are expecting trouble they can watch both ways at once. Makes sense."

"If it's so sensible, why hasn't anyone else taken him up on the offer?"

"Probably because there isn't one guy in ten thousand dumb enough to fall for it."

"Do you suppose his gold strike is all in his head? Brains leaked out, fantasies leaked in. He was in a coma for months, he could have imagined anything."

"Could have, but someone thought he'd found gold, enough to kill two men for."

"Yeah, but the guys who jumped him may have been just as crazy as he is. If I'm not back in Fox in the morning I'll lose my job and have to wait in line again. I could be out of work for two weeks. Besides, this is going to cost a bundle if we don't get lucky. You got any money left?"

"If I had any money left, we'd still be in Joanne's apartment, but don't worry about that. Just think of your hide, and how much it's worth to you. You have to make the decision, Stew. If we get rich, it's fifty/fifty. If you get killed, you're on your own."

We walked back toward the airplane in silence, and Alex paused with his hand on the fuselage to look at me. It was decision time.

"Well, I guess there are two guys in Alaska crazier than K.J. That's us."

Alex nodded and opened the baggage compartment. He'd known what the decision would be from the start. First he tossed K.J.'s shoes out into the snow, then he dragged out his emergency gear. He loaded me up with socks, shoepacks, mitts and parka, and then put his pistol and a box of ammunition on top of the pile.

Loaning me his gun was so intimate, such an expression of solidarity that it almost brought tears to my eyes. There's a saying in the Arctic: "You may borrow my car, my snow machine, my boat, my dog, or my wife, but you may not borrow my gun." When Alex handed me his pistol, it was like giving me a part of himself. It's the patrolman model, .357 magnum, Smith and Wesson revolver with a six-inch barrel, but this one was also part of Alex's identity. I'm as good as the next guy with a pistol, most Alaskans are, but Alex is the only guy I've ever known who can put all six shots through the same hole at thirty feet. It's uncanny, it's magic, it's a partnership between Alex and the gun that goes beyond human bonds. When he handed the weapon to me, the word elook took on a whole new meaning.

He closed the baggage compartment, opened the pilot's

door and rummaged around in the map case. He pulled out a ledger-type book and I followed him back into the lodge. He walked up to the registration desk, and Andy deserted K.J. to join us.

"How do you feel about a check from Bushmaster Air Alaska?" Alex asked.

Andy nodded. "I like it a heck of a lot better than promises of gold."

Alex tore a check out of the book and signed it. "Let's leave it blank for now. If Stew comes back with a bucket of gold, tear up the check. If he slinks back to Fairbanks with his tail between his legs, fill out the check for whatever he owes you, and Johnson's bill for this year, of course."

Andy took the check and stuck it into a pigeonhole.

Alex turned around and almost ran out the door. He charged straight to the airplane, fired it up and took off in a cloud of exhaust and snow. That wasn't so unusual. Alex had left me to moil for gold and flown away many times before. We knew that in the Arctic when two people part, even for a week, they may never see each other again. This time had some earmarks of a final one. We were either going to get rich, or I might get dead, and Alex might have to explain an un-stubbed check for several thousand dollars to his partner.

In any case, when we parted at such times, we didn't do a lot of handshaking and speechifying. It would be too easy to get maudlin if we ever stopped to think, so, maybe, like this time, that's why we never stopped to think.

Chapter 5

Drink to me only with thine eyes, and I will
pledge with mine.
To Celia—Ben Jonson

KJ was no longer hoisting the glass. His head had drooped down so close to the table that he was just tilting the glass to drink. Andy took the bottle and the three empty glasses back to the kitchen. He came out wiping his hands on a dishtowel, and tossed the towel on the table, preparatory to swabbing up the liquor that K.J. was spilling. Then he noticed I was standing there with my arms full of Alex's emergency winter clothes.

"You're in the second room on the right, upstairs. Stash your gear, and we'll put K.J. in that room behind the pantry."

A hallway led between creaky wooden stairs on the right, kitchen on the left, emitting an aroma from heaven.

The hall continued past the kitchen. The pantry was under the stairway; behind that was one bedroom meant for overflow on the right, and Andy and Stella's bedroom on the left. I tromped up the stairs, found the second door on the right open, and tossed Alex's largess onto the bed. Socks and shoepacks would fit fine, parka just a little too big and wolf mittens a bit tight, but all very welcome. The first door on the right was closed; the open door on the left was the communal bathroom. My room had no lock because there are no keys or locks in a bush lodge. Maybe that's because everyone is trustworthy, but also because no one could go anywhere if he tried to run away.

I always shiver when I think of the ancient punishment for capital crimes. It was to drive the miscreant out of the village without a shirt. He'd be dead in three days, either from freezing in winter or mosquitoes in summer. If someone tried to run away from Bettles, after absconding with the crown jewels for instance, he'd probably wear his shirt, but that would just stretch his ordeal to six days.

When I got back downstairs, Andy was wheeling K.J. down the hall, holding him by the shoulders to keep him in the chair. I followed along. K.J.'s room was the same as mine, a single bed, a chair, and a dresser with an enamel washbasin perched on top. Andy wheeled the chair right up to the bed. Our host kept K.J.'s shoulders, I grabbed his hips, and we hoisted the body on top of the patchwork quilt. The body didn't move, so we left the chair and returned to the dining room.

"Dinner at 6:00." Andy said. "Not 5:59, not 6:01." He nodded toward the big clock that hung on the wall at the end of the room, snagged a chair from the dining table, and carried it back behind the counter to attend to his radio traffic. The clock read 5:15, and it matched my Casio, so I wandered back upstairs. The door on the right was still closed. I checked out the community bathroom, a lav, a conventional commode, and a steel shower. I rinsed off the dust of travel and stretched out on my bed to wait for the magic hour.

I was awakened by the sound of something heavy sliding across the floor in the room next door. While the outside walls are log, ten inches thick and impervious to sound or weather, the inside walls are just framed, with Celotex, a fiber wallboard, on both sides. You can carry on a conversation with someone in the next room in a normal tone of voice. I didn't stop to wonder about the scraping sound. I wouldn't have cared if it were a stack of bodies being dragged. It had been ten hours since the nauseating eggs in the Model Café. Nothing wrong with the eggs, the nausea was internal, but it seemed longer. Breakfast was in a different world and a different chapter in my life. Also, I had faith that even if Stella served moose meat and beans, they would not be recognizable as the humble fare I was accustomed to.

I made it downstairs at 5:58, Andy came around the end of his counter and strode to the head of the table, but he didn't sit down. He motioned me with a jerk of his head to the chair on his left. That was the chair I would have chosen because it put my back to the wall. That's paranoia without cause, but I do feel better knowing that no one is behind me. It also gave me the view of the door to the kitchen and the stairway.

I started to sit, but there was something purposeful in

the way Andy was standing, so I stood behind my chair and waited for a cue. At 5:59 there was a rustle from the stairway, and then the unmistakable click of high heels marching downward. One may see a pig riding to market in the queen's ceremonial carriage, or a snowman on the beach in Miami in July, but one does not hear high heels on the stairs in a remote lodge above the Arctic Circle. I glanced at Andy. He had rolled his eyes to the heavens, apparently inspecting the underside of his white caterpillar eyebrows.

The woman who emerged from the stairway might have just stepped out of the queen's carriage. I guessed her age to be near fifty, iron gray hair severely coiffed, a ramrod up her back that robbed her champagne-colored evening gown of any hint of femininity, and the eyes of a judge who is pronouncing a death sentence. She glared around the room, assessing its worthiness to receive her august presence, but if she noticed me, she took me for part of the furniture.

We passed inspection, and she marched sedately to the chair on Andy's right. He rushed to pull the chair for her, but I was distracted. The girl who materialized from the stairway wafted in like a bright summer day. Honey blonde hair framed an oval face and cascaded down her back. Blue eyes had been plucked from the clearest and brightest of Alaska skies. She wore a long-sleeved burgundy gown that swept in graceful curves to the floor and moved with a vitality that may have been the cause of my mouth hanging open. I snapped it shut. Andy seated the girl and returned to stand behind his chair again.

"Mrs. Whidbey, may I present Mr. Benjamin Stewart? Stewart, Mrs. Whidbey and her daughter, Carolyn."

"Hi," I said. "Please call me Stew."

"No, thank you. Mr. Stewart will do nicely. Are you a rapist, Mr. Stewart?"

That question flummoxed me. Could she have seen my appraisal of her daughter and read my mind? Probably, but rapist was a little over the top. Honestly, it was seduction that came to mind. I was saved by Stella, carrying a steaming platter of meat into the room. Stella is past sixty, but with the vitality of a twenty-year-old. She'd been a raven-haired beauty in the recent past. Now she was a gray-haired beauty and the smile lines that were etching onto her delightful visage had an impish quality to them. I couldn't remember ever having seen her in a dress before, but she was wearing a flowered number, classier than a housedress, and covered by a white apron with frills on it. One doesn't normally associate frills with Stella.

"Good evening, Mr. Stewart. Ladies and gentlemen, tonight's entrée will be veal cutlets Savoyarde." Stella nailed me with a steady stare that told me plainly I was not to contradict her. I nodded in understanding. She set down the platter of moose cutlets, smothered in melted Gruyere cheese, redolent of vermouth and paprika, with corners of ham slices peeking out of the cheese.

She went back to the kitchen for salad. Andy sat, so I followed his example, and Andy decanted the Merlot that had been open and breathing. He didn't just pour the wine; he decanted it, starting with Mrs. Whidbey, then Carolyn, the vacant place beside me that was set for Stella, then me, and himself. Everyone else had removed napkins from the table and spread them in laps, so I did that, but I was pinching myself, trying to wake up from a dream.

Stella's speaking words in a foreign language was a

shock, and the formality in the air was disorienting. Normally, Stella would have come out of the kitchen, already quaffing her second glass of wine, probably with her shoes off, and shouting the latest gossip to any new arrivals. By now, Andy should have snared one of the disguised moose steaks and been half through it, but he was sitting like a statue, hands in his lap. I was starting to wonder if Andy and Stella had got religion, and maybe we were waiting to say grace.

My mouth was watering, and I admit it was about equally for the moose cutlets and Carolyn. She was sitting demurely, staring straight ahead with the classic expression of a cameo, but I had the feeling that she was barely suppressing giggles, if not a hearty guffaw. Her eyes sneaked over to glance at me, and her shoulders convulsed, but minimally, in a ladylike manner. Her eyes snapped back to the wall and I noticed she was biting her lower lip. I had a momentary flash of what it might feel like to bite that luscious ripe ruby lip.

Stella came back with a bowl of cabbage salad. Fanny, the native girl Stella had hired from the village, was right behind her with a platter of homemade bread, still steaming from the oven. I got a guilty stab of what might have been conscience when Fanny walked in. Stella set the salad on the table. Fanny gave me a shy smile and set the bread in front of me before she melted back to the kitchen. She's a pretty girl by any standards, half Indian, half Inuit, pleasant round face, eyes like Bambi's mother, and silky black hair she can sit on.

Andy leapt to his feet, so I joined him. Stella, sans apron, came around to my side of the table and I slid her chair for her. All was not lost. She elbowed me in the ribs as she passed, and then reached around to pat my backside when the tablecloth hid her hand. The same old Stella was alive and well somewhere inside that somber package.

Mrs. Whidbey raised her glass and proposed the toast. "To the beauty of God's handiwork. May we never despoil it." We all took a ritual sip, and started passing platters. I wondered if her reference to God's handiwork meant Carolyn.

That moose Savoyarde was the best dinner I'd ever chomped down on. It was hard to believe it came from the same kind of animal that was hanging behind my cabin, and if Stella wanted to call it veal cutlets, or emu steaks, that was all right with me.

My Merlot had evaporated pretty quickly and I was about to extend the glass to Andy for a refill when Stella's hand clamped down on my knee. I glanced around and noticed that everyone else still had a full glass, so I concentrated on the salad and the fresh-baked bread. It wasn't hard. Stella managed to have crisp fresh greens in the shadow of the North Pole, and the hot bread was to die for. If that turned out to be literal, I really didn't mind at that moment.

Mrs. Whidbey set the pace, chewing each mouthful forty times, and taking such tiny sips of wine that the level in her glass never went down. Carolyn matched her, each of them eating one chop, one slice of bread, and one little mound of the salad. I couldn't help myself. I speared another chop and a second slice of the bread. The butter on the table was real, and, next to the covert thoughts I was having about Carolyn, real butter on still-warm bread may be the greatest pleasure in life.

I finished my second chop and was eyeing a third when Stella's hand clamped down again. Mrs. Whidbey seemed to be finished, leaving a tiny bit of chop and salad on her plate. She sat back and sipped her wine. Fanny came from the kitchen and removed our plates, rubbing her breasts across the back of my neck when she reached for Stella's plate. Stella gave Fanny a whack on her bottom for the indiscretion, but that was behind my back. Stella was smiling beatifically, eyes straight ahead.

Fanny was back in thirty seconds with apple cobbler, smothered in whipped cream, and poured thick, black Yuban coffee into our cups. Mrs. Whidbey swirled a fork in her whipped cream.

"Well, Mr. Stewart, you haven't answered my question. Are you one of the rapists?"

I managed a weak, "No, ma'am," but I didn't sound very convincing. Andy took pity on me.

"Mrs. Whidbey is here representing The Green Army, watching over our fragile environment."

"Mr. Anderson, north of the Arctic Circle, I am The Green Army, and I assure you that there will be no rapine of our environment during my watch." She took one bite of her cobbler, and her body jerked as if she'd gotten an electric shock. The shadow that crossed her face looked human, like infinite sadness, but she reverted instantly to her drill-sergeant hauteur. I wondered why the apples cause such a violent reaction. I'd already eaten half of my cobbler and it was superb. She swirled her fork in the whipped cream, licked it, chased it with one sip of the coffee and stood.

"Come along, Carolyn," she marched toward the stairs. Carolyn had finished her cobbler and grabbed a sip of the coffee before she stood and followed her mother. She did sweep me with searchlight eyes when she turned, and I read all sorts of things into them, like humanity, for instance, but maybe that was wishful thinking. The high heels clattered on the stairs, we heard the door close, and then the scraping sound that had awakened me. I looked the question at Andy.

"Sliding the dresser in front of the door," he explained. "The environment isn't the only thing she's protecting from rapists."

"You, me, or Johnson?" I asked.

"Nothing so specific. The world in general, I think."

We'd finished the cobbler, and the wine lasted about thirty seconds after Mrs. Whidbey left, followed by her lady-in-waiting. Stella had slipped off her shoes and leaned back to put her feet on the table. "The way you devoured Carolyn with your eyes, if she were my daughter, I'd put a lot more than a dresser in front of the door, and then sit up all night with a shotgun. You're really not planning to despoil her, are you, Stew?"

I didn't have a chance to answer. Fanny came back with barrel glasses, a bowl of ice, and a bottle of Jack Daniels. She poured four generous shots, passed them around, and then plunked herself down in my lap.

"Don't you remember me, Stewie? That night in Fairbanks, you said we were made for each other."

I reached around her to pick up the bourbon. "Of course I remember you, Fanny. Why else would I come to the end of the earth? This is a sad day because I came to tell you that I've gotten religion. It broke my heart, but I took a vow of celibacy." I chugged the bourbon and she refilled my glass.

"That's okay, Stewie, I'll just cuddle up to you, and you don't have to do anything." She cuddled, I chugged.

Stella finished her bourbon and reached over me to take Andy's hand. "You kids work out the details, but for heaven's sake, be quiet about it. We're going to bed. Want to just cuddle, Andy?"

I made it up the stairs and into my room, but it wasn't easy because Fanny was hanging from my neck. The conversation from the room next door was plainly audible, and I realized it was the first time I had heard Carolyn's voice. That made me wonder how many more firsts we might share.

"Dammit, mother, you never want me to meet any real men."

"Hush, dear. Your father was a real man, and look where that got us."

"Well, those tutti-frutti friends of yours in San Francisco make me sick. Just once, I'd like to talk to a man who is more masculine than I am."

"Darling, that Stewart person is pure evil. You can see it in his eyes. I only want what's best for you."

I couldn't hear any more after that because I was trying to stifle Fanny's giggles without actually smothering her.

Chapter 6

Oh, what a tangled web we weave when first
we practice to deceive.
Marmion—Sir Walter Scott

Fanny was no longer snuggling when I regained
consciousness, but the redolence of coffee, bacon,
and waffles that drifted up from the kitchen suggested
where she had gone. I washed up, decided that I could go one
more day without a shave, and tromped downstairs toward
the aroma of coffee.

A dapper gentleman was sitting in my place at the table,
clean-shaven, fashionably long but well-brushed hair, and
I didn't recognize him until I noticed that he was sitting in
Andy's swivel chair. Stella must have cut his hair and shaved
his beard. His mustache had been clipped, so his mouth was
showing and the streak of gray hair I had first noticed was

darker, shoe polish, perhaps? Even his eyes were tamer. The left one that was looking at me had a civilized competence to it, and the right one had shifted several degrees closer to agreement with its mate and lost the predatory hawkish glitter.

"Good morning, Stan."

"Stew," I corrected him again. I squeezed behind him to sit, leaving a vacant chair between us for Stella. Fanny came out of the kitchen, beaming like a midsummer morning, and poured coffee. I tried to return her smile, almost made it, and beat my conscience down with an iron fist worthy of the Gestapo. She's a lovely girl, but not anything long term, so we needed to keep it cool.

Johnson sipped coffee, very genteel, thumb and two fingers on the handle, pinky extended, and retrieved the napkin from his lap to blot his lips before he turned to me.

"Will you be leaving for the mine this morning?" he asked.

I was so surprised that I choked on my coffee and was still gasping for breath when we heard the scrape from upstairs, followed by only one set of high heels descending. Dared I hope? I did not. It was Mrs. Whidbey who materialized from the stairway, dressed for the day in an L.L. Bean jumpsuit and engineer's boots, but joy incarnate, Carolyn was behind her, wearing the drumming heels, a swirling skirt, and a white peasant blouse.

Johnson reached over and punched my leg. I leapt to my feet, but he didn't. Instead he oozed a kind of sophisticated charm. "Madam, in the absence of our host, I fear that I must present myself. I beg your forgiveness for not rising, but I just walked here from Seattle, and I have frozen my feet. I am Hannibal Johnson, at your service, Mrs. Whidbey. You note that your reputation precedes you, but I was not prepared for such loveliness. The young lady must be your daughter, Carolyn; the resemblance is striking. The fortunate girl has inherited your eyes and your charming smile."

That was a new side of K.J. but it did fit his new appearance and I shouldn't have been too quick to guess his background. I looked quickly, and a semblance of a smile did flit across the dour visage. It hadn't occurred to me that was possible. The great lady was still standing by her chair and Johnson reached over to poke my leg again. I scooted around the table and slid her chair for her. Carolyn was also standing expectantly. I rushed to do the honors, and may have leaned a little closer than necessary. I suppose the emanation from her cloud of hair was soap, but it struck me as the most provocative of perfumes.

My fingers were still grasping the chair when she sat, and she leaned back to rub her shoulders across them. First contact; electric shocks ran up my arms. I was just stepping away when Fanny came in, brandishing the coffeepot. She accidentally stepped on my foot and ground her heel in before she leaned to pour Mrs. Whidbey's coffee. I limped back to my chair just in time to see the hot coffeepot graze Carolyn's shoulder. Carolyn flinched, but kept smiling while Fanny filled her cup and then dribbled a tiny string of hot drops toward the edge of the table. The droplets ceased, one inch before they would have landed in Carolyn's lap.

"You say that you walked here from Seattle?" Mrs. Whidbey asked. "That is a remarkable feat, Mr. Johnson."

"Certainly, madam, I wouldn't dream of polluting this pristine atmosphere with the noxious fumes from internal combustion. Unfortunately, the feat was more remarkable than the feet. The spirit was willing, but the flesh was vulnerable."

"And what business brings you to our outpost of nature?" Mrs. Whidbey. sampled her coffee, wrinkled her nose, but took another sip. Fanny was bringing platters of waffles, a plate mounded with butter, and little pitchers of homemade blueberry syrup. When she came back with the platter of bacon, she started to place it in front of me, then treated me to a scowl and put the dish in front of Johnson.

He helped himself to the two strips I had been eyeing. "It has come to the attention of myself and my brash young assistant that a landslide has marred the banks of the wild and scenic John River. It is our intention to clean the bank and restore it to its original pristine glory."

"Very laudable." Mrs. Whidbey had helped herself to the next two rashers and passed the bacon platter to Carolyn. She picked out a waffle and started buttering. "Naturally, I shall accompany you on your quest to monitor and document your efforts."

Carolyn slid the platter toward me. I stopped buttering waffle to cadge the last two strips of bacon. I was so intrigued by the image of Mrs. Whidbey in that Hell's Canyon we had flown through that it took a moment to realize she represented utter disaster. How the heck was I going to gather up a basketful of nuggets without her noticing?

She poured a generous puddle of the blueberry syrup onto her waffle, and when she tasted it, she very nearly smiled again. Blueberries on the tundra are half the size, but twice the flavor of any domesticated variety.

"This is the way the bounty of God's earth was meant

to be used, Mr. Johnson. An infinitely renewable resource, lovingly harvested for the enrichment and edification of His children." After that, she got busy with her fork and neglected to enlighten us further.

Apparently, talking with our mouths full was not part of the new regimen, and we did keep our mouths full until the last bite of the last waffle had been saturated with blueberry nectar and consumed, by me, of course. Fanny removed plates and poured more coffee, this time without injuring anyone.

"If you gentlemen will excuse us, I must get to my journal. I'm happy to have made your acquaintance, Mr. Johnson, and I assure you that your worthy project will get a favorable mention in my logbook. Come along, Carolyn."

"The pleasure was all mine, madam. I look forward to a mutually beneficial and pleasurable association." Johnson reached over and punched my knee. He was obviously far more sophisticated than me and knew the proper procedures in this case. I shot to my feet and hurried around to pull chairs. I did notice that Mrs. W. had expressed no pleasure in meeting me. Carolyn was careful not to touch me, although I gave her every opportunity, but then I noticed that mama was watching. When she was safely out of the chair, and mama had turned toward the stairs, Carolyn did sneak a sly little smile in my direction, which I treasured.

Two minutes after the upstairs door closed, Andy and Stella came straggling out of their bedroom, yawning, stretching, and scratching, pleasures that we had been denied. Fanny brought more waffles, more bacon, more coffee. I started all over, and this time talked with my mouth full. It was a relief to lose the act we'd been putting on for the ladies.

"What the hell did you mean, going to the mine this morning? There's ten feet of snow up there. I'd be lucky to find the Hippodrome in that canyon."

"Well, what I been thinking, Stan...

"Stew."

"Stew, is that if I drew you an exact map of where we buried the gold, and if Andy loaned you a snow machine and a shovel, you could dig up the gold in an hour or so and we could fly first class to Las Vegas while we wait for breakup."

Andy did swallow waffle before speaking. "Happy to oblige. You can take my Arctic Cat. It's a Bearcat, good old workhorse, can go anywhere. Incidentally, if you settle K.J.'s bill for last year, Stella and I will join you in Las Vegas."

Fanny must have been listening because she was out of the kitchen like a shot and parked in my lap again. "Do it for me, Stewie. I've always wanted to see Las Vegas."

An hour later I was on Andy's Cat, and heading out into the wilderness. There is no convenient way to carry a shovel on a snow machine. I solved that problem by sitting on the shovel and letting the handle stick out behind.

What was less predictable was that Mrs. Whidbey and Carolyn were right behind me, riding a Polaris and an Elan, respectively.

Chapter 7

The best laid schemes o' mice and men gang aft a-gley.
To a mouse—Robert Burns

May Day was appropriately glorious. Bright sunshine streamed from a cloudless sky and glinted off the snow with the brilliance of diamonds. The temperature hovered at fifteen degrees above zero, and the arctic winter wind had been replaced by the unmistakable ambience of springtime.

I was comfortably ensconced on Andy's Bearcat, even though I was sitting on a shovel. The basket he had attached behind contained the usual emergency gear, hatchet, rope, tarp, candle, sleeping bag, and the lunch Fanny had packed for us. I thought the lunch was superfluous, but it pleased Fanny to be participating in the preparation for our wealthy future together.

Andy's Cat purred like the well tended, if antique, pet that it was. I figured one hour for the twenty-mile trek to the mine, twenty minutes to dig up the gold, and an hour to return. K.J.'s map was drawn with reference to the cut bank I'd seen. One hundred paces downstream, twenty paces in from the river, and six inches under loose dirt behind a boulder.

With no airplanes in sight, I zipped across the runway, shot over the berm, and floated over three feet of loose snow at twenty miles per hour. After a hundred yards, I looked back to be sure my entourage was intact. It wasn't. I had used the berm at the edge of the runway for a ski jump and flown ten feet. Mrs. Whidbey came chugging slowly up the berm, and slowly down again. With the machine pointed straight down, she buried the tips of the machine's skis. I was sorely tempted to leave her there. Maybe I could protest that I hadn't noticed her predicament.

Aside from my natural chivalry, what made me return was Carolyn, sitting with her machine perched on top of the snow berm behind the disaster. You have to take my word that the padded figure in snowsuit, parka, and helmet was Carolyn. Try to remember the figure she had cut at breakfast, and if you're a gentleman, let it go at that.

I swung a wide circle through unmarked snow and returned to the scene of carnage. Riding a snow machine on deep snow is very much like riding a motorcycle. One leans to bank the curves and stability comes from speed. A machine that's up to speed floats over any depth of snow, not unlike a boat that is planing. If you're stopped in deep snow, the process of getting up and running again is a challenge similar to a water skier who is starting out.

Mrs. Whidbey putting along at minimum speed was an invitation for disaster, and driving straight down a bank where skis were obviously going to dig in was disaster incarnate.

I rode past the tips of the buried skis to pack down the snow, and back to park on the trail I had blazed on the first pass. Shovel in hand, I waded through the snow to the scene of the disaster. She was sitting on her machine, staring straight down at the snow, and darned if she wasn't feebly revving her engine, spinning the track to dig herself deeper. I used the shovel to dig down, grabbed the handhold on the front of her skis, and used the skis for levers to pull them out of the snow. She revved her engine again. The machine nosed up onto my packed track; I dove to the side, and she chugged slowly onto the trail. I climbed up the berm, grabbed Carolyn's skis, and turned her around toward the runway.

"Hit the berm at fifteen miles an hour and jump over the canyon," I instructed.

Her helmet nodded. I waded back to my machine, swept in a circle to get back on the trail in front of her mother and led her away from the berm. I heard the engine on Carolyn's Elan scream, even over the purring of Andy's Cat. Carolyn hit the berm at forty miles an hour, stood up like a ski jumper to control her flight, and sailed right past us.

She hit, and skipped like a flat stone on water, threw all of her weight to the left, banking almost ninety degrees for a high-speed turn, and floated around to come chugging sedately up behind us on the packed trail. Carolyn had the idea.

We headed toward the river, but angled upstream, which was the direction of Bettles Village. I needed to keep my speed up to break trail, but mother was back there, chugging along at a speed that would bury her if she strayed off the trail. I let her get a hundred yards behind, then made a circle and came back to park on my own packed trail to wait.

The second time I pulled that maneuver, I heard Carolyn's engine scream again. She shot out of the trail, made a couple of sweeping turns, obviously enjoying her freedom, and came back to the trail ahead of her mother. That did it. Mrs. Whidbey was not about to let Carolyn and me disappear into the distance together, so she picked up her pace and we rumbled right along toward the village.

Villagers had made several trails, and when we started meeting those, I picked one that busted through the line of trees on our left and led down toward the river. That trail was packed a couple of feet deep, as hard as concrete. We wound between spruce trees, and down a toboggan run to the river ice. That is, Carolyn and I did. The river was packed like a highway where hundreds of machines had plied it all winter. We fetched up as soon as we got out of the tree shadow into sunshine, took off our helmets and waited for mama, and waited.

When my conscience insisted, I drove back up the trail into the trees. I came to the bottom of her machine, which was lying on its side crosswise to the trail, track turning lazily, and one shoepack protruding underneath the running board. I shut off her engine. I could tell she wasn't dead because of the stream of spluttering that was spewing out of her helmet. If she hadn't been such a lady, I might have taken some of it for profanity.

I picked up the rear of her machine to release the foot. She scrambled up and jerked her helmet off.

"You certainly took your time about coming back. Are you trying to kill me, Mr. Stewart?" Her predicament was my fault. Guilty without trial, no defense permitted.

I dragged the machine's rear bumper around into the trail. She had let her right ski wander into the bank and had hooked a bush. It took three heaves, holding up the track and straining backward, to unhook the ski, and I was sweating when it came free. Working up a sweat is not a good thing to do in the Arctic. You're dressed so warmly, thermal underwear, cotton, then wool socks, shoepacks, snow machine suit, and parka, that the temperature becomes irrelevant. However, all of that insulation depends on your staying dry. If you work up a sweat, soak your socks and underwear, and then stop, you can get in trouble.

I grabbed the handholds on my own skis and pulled my machine around. The trail wasn't wide enough for passing, and the machines didn't fit in it sideways. Trees were too close to make a detour. I pulled until the machine was jammed, then stepped out of the trail and sank into loose snow to my waist to lift the track around. By the time I got through thrashing and crawling in the snow, and was back on my machine again, I felt as if I had been in a steam bath.

Carolyn was sitting sideways on her machine, helmet off, enjoying the sunshine. We passed her, but in a moment she was beside me, and we cruised up the river, three abreast. It was like driving up a country road, altogether pleasant. That may explain why some people go snow machine riding for pleasure. I was starting to think our expedition was back on schedule.

The village went by above us on the right bank. The smell of wood smoke and fur drifted down. A few log cabins with corrugated metal roofs were visible through the trees. Several dogs were barking; a chain saw was whining somewhere. We glided by.

The river widened, and a gravel bar jutted downstream in the middle of it, like the prow of a ship. Most of the tracks went straight ahead, up the Wild River. We swung to the left and followed the John River. Our trail began to taper off, tracks veering to climb the bank on either side. We passed some pole-and-canvas shelters where people had been ice fishing, but most of the previous expeditions had been gathering wood, or, don't tell Madam, hunting moose illegally.

Our final predecessor had swerved out of the river and climbed the left bank into a grove of scrub alder trees, almost certainly for a moose. We were riding single file on unmarked snow, and Carolyn had cut her mother off to get behind me. Mountains were beginning to crowd the river. It narrowed to a hundred feet, then spread out to a hundred yards. When cliffs blocked the sun, the temperature immediately dropped to zero, but soared to fifteen above when the sun reached us.

We'd been following the middle of the river, but it widened out ahead of us, and I noticed a depression--maybe even a darker color--to the snow in the center. I didn't even think about it, just swerved toward the right bank and kept on trucking. I could hear Carolyn right behind me, but all at once I got a premonition of doom. I slowed and looked back.

The trail Carolyn and I had made was a radical turn. I watched in horror when Mrs. Whidbey continued straight ahead. She was driving fast enough to make her own trails now, but there are limits. She sailed right into the open field, disdaining our detour. We watched her inexorably slowing, and the machine steadily sinking into the snow. When it stopped, only the windshield was showing, and the great lady was standing on the seat.

Carolyn had taken off her helmet to watch the show. "What's the matter, what's happening?" she asked.

"Caroline, our present predicament is called overflow. It can happen on lakes or rivers and it's because snow is a wonderful insulator. Something, maybe a hot spring or a creek, causes water to flow on top of the ice and it stays liquid."

"I don't see any water, it looks normal."

"Yes, it looks normal, but snow absorbs water like a sponge. If you reach down a few inches and gather a snowball in your hands, water will run out of it until you're left with a teaspoon-sized kernel of slush."

We shut off our engines. Normally, that would have produced the profound silence of the un-peopled arctic, but in this case we were assailed by screams that awakened the echoes of the hills.

Another echo caught my attention for a moment because it didn't seem to fit. The sound of our running engines echoed for a moment too long, and the echo came from across the river where the terrain was relatively flat. Mrs. Whidbey's screaming was echoing from the hills behind us.

Caroline still didn't appear properly alarmed. "So she has to back up?"

I took the opportunity to pontificate. "Caroline, if only it were that simple, but here's the problem. One time I was crossing a tiny lake down in Kuskokwim country. I was on snowshoes, attacking Barometer Mountain above the Red Devil mine. The trip had to do with a lack of meat in the cache, but that is beside the point. I had done my snowshoe shuffle, twenty feet across this little lake, when the lake gurgled and grabbed me. One step I was on top, the next I was standing in two feet of water. The ice hadn't broken, or I'd have been gone. The water was overflow, in that case very probably from a hot spring because the water was dark brown and smelled of sulfur.

"The air temperature was fifty degrees below zero. The standing joke is that if you spit at that temperature, it will freeze on the way down and shatter like glass when it hits. I haven't tried that. What I did try was struggling to pull one snowshoe up out of the slush. That's a good trick under any circumstances, but in this case, the second the shoe broke the surface the water froze and the shoe suddenly weighed ten pounds. I got the other one up, and was turned around in the process, but that one, too, was already straining the binding strap. I made six steps back toward shore, shoes getting heavier, ten pounds per step, before the bindings broke.

"Obviously I made it out and back to the Red Devil Mine, but it was an ordeal like the rusted Tin Woodsman went through, pounding on my legs to break the ice so I could bend my knees."

"Wow," Caroline said, "I see what you mean."

Carolyn and I sat sideways on our machines to consider the situation. That did not alleviate the screaming.

"Maybe we should just leave her," Carolyn suggested. "Isn't the custom to put old people on ice floes when they're of no further use?"

"Well, yeah, that is the custom with old people, but they don't usually send them out on new snow machines. Shall we have lunch before we attempt the rescue?" I was kidding, of course, this was a full scale emergency.

My suggestion was nixed by a new crescendo in the screaming. I started my machine, struggled up onto the snow to plane, and came back to skirt the edge of the dark area. I zipped right on by, made a circle, and came back one machine width closer. That time, my right ski was grabbed by a monster from below that tried to jerk me into the swamp. I wrestled it back and kept going, but the edge of the overflow had been defined.

Carolyn and I walked out onto the last solid track in the snow, and the screaming tapered off. We were thirty feet from the refugee on the island, close enough to shout at more conventional volumes.

"Mr. Stewart, what have you done to me? I'll prefer charges for this assault. I demand that you get me out of here right this minute."

I shouted back. "We can probably rescue you, or at least recover your body in the springtime, but this would be a good time for you to start calling me Stew...maybe even admit that the idiot who drove into the overflow was not me."

"Get me out of here this instant, you sniveling nincompoop. If The Green Army hears about this, they'll have you shot at sunrise." I glanced at Carolyn, and her solemn nod seemed to convey that her mother was not making an empty threat.

"We need some logs or poles to make a bridge. I would not want to cut any of these lovely spruce trees on the bank, so I'll drive back to the lodge and see if Andy can spare some lumber."

"Screw the damn trees; just get me out of here! I'm being grossly inconvenienced. My feet are wet, and if they freeze, I'll hold you personally responsible."

"Well, all right, I'll despoil the forest, if you insist. After all, they are your trees, but cutting them down in their prime pains me deeply."

I left Carolyn to suffer her mother's abuse and walked back to Andy's machine. A good stand of spruce on the right bank ranged from Christmas trees to lodge poles. I used the hatchet, and started despoiling nature. I was hacking and slashing frantically, because this really was an emergency. With wet feet, she would very soon be in serious trouble, in spite of the way she was stomping on her snow machine seat.

I whacked down six trees of the twenty-foot variety, cut them into ten-foot lengths, but left the branches on, and used the machine and the rope to drag them back to our staging area. Mother had wound down, was now sitting on top the seat, and Carolyn did look genuinely worried. We slid and tossed my poles out onto the snow, trying to make a solid mat, and I walked out on the first few to toss more poles and branches.

A light, brighter than the snow, flickered from the tree line across the river. It could have been a reflection from a discarded Coke can, but then it flashed again. It was the reflector, not me, that was moving. I didn't stare, but I pondered. The reflection was probably from the visor on a helmet, and that explained the strange echo I'd heard when we shut off our machines. There was nothing wrong with that, maybe a moose hunter was waiting for us to go away, but most hunters would have come around and offered to help. This one was just watching us, and from the trees, out of sight. I didn't like that at all.

Our bridge sagged and threatened, but I made it back to the solid snow with still-dry feet, and raced back to continue despoiling. The bridge building was a three-prong affair. It didn't displace quite enough water to float, and didn't disperse weight over enough area to stay up on the snowshoe principle, but it did some of each, and most important, it broke up the insulation and let water contact the air where it froze the whole mess together.

It was an hour later when I reached over the windshield to grab the lady's hand and the two of us scampered back across our bridge. I checked her feet, wet to the knees, with a skim of ice frozen over her boots.

"Get on," I commanded. She sat behind me on the Cat. I drove up onto the edge of the now-barren bank. Carolyn followed. I spread Andy's tarp on the ground, gathered an armload of dry branches that had broken off the bottom of the trees, and built a bonfire next to the tarp.

"Get her boots off, dry her socks, rub her feet until they turn pink, and for heaven's sake, do not let any of her clothes catch fire." Carolyn took over the rehabilitation of mother. My job was the machine, still poking a little crescent of transparent windshield above the snow.

I drove a decent interval up the bank, in case disrobing were required, and cut another load of poles, this time trimming off the branches. I used most of my new poles and branches to shore up the bridge, but arrived at the edge of the abyss with two good stout poles, each ten feet long. I laid one crosswise at the end of our bridge for a fulcrum, got the other one jammed down under the front of the machine and pried.

The fulcrum and the end of my bridge went down; the machine didn't budge. I went back to shore for the rope, used my useless lever pole to bridge the gap, and walked the plank onto the machine seat. A skim of ice was frozen behind the seat. I took off my mitts, beat on the ice with my fist, and when it gave, I grabbed the trailer hitch and attached the rope.

The sun had moved to the west and was starting its ellipse to the north, almost behind the hills, so the trees across the river cast exaggerated shadows onto the ice. The shadows were lacy and indefinite, except for one, solid black, and it moved. It was the shadow of a man, and he was holding a rifle. Surely a moose hunter? I walked back to solid snow, uncoiling rope, and then down the track until I was almost behind the submerged machine.

Several passes with the Cat packed a solid trail. I tied the rope to the hitch, and let the Cat pull. It moved ahead several inches while the rope disappeared under the surface, but then the track spun and dug down. I abandoned a straight pull in favor of several jerks, expecting one of the hitches to detach and go flying, but they didn't, and the Polaris moved backward a foot.

That was good because snow machine skis swivel from a point toward the rear of the ski so the weight of the machine forces the tips up. For going forward, that is ideal. When I dragged the machine backward, the rear of the skis went down, dug into the ice, and the ski tips appeared, sticking straight up in front of the cowling, but their pivoting had also pried the machine up several inches. I untied the rope and rushed to cut more poles.

I was dashing like a madman because by that time my feet were wet above my boots, my arms wet to the elbows, and with the machine momentarily loose, I didn't want it freezing down again. I shoved poles under the skis, and that time when I pried, the machine budged upward. More poles, more tamping, more prying. I got the rope off the rear hitch and tied it through the handholds on the front of the skis. The rope was wet, and parts of it frozen as stiff as a rod. I whipped those back and forth to break up the ice, strung the line back to shore and shouted for Carolyn. She came bumping down the bank on her Elan. I rigged a bridle so both machines could pull.

Rubber belts screamed, tracks spun, snow flew, smoke billowed, but we were moving. We kept sliding back, charging ahead again, and finally the Polaris was on top of our bridge and creeping forward. It didn't stay up, it wallowed and dove, but we kept pulling and it kept moving.

When the machine beached on the now-packed highway, I untied the rope from our hitches and thought to ask. "How is la mère?"

"Warm, dry, and complaining that your plan is to starve us to death." I dug the lunch out of Andy's basket and handed it to Carolyn. I ran back to the Polaris, tipped it on its side, shook and banged it, and kicked the track, knocking off ice and shaking off any water that hadn't already frozen. Water had not breached the gas tank. I pulled the starter rope. The rope is attached to the engine with a clutch and pawl mechanism so it disconnects when the engine starts, but the pawl wasn't connecting, and the rope didn't retract. I banged the side of that housing a few times. The rope reluctantly pulled back in. It pulled out and back several times, still not connecting to the engine, so I banged the housing a few more times. The pawl caught, the rope stretched, but nothing turned.

I kicked the hood to break off ice, swung it open and

administered several sharp if soggy kicks to the engine. I pulled the rope again, letting the nylon stretch and my back throb. Very slowly, the rope began to inch longer. I kept pulling the rope, but reached to turn the key and let the electric starter help. The rope moved; the engine turned. Suddenly the rope gave way and I almost fell over backward, but the engine came sputtering back to life.

I slammed the hood shut, stood beside the machine and pushed while I revved the engine. The drive belt screamed and smoked; I shook the machine and shoved. The track moved an inch, then another. Ice that was caked on the track and sprockets cracked like the sound of a hammer hitting steel, and spewed out behind. The track dug in, and the machine left me lying on my back in the snow, but, I was lying there very, very happily.

I scrambled and chased down the machine that was idling steadily away from me, drove it up to park nose to nose with the Elan, and ran back down to retrieve Andy's machine. I parked the Cat right behind the Polaris, like wagons circling before an Indian attack.

The sun had dipped below the bluffs across the river, and the temperature was dropping like the Times Square ball on New Year's Eve.

Chapter 8

A little warmth, a little light, of love's bestowing
—and so, good night.
Trilby—Du Maurier

I was surprised, and more than a little relieved, to see Madam sitting in a sleeping bag that was pulled up to her belligerent chin. Carolyn was kneeling on the tarp, feeding branches into the bonfire.

"Hey, you brought sleeping bags with you."

Carolyn answered; Mama wasn't speaking to me. "Yeah, the guidebook said that in the Arctic, you should never leave home without them."

"Good, so you each have one?"

"We did, but Mother's was soaked, and now it's a solid block of ice. Those little duffel bags are supposed to be waterproof, but Mother's held the water in."

"Gee, that's too bad. You and I each have sleeping bags, but your poor mother is out in the cold."

"Don't talk nonsense, young man. You will immediately produce your sleeping bag, and if it is suitably sanitary, present it to Carolyn. I do not appreciate your attempts at levity when we are all about to die of exposure."

"Right." The final item in the basket was the sleeping bag Andy kept there. I sniffed it, gave a so-so hand wobble and tossed it to Carolyn. I rummaged deeper, but the box was empty. "Darn, there is supposed to be a trumpet in here. At times like this, it is customary to play a few choruses of 'Nearer My God to Thee'. In the meantime, please scoot your august ass off the tarp."

That remark earned me a glare that singed my eyebrows, but madam managed to stand and did a bunny-hop, bag and all, to sit on the Polaris seat. The rope was a wad of wire by that time, but I beat it against a tree until it shed most of its ice cover. The fire was crackling between two trees that were fifteen feet apart. I stood on my soggy and rapidly freezing toes to tie the rope as high as I could reach in one tree, then stretched it past the fire and tied it to the other.

Carolyn saw what was coming. She stashed the sleeping bag on the Elan seat, and grabbed a corner of the tarp. We pulled it over my rope, and down toward the machines. When there were three feet of tarp left on the ground at the back, I tied our two corners to the machines. Madam debated whether or not to move, but since I didn't stop pulling tarp, she slid down to sit on the running board. I caught the tarp at the center of the back, pulled it toward a tree and tied it there, letting the two ends flap down for a teepee effect.

Working fast helped, mostly to keep up the circulation,

but my feet were gradually checking out. I used the shovel to scrape some snow from inside the back of our new tent, and used the snow to weigh down the flaps, then ran back outside and whacked off spruce boughs until I had enough to make a double bed. Those spread at the back of the tent and I dashed back out for firewood. It was on my second armload that I realized it was now too dark to see, even branches that were silhouetted against the snow. By the end of May, there would be no dark nights at sixty-seven degrees north latitude. Even at the first of May, if we'd had an unobstructed view to the north, there would have been sunset colors in the sky all night, but our northern exposure was the four-thousand-foot curtain of the Endicott Mountains. The tarp was glowing a cheerful orange from the fire, and it actually looked warm. I stumped in on my now missing feet.

Carolyn had spread the second bag on the spruce boughs, but was hovering by the fire, keeping it contained with a stick, and feeding on branches. I plunked down on the end of her bag and ripped off my shoepacks. I banged the canvas on the ground a few times to break up the ice and peeled the felt inner liners out. I tried wringing them, but the half-inch-thick felt held the moisture. Wool socks hadn't completely frozen. They wrung much better, about a cup each, and finally the cotton socks that were sticking to my skin came off. Those wrung too, and I rubbed my feet like a Boy Scout trying to start a fire by friction.

It took a few minutes for the feeling to come back; then I wished it hadn't. There is no way to describe the pain when frostbitten feet begin to thaw. A normal reaction would have been screaming, but with Carolyn there, I had to maintain a stoic image. I screamed on the inside only, and kept rubbing.

I hadn't realized how frantically I was working until the pain began to subside and I looked up to find both women staring at me. I gave the feet a couple of more symbolic pats, and stood up barefoot on the sleeping bag to unzip and remove my snow machine suit.

I worked the suit over the rope, letting the arms and legs hang down toward the fire, put my parka back on, grabbed the shovel, and sat down again. First I laid the cotton socks flat on the shovel blade and held them over the fire to toast, like hot dogs.

When I took the suit off, Alex's pistol that was stuck in my belt was exposed, and Mrs. Whidbey was staring at it.

"Mr. Stewart, I cannot approve of guns under any circumstances. You will immediately toss that hateful object out into the snow. I will not cohabit with it."

My cotton socks had stopped steaming. I pulled them back from the fire and slipped them on. They were almost hot enough to burn me, and they felt wonderful. I spread the wool socks on the shovel and extended them. Carolyn slipped a couple more branches under them and raked an errant coal back into the fire.

"Gee, Mrs. Whidbey, it's either you or the pistol, huh? Rarely has my young life been faced with such a difficult choice." I was still holding the deep furrows in my brow, pretending to consider, and Carolyn was almost choking, trying to suppress giggles. Fortunately it was during that interlude that the first wolf belted out his mournful howl from across the river. The howl must have startled a bear or moose, because the crashing through the brush behind the tent sounded like a bulldozer.

I was happy to hear those four-legged wolves across the

river, because that meant that the two-legged watcher was gone. He hadn't threatened us in any way, but he had stood watching entirely too long and must have driven his machine away when he could hear me making noise.

I wasn't worried about the wolves because with good luck and a few tools, humans have arrived near the top of the food chain. With our faculties about us, and with some version of Alex's pistol in our belts, we have very little to fear from any animals except other humans. Other humans are usually benign and helpful. However, when you're twenty miles from the nearest village, you are on your own. If the situation gets out of hand, one does not call the police. Your life may depend on your pistol. I didn't share those thoughts.

"You know, Madam, if you would scoot a little closer to the tent flap, and maybe hold your hand out for bait, I could shoot a few wolves. Then we could toss the gun away, and I'd have a nice warm pile of wolf hides to cuddle in tonight. No. On second thought, those are probably gray timber wolves. They are an endangered species, so I shan't shoot them. I'll toss the gun away, and we'll die happily, knowing that our passing will be an addition to nature's bounty, and a boon to God's furry little woodland creatures."

I pulled the shovel handle back and turned the wool socks. They had stopped steaming, and were starting to smoke, but were still damp on the other side. I extended them again, but held the shovel a little higher. Conversation had tapered off, so possibly mother had forgotten the gun.

She had, and she mentioned what was distracting her. "What provisions have you made for our sanitary requirements, Mr. Stewart?"

"No problem at all, madam. Right behind this tent are

several million acres where privacy is ensured. Nary a Tom shall peep, from here to the North Pole. Please note that it was God, not I, who designed the female anatomy."

"I'll just bet you're an expert on that," she growled. Carolyn blushed. I pulled the shovel back; my socks were toasty and I put them on. Pure heaven. "Would you like to borrow the shovel, so that no raw effluent will mar the wilderness?" She didn't seem to think that was funny.

"There's a roll of toilet paper in my duffel bag, Mama, just like the guidebook recommended." Carolyn opened the bag that was strapped to the seat of the Elan and pulled out a fresh, still-wrapped-from-the-store roll of Scott tissue. The great lady grabbed the roll and stood. For a moment I thought she was going to do her bunny-hop, bag and all, but she let the bag drop. "What sort of animal was lurking behind the tent when the wolf howled?"

That question strained my self-control. Should I tell her it was a grizzly bear, a saber-toothed tiger, or a moose, which was almost surely the case? Once again, my chivalry saved the day.

"I believe that was a snowshoe hare, madam. They are extremely shy, so she's miles away by now." I made the hare female, to protect madam's modesty. Madam stomped out of the tent, tissue in hand, but not the shovel. I set the felt boots on the shovel blade and went back to toasting. Carolyn came to sit beside me on the bag, another first, and this one was finally getting somewhere. She dug into her pocket and produced half of one of the sandwiches Fanny had packed.

"I saved this for you. Mama said real men don't require food, but I thought..."

I grabbed the sandwich, ripped off the plastic wrap and

wolfed it down. The sandwich was a little squashed from hiding in Carolyn's pocket. Egg salad had oozed out onto the Saran Wrap, and I licked that clean. We heard a rustle and a mild oath from behind the tent. Carolyn leapt up, grabbed the incriminating plastic wrap and tossed it into the fire. I put the felt boots back to toasting, and mother crawled in, red faced, and furious, but maybe for a change her anger was at God, instead of me. She stepped into her bag again and pulled it up, then did two hops and fell over onto the spruce-bough mattress. She stayed there.

"Will you come outside with me, Stew?" Carolyn asked.

"Sorry, but I wouldn't dare. Your mother would much rather you were eaten by wolves than accompanied on a personal errand by me. Were I to step outside with you, she'd run all the way back to Bettles and have me arrested for perversion. You go ahead, and if that mountain lion comes back, scream, but be sure you're decently covered when I come out to shoot him."

Carolyn looked to see if I was kidding, wrinkled her pixie nose at me, picked up the roll of tissue, and disappeared into the darkness. One minute later, the wolves set up a chorus of howls. Two minutes later, Carolyn was back, still tugging zippers. She crawled into her bag. I was sitting on the end of it, so she rested her feet, shoepacks and all, of course, inside the bag, on my thigh. Neither of us mentioned the contact. I pulled my felt boots back and slipped them on. My snowsuit was still hanging over the rope but no longer steaming. I stood to work it down, then took off my parka, put on the suit, and slipped the parka on again. The suit had the full-bodied aroma of smoked salmon, the smoke, not the salmon, but it was warm and dry.

"How will you sleep, Stewart?" Carolyn was already sounding drowsy, her voice soft and furry.

"Oh, don't worry about me. Real men never sleep, and I must keep the fire going. Were the fire to die down, the wolves would be on us in a second, so I shall spend the night in constant vigilance." That heroic speech was met by a gentle snore from Carolyn, and then a couple of derisive, but, I think, sleeping snorts from Madam.

I did tend the fire now and then. As arctic survival goes, we were pretty comfortable, but I expect the outside temperature was well below zero, and our little tent was mostly open above the machines. Each time I had a good blaze going, I leaned back against the back of the tent, burrowed my feet under Carolyn's bag, and napped until Jack Frost nipped my nose and woke me.

Chapter 9

It's not the gold, so much as just finding the gold.
Spell of the Yukon—Robert Service

"Aw, Mama, let's go on. It's just a few more miles, and it's such a beautiful morning."

"Nonsense, Carolyn. Mr. Stewart has seized every opportunity to try to rid himself of us permanently. It is obvious to me that his business on this river is nefarious, if not actually larcenous. It is imperative that I return to Bettles immediately and chronicle his treachery in my logbook."

"Aw, Mama..."

"Hush, child. Remember he is carrying a gun, and may have the intention of... heaven knows what. It is well past time for my morning coffee, and as you notice, Mr. Stewart is not providing that. He's torturing us with the rigors of arctic survival."

I was sitting on the Cat, waiting for the outcome of the argument. The tarp was folded, bags rolled, rope beaten into submission and stored. On the right, I could see the cliffs where the canyon narrowed. The mine was two minutes upriver from that spot by air, maybe ten minutes by snow machine. On the other hand, with Mrs. Whidbey in tow, it might take the rest of our lives. Much as I wanted Carolyn to stay with me, I was also thinking that I had every intention of despoiling some nature, and these particular witnesses, I did not need.

Mother won the argument with sheer force of personality. She could have repulsed an attack by the marines as easily. I drifted down the bank and turned left toward Bettles. The ladies stayed right behind me, Mrs. Whidbey never varying from my tracks by so much as an inch, and in an hour we pulled up in front of the Bettles Lodge.

We left the machines by the door and marched up the steps. Breakfast was over, but K.J., Andy, and Stella were still drinking coffee at the table. Stella ripped her feet off the table and sat up. I peeled off parka and snowsuit as I ran, leaving them on the floor. I headed straight to the table, but Madam and Carolyn disappeared up the stairs.

Fanny came from the kitchen with a steaming cup. I grabbed it, and then her hand. I was nibbling her arm, headed for her elbow, ready to eat anything.

"Hungry, Stewie?"

"If I'd had a team of dogs, I'd have eaten one. I've had exactly one half of a sandwich in twenty-four hours." Fanny pulled loose and headed for the kitchen, I buried my nose in the coffee.

"Why do I perceive that you did not find the gold?" K.J. asked.

"Did you keep that little girl out all night in order to despoil her, Stew?" That was Stella.

"Is my Cat still in one piece?" Andy wanted to know.

Fanny came back with a plate of biscuits, buttered, and smothered in brown gravy with bits of floating corned beef. I answered all further questions with my mouth stuffed full.

"In the first place, that woman is a one-person disaster area. We probably qualify for federal disaster relief funds. Yes, the machines are all in one piece, no thanks to her, and no, we turned back three miles downriver from the mine."

I gulped coffee and refilled my mouth. "I did not spend the night despoiling anything but a pack of wolves. Herodias and Salome will come down in a moment, demanding my head on a platter, and I didn't even get the dance of the seven veils. Meantime, she's upstairs, writing in her journal that I tried to kill her at every turn, and The Green Army is on the way here with machine guns to execute us all."

"Well, that's a relief." Stella reached for the coffeepot and refilled her cup. "When you didn't come back last night, I was afraid something bad had happened."

The two women who marched sedately down the stairs bore no resemblance to my traveling companions, except for the dour expression on the leader.

"Good morning, Mrs. Anderson, Mr. Anderson, Mr. Johnson." Madam did not notice that I was sitting there. Andy jumped to pull chairs for the ladies.

"Fanny, a cup of coffee would be most welcome. We have been severely deprived during our arctic survival ordeal." She gave me her beneath-contempt dismissive sniff. She was dressed in an L.L. Bean contraption, suitable for safari. Carolyn rivaled springtime in a yellow pinafore over ruffled white blouse. Neither showed permanent scars from their harrowing ordeal.

Fanny served the coffee and set plates of the biscuits and gravy. Mrs. Whidbey did not wolf them down, but she did break precedent and chew each bite only twenty times. Carolyn dug in like a farm girl during threshing season. As usual, all conversation ceased until Madam pushed away her plate. She shoved back her chair and stood without waiting for Andy. He was left halfway out of his chair, arm extended toward emptiness.

"Come along, Carolyn. I have absolutely volumes to write in my journal." She gave me the dismissive sniff again, and strode away to implement my execution. The door upstairs slammed.

"You'll be going back for the gold, of course?" K.J. grimaced and wriggled his legs to remind me that his feet were still paining him.

Fanny topped off my cup and plunked down in my lap again. "Oh, Stewie, I'm so proud of you. You are so strong and so brave. Bring back buckets of gold so we can live happily ever after." She was snuggling, a bit more provocatively than I found comfortable in company.

"Run fix him a lunch, Fanny. I'll gas up the machine." Andy detoured around my suit and parka that were still crumpled on the floor and strode out the front door. We heard the Cat start and roar away.

"Do you still have the map?" K.J. asked. I nodded.

It did seem to be a forgone conclusion, at least by everyone but me, that I was going back. Fanny heightened the impression by holding my lunch under her arm while she picked up my snowsuit, shook it out, and handed it to me. I pulled it on and zipped while she picked up my parka. I pulled on the parka. Fanny stood on tiptoes to buss my cheek and handed me the lunch. Outside, the growl of the Cat, returning from the gas pumps, stopped in front of the door. Fanny pulled me around toward the exit and shoved.

Well, as Carolyn had observed earlier, it was another glorious morning. I racked the Cat wide open and hit the snow berm at our former spot. I was trying to best Carolyn's jump, but hit the snow ten feet short, and my skis weren't quite straight when I landed, so I did a dangerous dido, but recovered and raced away to seek my fortune.

I was breaking only one hard-and-fast rule of the Arctic: "You must never, ever, under any circumstances, venture into the wild with just one machine." Other than that, I was cruising.

Our previously packed trail was meant for speed, and in forty-five minutes I was passing the scene of our Waterloo. I did have a touch of nostalgia, remembering the way Carolyn had tossed her golden hair in the sunshine while she suggested that we leave her mother on the ice floe. I sailed on by, followed a couple of wide bends in the river, and dived into the canyon.

I was in deep shadow, a blue and lifeless void with ancient rock walls towering above me. Gollum caves came to mind, but I booted them back to Tolkien. Boulders the size of cars had rolled down to line the riverbanks, but I dismissed them as part of the geologic past, some upheaval of the primordial earth before time began.

It was partly the sun's approaching its zenith, partly the way that the river turned, but I spotted the cut bank ahead glowing a light brown in sunshine. For a moment it appeared that the entire bank was gold. I took that as an omen, perhaps the first good omen I'd ever noticed. I ran the machine back and forth a few times to pack down snow, but actually there wasn't much in the canyon, maybe one foot and some drifts instead of the three feet that blanketed the open country.

I parked the machine near where I judged the box might be buried, and walked to the cut bank to pace the distance. Johnson was two inches taller than me, so I counted off an extra pace and a half to compensate. The indicated distance was a few feet short of the spot where I had parked the machine, and the snow between the river and the cliff was fairly shallow at that point. Below the machine stood a massive drift that reached a long way up the cliff, but, another omen, I paced in from the river twenty and a half paces in less than a foot of snow.

There should have been a boulder there. There wasn't. I walked back to the edge of the ice. The river had dropped since freeze-up, so there was a sheet of ice lying on gravel with no water under it, but then I figured that Johnson's measurement was in the fall. The water would have been low, probably about where the ice started. I turned back toward the cliff.

At that point the canyon was running east and west and the sun was still winging its way down from the north, so the shadow of the north bank slashed across the south bank I was facing. The snowdrift just downstream from the machine was impressive, at least forty feet tall, and reflecting the sunshine above the shadow. It was dumb luck that had put the monstrous drift downstream from Johnson's measurements. I was looking up at the drift when a moving shadow flickered across it. Probably a moose on the cliff behind me, and my imagination made it into a man with a rifle.

From the edge of the cut bank, one hundred one and a half paces brought me to the point where I had turned. I faced the bank and counted twenty paces again. No mistake and no boulder.

I had been carrying the shovel, and I whacked the ground in frustration. The shovel hit wood, not rock. Under the snow was more wood. I dropped to my knees and scraped the snow away with my mitts. What I uncovered was not the top of a box, but the bottom of a box. It had been sheered off, an inch above the bottom, and nestled in the corner of the remains were five of the biggest, most beautiful nuggets I had ever seen. I jammed those into my pocket. The weight pulled me off kilter, and the feeling was glorious.

The scenario was obvious. Ice had come down river at breakup, removed the boulder, and sheared the top off the box. That meant Johnson's nuggets were scattered down the bank. I grabbed up the shovel and started throwing snow, making a path, then turning the shovel on edge to scrape the rocks clean. I had almost reached the big drift below the machine when I uncovered another nugget; gleaming, glistening, sparkling, beckoning. I pocketed it, and attacked the snowdrift.

I got carried away with the thought of what was under that drift. I was so distracted that I paid no attention when a few snowballs rolled down the drift from above. The drift was four stories tall and almost vertical, but that didn't register. I was shoveling under the drift and sweating, almost tasting the gold. The whisper when the drift moved was loud enough to get my attention. The entire snowdrift slumped and settled. By the time the whisper became a roar, I had forgotten gold and was running toward the center of the river, dragging the shovel, leaping tall drifts in a single bound. I didn't look back.

Snowballs were passing me on both sides, then the snow I was running on was moving along with me, like running in the edge of the surf. Something grabbed the shovel and jerked it out of my hand. I gave a final, mighty leap, tripped on a berm, and rolled to face my fate. I opened my eyes and saw–sunshine. The roar I was still hearing was blood pounding in my ears. Everything had stopped. I stood up and brushed off snow.

The shovel was twenty feet behind me, buried almost to the tip of the handle. The snowdrift that had reached up the cliff was now spread across the river. I heaved on the shovel handle, working it back and forth, and finally pulled it loose. The snow pile reached from the middle of the river to the cliff, getting deeper as it went, and was packed almost as hard as concrete.

Chapter 10

The snow shall be their winding sheet.
Hohenlinden—Thomas Campbell

The place where the machine had been parked was under a gentle slope of hard-packed snow maybe as much as eight feet deep. The shovel handle did go down into the snow when I shoved hard and worked it around. It eventually went all the way down to the blade, and hit nothing but snow underneath. I climbed down off the edge of the slide and tried to measure the depth with the shovel handle. Snow over the spot where I'd left the machine looked about seven feet deep.

The shovel handle is only five feet long, but if it came down on top of the cowling or the seat, it should hit them. I climbed back up and continued probing. In an hour, the top of the drift looked like a dartboard. I was exhausted, hungry, thirsty, and maybe getting just a bit frantic. I sat down on the snow, scooped up a handful and let it melt in my mouth while I tried to think.

Thinking never seems to occur to me until all else has failed, and once in a great while, thinking does pay off. I tottered back to my feet and started probing down the hill in the direction the slide might have pushed the machine. Holes two feet apart, in a line down the hill, finally paid off. The sixth hole hit something, five feet down. It seemed to bounce, like maybe the fiberglass cowling. A foot to the right and again, something was down there. I forgot about exhaustion and started shoveling snow.

If it had been colder, the snow might have been granular, but that slide was like shoveling dirt. The top of the slide had been in sunshine so that was part of the problem, maybe even the reason that the slide came down. The consistency was perfect for packing, and the slide had packed it, like making a snowball.

I'd taken my parka off a while before. The exertion had me sweating, and it was reminding me of driving steam points for F.E. Company, only this time the reward wasn't three dollars an hour. It was a ride home I hoped to earn, and the alternative, walking twenty miles back to Bettles, kept me shoveling with a will.

Hard snow or not, I didn't dare go down too steeply because a cave-in would be fatal. I was picturing the way the machine would be sitting, and digging a grave-sized hole with a reasonable slant to the sides. It was getting colder. I was digging steadily, but no longer frantically, and had stopped sweating. I climbed out of my hole, put my parka back on but left it unzipped, and went back to digging.

When I came to the cowling, the windshield seemed to have broken off, but then I realized the machine had rolled onto its side. I widened my hole around the machine, then noticed that the sides were getting too steep and climbed out to widen the top again. The safest way seemed to be going down in tiers, like the pictures I've seen of archeological digs. I borrowed the archeological technique for clearing the machine, too. It would not be good to punch a shovel through the fiberglass or the seat, so I brushed the snow away with my hands, and scooped it up at a safe distance. The only hard part was digging the snow out of the track and the bogey wheels, but whacking those with a shovel wouldn't hurt them. I was at the bottom of the hole again, actually standing on rocks beside the machine, when I noticed it was too dark to make out details. The sky was dark, too. My Casio said 10:00 p.m.

I had sat on the side of the seat to contemplate my sad fate and catch my breath, when I realized I was sitting next to the lunch Fanny had packed. I pried the box open. Fanny's lunch rolled out, and so did the sleeping bag. By the time I had scarfed down two corned beef sandwiches and blessed Fanny on her way to beatification for including a can of beer in the sack, it hit me that digging up the machine was just the first step. I couldn't lift it six feet straight up. I was going to have to dig a ramp.

That thought, and the total darkness, had me unrolling the sleeping bag and crawling in. I leaned against the side of my hole with most of my weight on the side of the seat, and was pretty comfortable. The last of the beer was a little slushy, not quite enough alcohol to prevent freezing, but it went down with a gurgle and I followed it with the contented belch that is only possible in utter solitude. Best of all, there was a whiff of Carolyn about the bag, and I was content to snuggle into that.

It may have been hours or minutes later when I woke up because my face was freezing. It felt like a swarm of gnats, buzzing and biting, but it wasn't; it was tiny snowflakes swirling around and stinging me. There was a vibrancy, a sound in the air that hadn't been there before. My first thought was a band of bagpipers, but then wailing banshees came to mind. I've never heard a banshee wail, but the moaning and screeching the wind was making might be what they sound like.

The Big Dipper's cup had been overhead when the sky first darkened, but it was gone, replaced by total darkness, and it didn't matter because I couldn't keep my eyes open in the swirling snow. The tarp was folded in the bottom of the box. I wedged the shovel handle between the bogie wheels and the track and stood it up to make a tent pole, then wrestled the tarp over the shovel handle and let it hang down to cover me and the machine. It rippled when the wind let out a particularly blood-curdling scream, but the swirling snow was on the outside.

Some say that solitary confinement is cruel and unusual punishment, and I could see their point. Also, the symbolism, buried in a hole three feet wide, six feet long, and six feet deep was poignant. If I were going to die there, I was already appropriately interred. Then I wondered if perhaps I was already dead. How different could it be? Total darkness, no room to move around, only the mind's eye functioning, and that threatening to get out of control.

I remembered the story by Ambrose Bierce about the

Occurrence at Owl Creek Bridge. A guy is about to be hanged, but when they shove him off the bridge the rope breaks. He falls into the river, wrestles his bonds loose, and swims under water, dodging bullets. He climbs out, and runs frantically through the woods. Just as he has made good his escape, the rope around his neck snaps taut, and he is dead.

Maybe something like that had happened to me. Maybe I had been caught and buried by the snow slide and was suffocating, or already dead, and my mind hadn't accepted it yet. Was the entire episode of digging for the machine a hallucination? Did anything that had happened prove I was alive? I wriggled around in my grave, and it was less confining than I thought a grave should be, but not by much.

Total darkness is frightening in itself. Close your eyes, open your eyes, no difference. Is that what it's like to be blind? Had I gone blind? Was the Big Dipper still up there? I pulled my arm out of the sleeping bag and felt the canvas and the shovel handle. They were vibrating, so my tent, at least, was real. If it never got light again, perhaps I could crawl and feel my way back to Bettles.

If I crawled into overflow and died along the way, would anyone care? I was providing a diversion for Carolyn, an interesting excuse to bedevil her mother for a few days. Fanny knew better than to count on anything beyond tomorrow, and like as not, if it took a week to crawl home, she'd introduce me to her new husband when I got there.

If another of Johnson's partners died, they might change his nickname. The K in K.J. might stand for Killer instead of Klondike. He'd probably like that. If they found the body with the six nuggets still in the pocket, Andy would be paid for K.J.'s grubstake, and Andy would be pleased. I was sorry that if Alex got his pistol back, it would be rusted.

Wind jerked a corner of my tent up and slapped me in the face with it. I wrestled it down and sat on it. That shouldn't happen to dead people. Still, my world was reduced to what was in my mind, and perhaps that is what death is, too. I thought about Descartes' reasoning: "I think, therefore I am," but that is only valid if thinking stops when we die, and how do we know that? Maybe the spark of consciousness is the spirit.

I read somewhere that victims of the guillotine rolled their eyes, looking around, after their heads were cut off, so maybe they were thinking the blade had missed. Maybe my mind was going to dim, perhaps gutter, like a candle going out. Would I recognize oblivion, if it happened? Would I be terrified if I felt consciousness slipping?

I pulled the sleeping bag flap over my head, it was pitch black anyhow, and breathed inside the bag. I wasn't cold, but I didn't want a chill to creep up on me gradually. I wanted to be toasty warm,the antithesis of death. I was getting sleepy, but it was the honest result of a hard day's work, not the insidious torpor of freezing.

I know people steeped in arctic lore would be thinking I was making several mistakes. I wasn't. If I got cold and lethargic, and then went to sleep, I would not wake up, but if I went to sleep warm, the transition to cold would get uncomfortable and would awaken Rip Van Winkle.

I've read advice in so-called arctic survival manuals that tells you never to breath inside your sleeping bag. I figure advice like that is written by well-meaning people who have thought about the situation, but have never slept out in the cold. My mind was skipping around through arctic lore but it was keeping me awake and I decided that was good. I'm always amazed by one very famous and well-documented misconception that wearing a beard will freeze your face. What the early explorers who started that rumor probably saw was men with frost and ice in their beards. What they didn't see was the half-inch of warm, dead air space inside the beard between the skin and the ice. Once the beard has a good layer of frost or ice on the outside, it stops the wind and you're good to go.

Even Billy Mitchell states the no-beard mantra as fact in his memoirs, and that is shocking. Billy should have known better, but there's his clean-shaven statement published for all to read. Moisture from your breath freezes the outside of your beard into a windproof shield and you keep a dead air space between your skin and the ice. Billy and his men wore beards in summer to ward off mosquitoes and shaved clean when the frost came.

I've tried to fathom the logic in the advice about not breathing into your bag, and the most charitable explanation I can think of is that the authors are worried about moisture in your breath. True, you don't want your bag getting wet, but there is a matter of degree. If you're breathing in and out inside the bag, it will take a week to breathe out a cup of water. It is also true that you breathe out carbon dioxide so if your bag were hermetically sealed, you might gas yourself. It isn't. In the meantime, your breath is around 90 degrees Fahrenheit, the equivalent of a small furnace, and if you're re-breathing the inside air instead of warming up outside air to body temperature with every breath you save a lot of energy.

Mistakes or no, I did wake up. I threw the sleeping bag flap back, and the canvas tent was visible. When the canvas slid off the shovel handle, six inches of loose snow cascaded over me. That woke me up. I pulled Mrs. Whidbey's trick of holding the bag up to my chin while I stood on the side of the machine to look out of my hole. When my head came up, my parka hood snapped back, and I nearly lost my cap.

The wind must have been blowing thirty miles an hour, and the scene on top was almost as white as the sides of the hole. I hunkered back down and thought about going to sleep forever. Then I thought about hot coffee and blueberry waffles, Carolyn's smile, and Fanny's cuddling. I dropped the bag and grabbed the shovel.

I didn't need to dig all the way down, just a ramp that wasn't too steep for the machine to climb. As long as I kept my head down in the hole, the wind didn't hurt too much. Snow was swirling around so I couldn't open my eyes all the way. I had to squint, but there was nothing to see, anyway.

I dug to the cadence of Robert Service's poem, The Cremation of Sam McGee. "If our eyes we'd close, then the lashes froze till we scarce could see. It wasn't much fun, but the only one to whimper was me." Time had no meaning, except that it separated me from a cup of hot coffee. I dug and threw snow. Snow swirled in, but I was winning. It took a couple of hours, but eventually a ramp burrowed up out of the pit. Close to the top, the wind was almost keeping up with me, drifting it over as fast as I dug.

I hunkered back down in the hole, dug another two feet all the way around the machine, and wrestled it upright. The starter rope was stiff, but it pulled, and the engine turned over. I pulled the choke and the rope again, pumped the throttle, jerked the rope, grunted, sweated, and heaved on the rope again. The first time the engine fired, it sounded like a cannon in the tight quarters and I feared for the sides of my refuge, but then realized it was carbon monoxide that was going to kill me. I jumped onto the machine, mashed the throttle, shot up the ramp, and out into space.

It was tempting to just head for home, but Bettles was too far away to go without the bag and the shovel; my life might depend on them again. I crawled back into the burrow, dragged them out, and struggled back to the machine. It was invisible in the swirling snow, but I could hear it idling. The bag stood straight out like a flag in the wind. I let it fly and rolled from the bottom until it was small enough to jam into the box. The canvas was too much. I held one edge and tried to fold, but it jerked me right off my feet and disappeared. I sat on the shovel, revved the engine, and then wondered which way to go; the whole world was white.

I figured, logically, that I was on the upstream side of the snow slide, and the wind had me crouched down behind the windshield. Turning the machine around put the wind at my back. Right or wrong, that was better. I eased forward and ran into the snow slide; that was good. Keeping the right ski up on the slide and the left ski down on the ice led me around the pile until the wind was behind me again. The machine chugged slowly ahead. As long as the track was smooth, it must be the river.

I know that judging directions by the wind has killed many a tenderfoot because wind swirls around, particularly near mountaintops. You can walk all day with the wind at your back, or front, and be making circles. I figured that would not be a problem in the canyon. The machine was running just above an idle, and when it bumped a bank, I adjusted and kept going. The inside of the windshield was caked two inches thick, but it didn't matter; there was nothing to see. The problem was to keep from being blown off the machine.

The wind shifted and shrieked from my left. My parka hood whipped across my face and the wolf ruff froze to my upwind cheek. I ripped it loose and let it flap. It must have been that the wind had shifted; I hadn't turned. If that was right, then this was the end of the canyon. I was contemplating that mixed blessing when the machine nosed down and immediately back up. I climbed off and felt around to see what had caused the dive, and it was a snow machine track. It was drifted almost full on the upwind side, but had the unmistakable tread riffles on the downwind side. I turned into the track, tilted at forty-five degrees, and followed it. Time was on hold. The machine was in a bubble, bumping along with no indication of speed, snow ripping past, but home had to be getting closer. Hang on, have faith, keep moving.

I know there's a common misconception that you don't have fog and wind at the same time. I can't speak for anywhere else, and I can understand that if the fog is coming from a river or a bay, wind is going to blow it away. In the Arctic, maybe it's because the entire Arctic Ocean or the Bering Sea is whiffing out fog. Also, fog can rise right up out of the tundra when the temperature drops, but for whatever reason, the wind can blow thirty miles an hour and the fog keeps coming for days.

Well, it hadn't been days, maybe hours. A black streak in the snow loomed ahead, and when it got closer, I realized it was the bridge I'd built to rescue Mrs. W. I gave that a wide berth to the left. Apparently it had stopped snowing because wind had blown the bridge clean, but visibility remained nil. White on white just doesn't show. The hole in the snow where the Cat had dug in when I had pulled the Polaris backward inched past. The machine dropped down again into the original track that came from Bettles. That track was deeper from our comings and goings. It was still drifted in, but I could follow it at a good clip. Two hours later, I parked in front of the lodge and crawled up the steps.

Chapter 11

But bringing money, thou shalt be always my
welcome guest.
George Barnwell—Anonymous

L unch was still in progress. I left a line of clothes from
the front door to the table, mitts, cap, parka, and
snowsuit. The clutch of diners that was gathered at
the near end of the table looked too formal, too intimate.
A chorus of "Hey, Stew," and one, "Stan, you made it."
Mrs. W. didn't notice me, but Carolyn's smile lit the room. I
bypassed them and sat alone at the far end. A beaming Fanny
brought the coffee that I had stayed alive for, and then a dish
of noodles smothered in gravy with mushrooms and chunks
of moose meat in it. Big spears of broccoli around the edge
of the platter were oozing melted butter.

"Beef stroganoff," Fanny whispered. The gravy turned

out to be sour cream, and I plowed into it with the same urgency that had kept me shoveling snow. It was fabulous, and my stomach stopped growling almost immediately. The broccoli had been a frozen package but was from heaven.

"Harumph." That was Mrs. Whidbey. I'd never actually heard anyone say that before. I'd always thought it was a comic strip word denoting stuffy, geriatric, British gentlemen's clubs.

"It was most inconsiderate of you to remain out all night with no word, Mr. Stewart. We might have worried."

I assume she meant that she might have worried if it had been someone else out all night. I couldn't answer, because my mouth was stuffed full and the shock of such atrocious manners might have killed the lady.

Andy and K.J. were about to bust with the question they didn't dare ask, both of them stealing glances at my trail of clothes, looking for a wooden box.

Mrs. Whidbey wrinkled her patrician nose and sniffed like a bird dog picking up scent. "What is that noxious odor? I fear that I have lost my appetite. Come along, Carolyn." She didn't wait for Andy to slide her chair. Apparently lunch was less formal than dinner. I did notice that her plate was scraped clean, so that may have contributed to her loss of appetite. Carolyn gave me a sunny smile that almost contained a wink, and followed the great lady up the stairs.

"Did you find it? Where's the box?" K.J. was looking pale from the strain.

With Mrs. Manners absent, so was the proscription on full-mouth grunts.

"I found where the box had been, but it went downriver in a spring flood."

"The gold was gone?" K.J. was thunderstruck.

"Well, the box went downriver in pieces, and it dribbled gold as it went." I scraped my plate, and Fanny refilled it from the platter she was holding.

"There are six nuggets in the pocket of my snowsuit." Andy bounded to grab the suit, and K.J. was right behind him, not bounding, but hobbling at a good clip. Fanny set the platter down and ran. Stella shoved the swivel chair halfway across the room, getting it out of her way. I was left alone at the table, with the rest of the moose, which was all I cared about at that moment.

Andy found the lumpy pocket and turned it out, letting the gold hit his counter with a series of clunks. He threw the suit behind him, and K.J. caught it. K.J. ran the suit through his hands, feeling for lumps. Maybe he was hoping that a few more nuggets were caught in the fabric. Andy ran around behind the counter, and carefully set his gold scale beside the nuggets. Fanny and Stella were each holding a nugget up toward the light, and even from my end of the room, I could see the reflections.

The nuggets were not smooth, so highlights were winking on and off, like from the facets of a diamond. Possibly because gold is soft, it gets mashed and mauled into irregular shapes, like three-dimensional inkblots, and many a nugget is treasured as a natural work of art, but not by us. It was the weight that interested us.

Andy wiped his hands on his shirt, perhaps so he wouldn't contaminate the process, carefully calibrated the scale, and stacked the nuggets on his tray, ripping the last two away from Fanny and Stella.

A reverent silence descended as each nugget was placed

on the plate and the pointer inched past the ounce marks.

"Seven ounces, 18 pennyweight," Andy announced.

Well, we weren't rich, but we sure weren't skunked, either. I did a quick calculation. Gold is measured in troy ounces, and there are only twelve of those to a pound. Twenty pennyweights equal one troy ounce, so we had very nearly eight troy ounces, or two thirds of a pound of gold.

Andy was paying $350 per ounce, and that was fair. The price of gold fluctuates, like futures in corn or pork bellies. At that moment, the going price was just over $400 per ounce, but the difference was Andy's shipping and handling charge. If he held the gold and got lucky on the market, he might make much more, but it is also possible that the price could drop below $350 and stay there for weeks. Both Andy and K.J. did the figures like lightening, in their heads: $2,712.50.

Andy ducked down behind his counter to fiddle with his floor safe and stood up again with a leather pouch in his hand. He carefully stacked the nuggets into the pouch, letting each one glitter and gleam for a moment before it disappeared. When the last of the pixie dust was concealed, Andy ducked down again. Stella retrieved the swivel chair and pushed it to K.J. who sat. She wheeled him back to the table. Andy was wiping down his gold scale with an oiled cloth. Fanny went to the kitchen and returned with a bowl of ice, five barrel glasses, and a bottle of bourbon.

I was stuffed so full that it was hard to walk, but I made it to the sociable end of the table. Now that I could concentrate on subtleties, I did notice the lingering essence from the last two days' perspiration that had sent Mrs. Whidbey to her room.

Stella and K.J. chunked ice from the bowl into glasses.

Fanny filled my glass with ice. I don't think she was being solicitous; she just didn't want me to dip my hand into the communal bowl. K.J. poured for himself and Stella, and shoved the bottle across to Fanny. She filled my glass and poured two fingers for herself, then did the honors for Andy, pouring his glass half way between her modest sampling and my gluttony.

Andy came from his counter carrying a sheaf of papers. We all raised our glasses, and Stella proposed the toast: "To the beauty of God's handiwork. May we rip the gold right out of its belly." We drank enthusiastically to that.

Andy pulled a pair of reading glasses out of his shirt pocket and perched them on his cherry nose. The Santa image was uncanny. "His eyes how they twinkled, his dimples how merry...."

"Congratulations, K.J., another $403.87 and your last year's bill will be paid." Mouths dropped open all around the table, and K.J. started to sputter, but Andy shoved the ledger out where we all could see it. The last entry in the ledger was $2,000 for a medivac charter. It hadn't occurred to us, or at least not to me, to wonder who had paid for K.J.'s trip to the hospital. It seemed to me that Andy had been downright altruistic, because at that point, he had thought K.J. was dead, and he still paid for the medivac.

It did seem like I, and therefore Alex, was getting shorted. On the other hand, I had only risked my life for the gold, not moiled in the mud for it. I wasn't worried about it, because I had a mental image of nuggets sprinkled like Hansel and Gretel's breadcrumbs, leading all the way back to Bettles, just waiting for the snow to melt.

Fanny picked up my discarded clothes and held them at

arm's length to carry them back toward the laundry room. She came out with a bathrobe, obviously hers, because it was going to end above my knees, and I'd be lucky if it reached around.

She handed me the robe, along with an order: "Hit the shower."

The upstairs facility has a screen-door-type latch, but I didn't bother with it. The protocol is that if the door is closed, someone is inside, and having the facility co-educational was unusual, so the latch seldom mattered. I stripped and climbed into a steaming hot shower. The soap in the tray smelled like Carolyn's hair, so I lathered myself with pleasure. A sudden draft told me the door had opened. I peeked out past the curtain to see Fanny collect my clothes and slip out with them.

Her robe did meet in front, but barely. It was a good thing Madam's door was closed when I passed. It wasn't bedtime for the rest of the world, but it was for me. I stretched out on the bed, and thumbed my nose at the fog and snowflakes that were battering my window.

Chapter 12

"Come, Watson, come! The game is afoot."
The Return of Sherlock Holmes—A. Conan Doyle

Sometime in the night I was almost awakened because my nose was buried in a cloud of soft hair that smelled like the shower soap, and a compact little body was making a warm streak down my front. I laid my arm across the intruder and gathered a handful of charms. They were B-cup, with a familiar pair of pencil-eraser-size nipples, so I hadn't died and gone to heaven, and Mrs. Whidbey hadn't relaxed her vigil. I cuddled the charms, and went back to sleep.

When I woke again, it was because of the rattling window sash. Judging by the snowflakes ripping by, I guessed the wind had escalated to over sixty, and wondered if glass can actually bend without breaking. Fanny was gone, but my clothes were clean and folded on the chair. The enticing aroma of fresh-ground coffee was a clarion wake-up call.

K.J. was already at the table, and Fanny brought coffee the moment I sat down. Her smile was as warm as the charms had been. K.J. had been doodling on a sheet of yellow legal pad, but he shoved the paper and a pen to me.

"Draw that snow slide."

I spent the next several minutes, into my second cup, drawing the site and the slide. I drew it plan-view, profile, and three-quarter, showing where the box had been, the spot where I'd picked up the last nugget, and where the slide was now. I may have exaggerated just a little, because I did figure that my life depended on convincing everyone there was no point in returning to the scene before breakup.

Stella and Andy emerged from their lair, so I moved down to make a place for Stella between me and K.J. That left K.J. sitting on Andy's left, and the two of them bent over my drawing. Fanny brought coffee for Stella and Andy and refilled my cup and K.J.'s. He and Andy were absorbed in my pictures and hardly seemed to notice the coffee.

Stella took a grateful sip, then turned and started firing questions about my night in the snowdrift. She used that female trick of pretending to hang on my every word, so I obliged, doubling the perils, of course. I had her wincing in sympathy, and squeezing my knee when I described the way the wind tore my tent away and buried me under two feet of snow. She gasped when I invented the growls and snarls of the vicious wolf pack that had circled my place of refuge all night. By that time, the drift had grown to fifteen feet deep, and I was thinking about tunneling to get the machine out, probably with a couple of cave-ins, but I was interrupted by a rustle from the stairway.

Andy and I leapt to our feet. K.J. shoved his chair back and struggled to stand, leaning heavily on an over-sized diamond willow cane. That was the first time I noticed that he was not sitting in Andy's swivel-chair-on-wheels. Mrs. Whidbey exchanged the appropriate pleasantries with everyone but me, and allowed Andy to seat her. Carolyn was dressed girl-next-door; frilly pink blouse, flowing tan skirt, and mid-heels that were strapped around her ankles so you had to notice and speculate.

"Please be seated, Mr. Johnson. Your gesture is gallant, but you must be in excruciating pain."

"Madam, with the pleasure of your arrival, all else becomes irrelevant." But he did ease back into his chair.

"Is that a map you have there, Mr. Anderson?"

I was surprised that Andy hadn't hidden my drawing, but maybe he hadn't had time. He covered admirably.

"Yes. Mr. Stewart has reconnoitered the disfiguring landslide that we intend to clean up." He turned the drawing so she could see it without breaking her neck, which was in danger. Fanny poured coffee and went back to the kitchen. Andy indicated my depiction of the snow slide.

"As you can see, the slide is much worse than we had thought. If this mass of debris is allowed to come down the river during the spring flood, thousands of salmon will be killed when they return to spawn. It is imperative that we clean it up right away, so Mr. Stewart, Mr. Johnson, and I will mount an expedition."

My mouth dropped open--that was getting to be a habit. I looked to see if he was serious, and he was. I couldn't believe that madam would swallow the line about debris endangering salmon, but she was lapping it up. Every spring, debris comes down every river, hundreds of thousands of tons of it. The salmon wait until the worst is over, then bust through it and don't even notice.

Then I saw that Andy and K.J. had been underlining the area on the downstream side of the snow slide. The old familiar itch grabbed me. Maybe they were right; maybe there was a line of nuggets sitting on the gravel below the slide.

"Surely you aren't going out in this blizzard, Mr. Anderson?" Mrs. Whidbey arranged her napkin. Fanny was bringing in platters of scrambled eggs and caribou sausages. We started passing and dishing. She brought hot biscuits, and set the plate in front of me, real proof that I was persona grata again.

Andy had filled his plate. "No, we can't leave this morning, because I have to clear the runway, but this storm should blow over by tomorrow morning." Mouths were filling up, and conversation ceased. Naturally I was watching Carolyn's long slender fingers buttering a biscuit, and the dainty, ladylike way she chewed. I wondered why that gorgeous creature obeyed her mother so meekly. Her actions suggested she might be retarded, but she was seeing right through the malarkey we laid on her mother so she was sharp.

I was half finished with my second helping when Madam pushed her plate away and drained her coffee cup. "Then we'll be leaving for the disaster scene in the morning? With mature adults in charge, I'm sure it will be quite safe. I shall immediately repair to my suite and begin preparations. Come along, Carolyn." We were all too stunned to rise.

The moment the upstairs door closed, I turned on K.J.,

mouth full of scrambled eggs and all. "What the hell are you thinking? I told you, we couldn't bust through that snow slide with a bulldozer."

"Quite true, I don't doubt your judgment for a moment, but look here." He was punching my picture with his finger. "The slide is only a hundred, maybe a hundred-fifty feet wide. If the gold went downstream, and scattered like you say, then most of it may well be below the slide."

"Wouldn't it be a lot simpler to just wait until the snow melts, cruise up there in a river boat, and gather the nuggets off the gravel?"

"Maybe, but suppose another ice floe comes down at breakup? It might scrape the nuggets into the river, or bury them twenty feet deep."

K.J. was pushing the right buttons. I pictured us scraping snow away and gathering nuggets in baskets. I grabbed another biscuit. "Are there any homesteaders living up that way?"

"Not likely." Andy looked puzzled. "Anyone living up there would get supplies through here, and I'd know them. What makes you ask?"

"Probably nothing, but I keep getting the impression that someone is watching when I go upriver. Maybe moose hunters?"

"How far up river?" K.J. asked.

"All the way. Before the snow slide, I thought I saw a shadow move on the cliff above me."

"Not moose hunters." Andy was shaking his gray mop. "We seldom venture more than five miles from here to get all of the moose we need."

"Damn!" K.J. slammed his fist on the table. "Same thing

happened before we were jumped. We never saw anyone, just an impression here, a suggestion there.... It might be those same guys, waiting for you to show them where the gold is hidden."

"Surely they haven't been waiting in the woods for two years. Where did they come from?" I turned to Andy.

"Only possibility is Allakaket. It's fifty miles down the Koyukuk, but there is a winter trail and it's an easy boat ride in summer. The bush telegraph has probably reported that Johnson is back... unlikely, but possible."

"Can you use that hog leg you carry, Stew?" K.J. meant Alex's pistol.

"Sure, I can hit anything I can see, but I'm not much good with shadows."

K.J. had not turned white with fear; he had turned bright red with anger. "If you see them, shoot them in the feet and drag them back here behind your machine. I want the pleasure of ripping their heads off in person."

Andy scooted his chair back and stood. "Well, that's a pretty far stretch, and in any case, Stew isn't in danger until he points out where the gold is. The way he's going, he may die of old age before then. I better get cracking on the runway."

"In this wind?" K.J. snared the last biscuit and reached past Stella for the butter. "Why bother? It will be drifted over again by morning anyway."

"Yeah, but the FAA called. Some cowboy took off from Galena and filed a flight plan for Bettles Field. There's no chance of him making it; he's surely already crashed in the mountains, but still, I have to do my part."

"What's he flying?" I asked. I think I was getting a premonition.

"It's a Beech 18, Zero-One-Victor. Ring any bells?"

"Oh yeah. Bells, whistles, and sirens. That's one of Alex's aircraft."

"Damn." Andy checked his watch and ran toward the den for his snowsuit. "He'll be landing in forty-five minutes."

"That would be our young benefactor?" K.J. asked.

"Yes, it would. Must be a medical emergency in the village. What else would bring him up this way in a blizzard?"

"Well," K.J. shrugged, "we'll find out in forty-three minutes. I think I'll repair to my suite and begin preparations for our visit to the disaster area." He stood, leaning on his cane, and marched determinedly back toward his room. He wasn't faking. He had to be in serious pain, but chose to ignore it.

I was reminded of those Mickey Spillane books where Mike Hammer walks around with half a dozen bullets in him, ignoring the pain, getting into fistfights, but trying not to leak blood on the carpets. Miners in the Arctic could have been the real-life models for Mike Hammer. If they had let little things like bullet holes, broken bones, or frozen feet stop them, there wouldn't have been any Alaska gold rushes.

I climbed the stairs and put on my snowsuit. Alex would now be landing in thirty-nine minutes.

It wasn't terribly cold outside, and the fog had thinned, but the snow was still belting down in tiny flakes, almost sleet, and it was going by at fifty or more miles per hour. Andy had turned on the runway lights, and they made a yellow glow, like a globe of snow over each light. I could see three lights at a time, and they're fifty feet apart. Andy came by on his snowplow, light blazing, strobe flashing, and going twenty miles per hour. There wasn't much snow on the runway, but he was breaking up drifts. He was moving fast because he needed to be off the runway before Alex arrived.

I knew there's an FAA radio at Bettles Field, but it's remote controlled from Anchorage. They can tell a pilot what the weather report is, and if there is any other traffic, but the airport isn't controlled, so landing is at the pilot's discretion. Andy had a radio in his snowplow, so he could have talked to Anchorage, or the incoming pilot, but he probably didn't want to mention that he was two hours late getting the runway plowed.

When he veered off the runway and started clearing a path to the hangar, I figured Alex was on the radio, and a minute later I heard the deep-throated booms of a pair of nine-cylinder radial engines. Landing lights appeared out of the snow. The Beech kissed the runway, rolled past me, then pivoted to taxi toward the hangar. Andy had the hangar door open, and Alex taxied straight inside. I made it under the hangar door while it was coming down. The props were still spinning, but Alex dropped the Beech's passenger door and climbed out.

"What the hell are you doing here?" I asked.

"Well, the weather was bad in Bethel, so I thought I'd come up this way and get out of the storm."

"That's all?"

"Not really. I've been thinking that maybe we could go up to the mine on snow machines. If Johnson buried a box full of nuggets up there, maybe we can find them. I brought a couple of snow machines with me."

"Oh, brother. Talk about needing to play catch-up. Let's go get some coffee while I bring you up to date on about a hundred developments."

By the time we reached the lodge, Alex was up to speed, and agreed that we'd assault the snowdrift with an army in the morning. When we stepped through the door, Fanny was out of the kitchen like a shot. She ran right past me and jumped on Alex. I mean, literally. She wrapped her legs around his waist, and hung on, smothering him with kisses.

"Oh, Alex, I was afraid you were never coming back for me."

"I wasn't." Alex kept walking, Fanny and all, and when we got to the table he peeled her off. I wondered if a swimmer getting untangled from an octopus might be like that. He stood her up, turned her toward the kitchen, said "coffee" and whacked her derrière a resounding smack. She didn't seem to mind. She trotted off to fetch coffee while we stripped off our snowsuits.

Andy was behind his counter, working his radio traffic, so I was surprised to see Stella and K.J. come out of K.J.'s room, until I noticed that Stella was carrying gauze and scissors. Stella walked over and joined us, K.J. stumping along behind with the cane.

Stella gave Alex a hug and a peck. "Hi, Alex, glad you could join us. Tonight's entertainment will be in the operating theater." Fanny brought two more cups. Stella sipped, K.J. waved his away.

"Something a mite stronger, my dear girl." He eased himself down into a chair.

Fanny took the extra cup back to the kitchen and returned with a glass, half ice, half bourbon. "Thank you, my dear child. You may save yourself numerous trips if you just bring the fountain and set it here." K.J. demonstrated his intent by draining half the bourbon.

"Operating theater?" I asked.

"Yep, 'fraid so. One toe has to come off."

"Can't it be saved?" I wasn't getting the picture.

"Stew, this little piggy has been dead for three days and it's starting to stink. It's time we gave it a Christian burial. Otherwise, it's gangrene city. K.J. is running a fever already, escalating while we dawdle."

"Want me to fly him into Anchorage?" Alex asked.

"Why? You got ten thousand dollars for an operation and a week to wait?" Stella raised her voice to be heard across the room. "Andy, it's amputation time."

"Just a minute, luv, I'm relaying Point Barrow weather. Almost done."

"Are we talking practicing medicine without a license?" I asked.

"The way I see it, Stew, it's a toss-up. Either we practice medicine without a doctor, or have K.J.'s funeral without a priest, illegal or immoral, take your pick."

K.J. had drained his glass, topped it off, and was well into his second. Andy came out from behind his counter and knelt to kindle a fire in the fireplace. He got a blaze going, and walked out the front door.

Stella sipped coffee. "Fanny, we need to boil half a dozen white towels." Fanny nodded and ducked back into the kitchen. K.J. was topping off his glass again.

"What do we do about anesthetic?" I asked. Then the truth dawned, and I wished I hadn't asked.

"The patient is being anesthetized at this time," Stella explained patiently. "After that, I figure you and Alex can hold him down." Stella went into the pantry and came out with a large sheet of clear plastic. She carried that to K.J.'s room. Andy came back in, brandishing pruning shears with two-foot handles. He propped it up on the hearth so the blades were in the fire, and came to join us.

"Can you spare a wee drap of that courage?" he asked K.J.

K.J. pushed the nearly empty bottle toward Andy, who tipped it up and chugged several swallows, straight from the bottle. K.J. retrieved it and poured the final dregs into his glass. Fanny came out of the kitchen with a dishpan loaded with steaming towels and carried them down the hall to K.J.'s room.

Stella came out of the room. "Showtime," she called.

We all stood, but K.J. came up at a forty-five degree angle, stumbling sideways. Alex caught him. I nipped behind Andy's counter and came back wheeling the swivel chair. The pruning shears in the fireplace appeared to be glowing red.

Alex eased K.J. down into the chair and held him there by the shoulders. I picked up his feet and followed Stella back to the bedroom.

"On his back."

Alex and I hoisted the body onto the bed and scooted it so the feet were on Stella's plastic. She unwound the bandage from K.J.'s left foot. It was an ugly sight, mostly bright red, but I got a glimpse of what Stella meant before I turned away. His second toe was mottled, black and stark white. Maybe I was seeing bone, but I didn't care to study it closely.

Stella looked at Alex and me. "Shoulders. Fanny, legs. Andy, ready." Fanny hiked her skirt up and sat straddling K.J.'s knees, leaning forward to inspect the operation. Andy came in carrying the pruning shears by a handle, blades smoking. He bent over the end of the bed. Fanny's back blocked my view, which was fine with me.

"Not that one," Stella screamed, "the next one."

Andy adjusted, and pulled the handles together. The blades met with a click, and something fell on the floor. Stella shoved Andy aside and went to work with a needle and thread, followed by towels and bandages. K.J. was snoring; the anesthetic had worked. Stella started taping, then gave us a head jerk that meant we were relieved of duty. Fanny climbed off the bed, bent to retrieve the severed digit, and tossed it into the wastebasket. We followed her back to the dining room.

Andy came in from outside. He had, no doubt, replaced the pruning shears on pegs in the garage.

"Fanny, perhaps one more wee libation is in order?"

Fanny came back with a fresh bottle and six glasses. She clunked ice into four and poured. Andy proposed a toast. "May all our fevers be gold." We drank to that.

Stella came out. "The patient is sleeping peacefully. I do believe the operation was a success." Fanny chunked ice and handed a glass to Stella. Stella noticed the sixth glass on the table. "I don't believe K.J. will be joining us just yet, Fanny." She took a healthy slug. "Alex, you're in the third room on the right, next to Stew. Dinner at six. I don't believe it will be necessary to mention this afternoon to our other guests."

"Other guests?" Alex asked.

"Brother, you haven't started to live yet. Did you say we need to unload some snow machines from that flying coffin of yours? I'll fill you in on the way."

Alex nodded. We finished our bottled courage and went out to joust with the wind.

Chapter 13

Let us eat and drink, for tomorrow we shall die.
—Isaiah 22:13

By five fifty-five, Alex and I were standing behind our chairs. Alex was behind K.J.'s chair; we didn't think he'd be coming to dinner. We had unloaded two new Panthers from the Beech; sleek, black, powerful, and obscenely phallic. Alex had presented me with a new pistol. It appeared identical to his, but it wasn't his. I ceremoniously returned his pistol, and the reunion was touching. He patted it, cracked the cylinder and spun it to check the load, then he stepped outside. A snowball the size of an orange was sitting on top of a runway light forty feet from the steps. Alex swung the pistol up, blew the snowball away, patted the pistol again and reloaded it.

I had also steeped Alex in the lore of The Green Army

and the mystique of its local representative. I left him to figure Carolyn out for himself. At five fifty-seven Andy got up from his radios. He stopped to stoke up the fire in the fireplace, added a log, and joined us, holding up the back of his chair. At five fifty-eight we heard the dresser slide upstairs. Alex looked the question at me.

"That's the door bolt," I explained. "It's the only rape-proof room this side of Seattle."

The ladies made their vinegar and spice entrance. They stopped behind their chairs, Mrs. Whidbey across from Alex, Carolyn across from the chair we were reserving for Stella, and me, across the social abyss.

"Mrs. Whidbey," Andy said, "may I present Mr. Alex Price. He is a well-known conservationist from the Bethel area who has heard of our emergency and rushed to our aid. Alex, Mrs. Whidbey, our ambassador from The Green Army, and her lovely daughter, Carolyn."

Alex used the smile that melts statues. "I'm delighted to make your acquaintance, Mrs. Whidbey. Your reputation is well known throughout the major river systems. I am overjoyed to find one of your expertise and dedication in charge of this expedition."

Carolyn let out a most unladylike snort, but covered it with a cough. Alex kept spreading his malarkey. "And you, Carolyn, we know what a help and support you are to your dear mother. What a joy it must be to her, having you follow in her footsteps."

Alex was just getting wound up, but Andy cut him off by sliding chairs for the ladies. The clock made its final tick to six and Stella marched in, carrying a shank from what must have been a very young and very, very illegal moose. "Ladies and gentlemen, a baron of beef, imported from the Highland herds of Scotland." She set the platter in front of Andy, and he jumped up to carve. Fanny carried a platter of steamed potatoes, carrots, and onions. Stella decanted the Mouton Cadet. Fanny ducked back to the kitchen and returned with two loaves of freshly baked bread. She carefully placed one in front of Alex and the other in front of me. This girl was hedging her bets.

Stella came to her chair; Alex leaped to slide it for her, and Stella pinched his tush below the table.

"How do you prefer your roast beef, Mrs. Whidbey?"

"Oh, I'm not in the least particular. A half-inch crust around a slightly pink center will do nicely."

Andy whacked off two slices, and the third met with her approval.

"Carolyn?"

"I'll take the first one. I can't stand the sight of blood."

"Where is Mr. Johnson this evening?" Mrs. Whidbey asked.

"Oh, the poor man has suffered a slight relapse and is confined with his feet elevated. I'll take some dinner to him later." Stella extended her plate; Andy whacked and served.

Plates were loaded, mouths filled, conversation stopped. That Scottish Highland beef was the best moose I've ever tasted. It positively melted in my mouth--both half-pound slices of it.

Fanny brought peach cobbler and coffee, and Mrs. Whidbey. actually ate that, too, before she sat back to cross-examine Alex.

"How goes the battle to save the Kuskokwim, Mr. Price?"

"We're winning that one handily, Mrs. Whidbey. Thank you for asking. Every man, woman, and child along the mighty Kuskokwim is dedicated to its preservation, so it flows with the same pristine clarity it had before man inhabited the planet."

Strictly speaking, Alex was telling the truth. The Kuskokwim is the same color as the dirt roads beside it. If you aspire to walk on water, that might be a good place to practice because it's almost thick enough. It has been depositing megatons of silt since water started running downhill. The Yukon/Kuskokwim Delta is larger than the state of Oregon, composed entirely of the silt from those two rivers, so mankind hasn't hurt them much.

"It's good to hear that we are making progress, Mr. Price. Do you foresee an equally idyllic future for the Koyukuk?"

"Certainly, madam. With dedicated conservationists like the Andersons here, and now that paragon of virtue, Mr. Johnson; with you in charge, I don't see how we can miss."

I thought Alex was laying it on a little thick, but he seemed to be getting away with it. I noticed that he didn't arouse controversy by including me in his litany of saints.

"Is your weather forecast still favorable for the morrow, Mr. Anderson?"

"I believe so, madam. This storm is moving through at fifteen miles per hour. Point Barrow cleared up this afternoon and the winds were dying down at Arctic Village before dinner. I expect we'll be clear and calm by morning."

"That is welcome news, Mr. Anderson. I shall continue my preparations for departure. Come along, Carolyn." Both Andy and Alex did chair duty. Alex made it to Carolyn's chair in time to let her hair brush his face when she stood.

"Mama, there's a lovely fire in the living room. Couldn't we sit there a moment, and perhaps have another glass of wine? It would remind us of God's bounty to His children."

"Nonsense, Carolyn. Moderation in all things. A little wine for thy stomach's sake, not for recreation. Need I remind you, that is wood being burned in the living room? That might be necessary to combat the storm, but it would be unseemly for us to enjoy it." Mama stomped toward the stairs. Carolyn gave a helpless shrug to the room in general, maybe most of it to Alex, and followed in her mother's footsteps.

In three minutes, the rest of us were ensconced on throw rugs in front of the fire, finishing the Mouton Cadet and starting on bourbon. Andy stretched out on his belly, facing the fire. Stella was using his back for a pillow with her legs draped across my back, all very friendly and comfortable. Fanny was snuggled between Alex and me. It was like a group hug at a therapy session. Firelight flickered on the dark wood paneling and danced from our glasses. The wind huffed and puffed, and the banshees wailed outside, but the solid log house was impervious.

I think it was significant that we didn't talk. We were enjoying a comfortable physical togetherness, but the dancing flames created a Rorschach test that was deeply personal and profoundly comforting. If mankind ever discovers the meaning of life, I think it will happen in front of a stone fireplace with a birch wood fire crackling, and a storm raging outside.

Andy and Stella got up, yawning and stretching, and wandered toward their boudoir, holding hands. Fanny hugged Alex and me for a moment, then collected empty glasses and went to clear the table. Alex and I climbed the stairs, flipped a coin for the bathroom, he won, and we retired to our respective rooms.

Wind was still rattling my windowpanes, but the quilted comforter did its job. I'd been dreaming of firelight, reflected in a mountain of gold, when the door to Alex's room slammed. A moment later, a naked Fanny opened my door and burst into the room. She was across the floor in three strides and launched herself onto my chest. My face was covered by soap-scented hair. B-cups mashed into my belly with a hint of nipples, but my chest was being puddled by a waterfall of tears. Her fragile little frame was wracked with grief. I wrapped arms around her and patted her back the way people do in movies.

"Oh, Stewie," she sobbed. "Life is so unfair. Alex has taken a vow as a Muslim priest and must never again have carnal knowledge of women."

I didn't have a response to that, so I made cooing noises. Her grief was real, and I genuinely wanted to comfort her.

"Thank heaven I still have you, Stewie." We clung together while she cried herself to sleep.

Chapter 14

The earth did quake and the rocks rent.
—Matthew 27:51

It may have been the lack of commotion outside the window that wakened me. The pane was covered by frost, but the frost glowed with a deceptively warm sunlight orange. The aroma of coffee beckoned. Alex came out of the bathroom and followed me down the stairs.

K.J. was perched on his chair and beaming.

"Good morning, Stan. Good morning, Alfred."

"Stew and Alex," I prompted. "Are you feeling all right?"

"Never better. 'If thy right eye offends thee, pluck it out.' Let that amputation be a lesson to you lads. If you have a bullet in your heart, or a pickaxe in your brain, you must remove it so healing can begin."

His cup was almost empty. He produced a bottle of

bourbon from between his legs and filled the cup to half. Fanny brought two cups and the pot from the kitchen. She finished filling K.J.'s cup, then served Alex and me, but reserved her morning smile for me. It was going to be several hours before Alex regained star status.

"Are you gentlemen ready for a ride on this glorious spring morning?" K.J. asked.

"You're not thinking of coming?" I blurted.

"Certainly. It appears that you cannot be trusted with the welfare of the esteemed Mrs. Whidbey, so I shall accompany the expedition to ensure that you don't drown the old bat."

Andy and Stella joined us, followed immediately by a whiff of Deep Woods Off, the most aromatic of mosquito repellents, from the stairway.

Mrs. Whidbey appeared to have doubled in girth overnight, and even Caroline was looking chunky. They wore camouflaged survival suits, covered with zipper pockets. We all rose for the entrance. K.J. surreptitiously set the bottle on the floor beside his chair, and stood with amazing alacrity. He was the first to find his voice.

"Good morning, madam, I see that you are prepared for a sojourn into the wilderness."

"Precisely, Mr. Johnson. I have found the preparations by inexperienced locals to be woefully inadequate, so I shall demonstrate the proper way to travel." She waddled toward the table, forcing each step as if she were already wading in deep snow, and clanking as she walked. Andy pulled chairs, but madam wasn't ready to sit. She continued our education.

"I have here," she said, patting pockets, starting just below the knees, "coffee, tea, sugar, salt, pepper, Tabasco, knife, fork and spoon, topographic map, compass, blackberry brandy..."

"Blackberry brandy?"

"Certainly, Mr. Anderson, in case of snakebite." She was prepared to continue for several more minutes, but Fanny came in with a platter of pancakes, followed by more little pitchers of the blueberry syrup that makes life in the Arctic worthwhile. Mrs. Whidbey allowed herself to be seated. In truth, she sagged into her chair, dragged down by the weight of travel necessities.

An hour later we were lined up in front of the lodge, billowing exhaust like a pack of Hell's Angels preparing to rumble. Andy was riding his Cat, K.J. on Stella's matching machine, Madam and Caroline on their former mounts. Alex and I were bringing up the rear on the new Panthers. Each traveler of the male persuasion was seated on a shovel that jutted suggestively out behind.

The landscape gave new meaning to pristine. Snowdrifts sculpted all features to voluptuous curves and undulating designs. It was clean, clean, clean. The woods reminded me of James Russell Lowell's poem, The First Snow-Fall. "Every pine and fir and hemlock wore ermine too dear for an earl, and the poorest twig on the birch trees was ridged inch deep with pearl."

Andy led us around the airport and down onto the river by a much simpler route than the one I had taken. Madam was no doubt congratulating herself on her choice of traveling companions.

We swept past the village and arced onto the John River. Andy, breaking trail, was climbing drifts and jumping off, but with each machine's passing, the trail deepened and smoothed. When we approached the glen where the overflow lurked, I punched the Panther and pulled out to pass. We were no longer in Andy's front yard, so it was politically acceptable for me to lead.

Mashing that throttle was an experience. This was the new, 500cc model, and it was a good thing I was hanging on, because it leaped like a thoroughbred from the starting gate. Wasn't there a teenage cult song a while back about a motorcycle rider with "a quarter-ton of steel between his legs?" That's how the Panther felt. I ripped past the line, and Carolyn leapt the trail to follow me. That was legitimate; she too was a pioneer of this terrain. I passed Andy and made the detour around the overflow, which was again invisible, seductively flat and smooth. The only sign of our former encampment was a gap in the trees, like a front tooth missing in a Pepsodent smile.

We weren't worried about an ambush because we were all armed---except the ladies, of course. If the stalkers had been confrontational, they could have held me at gunpoint, and toasted my feet over a campfire until I gave them K.J.'s map. They hadn't done that, and if they had been watching, they would now conclude, correctly we hoped, that the nuggets were under the slide. If we came out of the canyon with a basket of nuggets, we were prepared to shoot our way out.

The river funneled us into the canyon, but canyon walls kept the sunshine outside. Wind had scoured the canyon floor, leaving patches of clear ice in the center of the river, but packing a drift on the right-hand bank. The left-hand bank was plastered with snow that clung in depressions and behind outcroppings, but those would melt and come down when the sun topped the canyon's wall.

Drifts were built behind boulders on the banks, reaching

downstream for twenty or thirty feet, and that was a bad thing, because the precise area we were aiming to dig was on the downstream side of my fateful snow slide. I parked at the foot of the slide, and machines lined up behind, shutting off engines.

K.J. walked toward me, carrying his shovel and not limping much. He seemed to be taller than I remembered, so Stella must have rigged some traveling bandages and covered them with the canvas from snow packs. Carolyn had walked back to her mother and there was a flurry of tugging and grunting going on. K.J. tossed me his shovel and crow-hopped back to the great lady's machine. She was attempting to stand, and Carolyn was struggling to pull her up. K.J. took an arm, and he and Carolyn pulled mother to her feet, but she sagged backward and sat sideways on her machine. Apparently her travel preparations were for everything but walking.

"You go ahead," she announced. "I shall supervise from here."

K.J. came back and retrieved his shovel. Carolyn started emptying her pockets, making a pile on the Elan's seat. We trekked to the upwind side of the slide and I pointed out the remnants of the box, and the path it had taken. As snow drifts will, mine had migrated downwind, snow blowing off the leading edge and stacking up behind.

Rocks on the upwind side were bare. The slide had moved several inches downwind and uncovered the spot where I'd been standing when it all came down. K.J. dropped to his knees and scooped up a nugget. It was the size of a large peanut, and for a nugget that is gigantic. He lost control for a moment and started whanging the side of the slide with his shovel, but it was cement-hard. Andy took charge of himself, Alex, and me. K.J. was attacking the slide, and it appeared he was going to stay there. We three walked back around the slide and passed the command post. Carolyn joined us, looking much more svelte.

"Are you quite comfortable, Madam?"

"Yes, thank you, Mr. Anderson. Are you planning to shovel this monstrous protrusion away?"

"Well, perhaps not all of it, ma'am. We're still reconnoitering, but it seems likely we'll be able to attack its flanks and weaken it so that when the water rises it will slough harmlessly onto the bank. Mr. Johnson is working on the upstream side and we three shall attack it from below."

Carolyn was wavering, thinking of accompanying us. I had a better idea.

"Carolyn, I noticed several dead spruce branches across the river. They should be removed, lest they enter the water. Perhaps you could drag them over here and burn them, even brew coffee in the process. You'll find a coffeepot, a jug of water, and paper cups on my machine." Bulky though Mrs. Whidbey was, I hadn't spotted any bulges that appeared to be the supplies I was offering.

Carolyn looked skeptical. Maybe she realized she was being third-based. I winked and handed her my lighter. She shrugged and set out in search of dead spruce boughs. We walked on around to the downwind side of the drift.

It tapered off to bare gravel, but sloped up fast toward the original slide. It was Andy's opinion that Alex and I should dig into the drift while he searched the gravel downstream. If they ever decide to move Mt. Everest, Andy will send Alex and me to dig it up. However, each time we dug down to gravel, and then scraped it clean, there was a chance of finding nuggets. If you have the fever, it keeps you digging.

The sun topped the ridge and worked its way down the western wall. Plastered snow and loose gravel fell down, making clatters that echoed through the canyon. Andy had been downstream half a mile and came back, skunked, to sit on the edge of the drift. Alex and I had dug a swath ten feet wide, which was now five feet deep, and had found nothing but gravel. Carolyn came around to our side of the pile to inspect our efforts and announce that lunch was served.

Alex and Andy followed her back to the campfire; I walked around to try interrupting K.J. He was digging a tunnel, about the right size for a grizzly bear and deep enough that I reached in and whacked his leg to get his attention. I had started to drag him out by the feet, but caught a macabre image of them pulling off in my hands.

He crawled out backward, a skinny snowman with a big grin, and displayed two more gigantic nuggets in his hand. "You havin' any luck?" he asked.

"Nary a nibble. Digging is easy now. In a couple more hours, we'll get to the slide, and that will be tougher, but the pot of gold must be between us."

He pocketed the nuggets, and positively strode to the campfire. Carolyn was handing out Highland roast beef sandwiches and paper cups of coffee. We sat on our machines and devoured.

"How is it progressing, Mr. Anderson?"

"Very well, madam. I believe that a few days may accomplish our objective."

"Days, Mr. Anderson?"

"Well, as you see, it is a rather large collection of debris, but we shall conquer."

K.J. spoke up. "You gentlemen seem to be getting ahead of me. I believe it might be more fruitful if you joined me on the upstream side." He gave Andy and Alex broad winks, and they both perked up.

"Certainly, Mr. Johnson." Andy had caught Johnson's implication and was almost rubbing his hands in glee. "If we all work on the upstream side until dark, perhaps we can sufficiently weaken this abomination."

Madam set her coffee cup on the seat and picked up a notebook. "Would you outline your plan for me, Mr. Anderson?"

Andy chewed and swallowed. "Certainly, Madam. We are usurping a technique from our enemies, the loggers. When it is their intention to vandalize and steal a large tree, they first make an undercut on the side toward which they wish it to fall. They then make a straight cut in from the opposite side until the victim is sufficiently weakened.

"We are employing such a two-pronged approach. Mr. Price, Mr. Stewart, and I have been working on the undercut, while Mr. Johnson is making the straight cut. If we are successful, when the water rises the pile of debris will fold toward the undercut, and be harmlessly deposited on the bank, thereby saving the salmon runs for years to come." He filled his mouth with sandwich again to preclude further questioning. Madam was busily writing and sketching in her notebook.

"Shall we get back to work, gentlemen?" K.J. picked up his shovel.

That was when the earth shook, thunder erupted, and a chunk of canyon wall that looked like Hoover Dam crashed into the river half a mile below us. Rocks the size of automobiles slid and tumbled, grinding and screeching. The ice didn't even slow them down. A fountain of water splashed up, almost to the top of the canyon walls, and a cloud of snow belched upriver toward us.

"Go!" Andy shouted. "Go! Go! Go!" He leapt onto his Cat and threw a rooster tail of snow, sloughing away up river. Carolyn and I swung Mama's feet astride her Polaris. I punched her starter, put her thumb on the throttle, and gave her a shove. Her eyes had gone super-sized, but K.J. raced by after Andy, and Mama followed him.

Carolyn had started toward my machine with the coffeepot. "Leave it," I screamed. "Just go." I realized that the river probably appeared static to Carolyn, but the rest of us knew that a millrace under the ice had been blocked. She caught the panic in my voice, dropped the pot and ran. Carolyn and Alex raced up the river after Andy, and I was twenty feet behind them, but already the ice was shifting and cracking under me.

When that rockslide dammed the river, it was going to back up water instantly. Rising water rips ice out of its way like a bulldozer through whipped cream, and water was going to rise until it spilled over the rockslide. I hadn't stopped to measure, but the slide looked fifty feet tall to me, and the river was going to fill our canyon in minutes.

Alex and Carolyn were riding side by side, but he took the inside of a bend and pulled ahead, so he could be forgiven for not noticing that the Elan couldn't keep up. He whipped around the next bend, and was gone. The ice rose up behind me, and I was sliding downhill like a surfer on a wave, the crashing and grinding so loud that I couldn't hear my engine. Carolyn was ahead of me, hunkered down behind her windshield, and squeezing the throttle with both hands, but the Elan was going nowhere. I pulled up beside her, bumping skis.

"Get on," I screamed. She stood up on the running boards, holding the throttle with her right hand, grabbed my shoulder with her left, and jumped onto the Panther behind me. She will never know how close she came to jerking me off that machine. I punched the Panther, and it leaped, but this time it didn't seem so fast.

We were on solid ice in a foot of snow, the sound of thunder behind us receding. We rounded a bend and I saw the other machines ahead of us, Alex out front breaking trail and the other three pushing him. The canyon was tapering off, with walls down to ten feet high. I was starting to think we had cheated death again. I was leaning forward, down behind the windshield. Carolyn was flat on my back, her arms locked around my waist, and the Panther was screaming like the cat it was named for. I noticed the speedometer flicking past ninety-five. The quartet ahead swept around a bend to the left, half a mile ahead, and we blasted into the straight stretch, skimming the snow.

Krakatoa may have sounded like the explosion that deafened us. The entire straight stretch broke loose in one chunk and we were on a fast elevator, going up with Old Faithful erupting all the way around us. Our chunk was climbing crazily, banging against the walls, trying to surge upstream and grinding off edges with shrieks and howls. Suddenly water shot out from under our sheet over the ice ahead of us, like Niagara on tourist day. To drive off the end of our sheet would be to die horribly, but quickly.

We were so close to the top of the canyon that I could

see over rocks in spots. I picked the lowest spot I could find and laid us on our side for the turn. A solid rock wall three feet high stared at us, then a fountain of water spewed up between us and the rock. The edge of the sheet crumpled to make a ramp, and the water threw us over the rocks. Suddenly we were whipping between trees, climbing a gentle hill, and I was squeezing the brake. I rolled off the machine onto my back in moss and snow, dumping Carolyn in the process, and the two of us lay there gasping.

Chapter 15

None but the brave deserves the fair.
Alexander's Feast—Dryden

Carolyn stopped gasping and caught her breath, but she was pale. "Golly, that was scary. I didn't realize conservation was so dangerous." Her voice quavered only slightly.

"Well, danger is a relative term. We're still alive, and a lot of people were killed in their bathtubs today."

"Why did the water run so fast?"

"It didn't. The water was already here. When it was blocked, it just went up."

"Do you think Mama and the guys made it?"

"Yes, I do. We saw them veer off the John onto Caribou Creek, so they were out of the canyon. They can't be more than a mile or two north of us."

"Which way is north?"

"Over that way." I waved vaguely upstream. We had gone a hundred feet up the hill, dodging and scraping trees before we stopped, but we could hear the ice crashing and grinding, and had to go back to look. Water had spilled out of the canyon and our sheet of ice was poking over the rocks along the edge.

"Will it keep rising?" Carolyn asked.

"It can't come much higher. It will rise until water goes over the dam, and then likely wash the dam away. The cliffs were higher downstream, but surely not much."

I've seen it many times but always have to stop and stare. When a river breaks up, it is an awesome sight. It doesn't matter if it's ripped out by the normal rising water of springtime, or by a cataclysm like ours, you can't help yourself, you have to watch. Chunks of ice weighing hundreds of tons are heaved around like toys, shaking the earth when they hit, or grinding up pressure ridges like continental drift forming mountains when they rub together. Sound is overpowering, from the deepest bass drums to tinkling cymbals. Groans and roars that we would call unearthly are being made by nature.

Our chunk, still the size of three football fields, began to tilt downward, away from us. Suddenly it shattered into a million icebergs, and a moment later it was rushing away down the canyon.

"What happened?" Carolyn was shouting over the din.

"The dam broke. Imagine the weight of water that was pushing on it."

"Are people downstream in danger?"

"Not much. Our problem was that we were in a canyon.

Below the canyon, the water will spread out and probably not get very deep."

"But what about the people in the village?"

"They're river people. The moment the John stopped flowing, ice by the village sagged down in the center, and they headed for high ground."

Water was running down the canyon walls and spray made rainbows. Chunks of ice raced away below us, rounded the bend, and the river was flowing clear and free. The show was over; we strolled back up the hill toward our machine.

"Shall we go find Mama?"

"I think we should let them find us, since we're between them and home. They may not be so sure we made it, but they'll know that if we did, we're on this bank. I expect we'll hear their engines in a few minutes. See that bare rock sticking up? Let's build a smoky fire on top of it that will make us easy to find."

I dug in the box on the Panther and pulled out the hatchet. Alex had made the usual provisions: sleeping bag, rope, hatchet, but no tarp. I hacked, and we each gathered an armload of dead branches from the bases of spruce trees. I was eager to climb the rock because it would give a view over the trees, just in case there was a distress fire burning upriver. There wasn't. We stacked our branches and I patted my pocket. No lighter. Carolyn laughed at my shocked expression.

"Looking for this? You gave it to me to make coffee."

We got a good blaze going, and I climbed back down for green boughs to make smoke. Carolyn stayed on the rock to feed the fire. I panted back up with an armful of green and sat beside her. We alternated green and dry to keep the fire up and make a column of smoke, but mostly we were straining our ears for the sound of snow machine engines.

"Would you mind telling me what you guys were really doing in the canyon?"

"Are you planning to follow in your mother's footsteps?"

"Good heavens, no. She's certifiable, you know, completely lost her mind when Daddy was killed. You guys have been super nice to her, and I really appreciate that. So, what was going on in the canyon?"

I looked into those glacier-blue eyes and saw honest, intelligent curiosity. I was pleased to realize she was not just a Barbie Doll. If I were wrong to trust her, well, I wouldn't be the first man to lose his judgment when a beautiful woman smiled at him.

"Gold," I said. "A box of nuggets was buried on the river bank, but it broke up in a spring flood and scattered nuggets downstream. We believe that most of them are buried under the snow slide where we were digging."

"So, all of the talk about polluting the river was malarkey?"

"Totally. That slide was purest snow, but more important, you just survived an example of how Mother Nature treats her rivers. 'If seven maids with seven mops swept it for half a year, do you suppose, the walrus asked, that they could get it clear?'."

Carolyn finished the quote, "I doubt it, said the carpenter, and shed a bitter tear'." She laughed; a delightful, warm little feminine sound. "Is the gold really so valuable?"

"Well, if K.J., that's Mr. Johnson, is correct about the amount he buried, then it's worth over One hundred and twenty thousand dollars."

"Wow, let's go back and dig. Why did you let a little water stop you? Shouldn't they be coming soon?"

"Yes, they should. If anything were wrong, if they were stranded, then Alex would have built a fire just like ours. No smoke is good smoke, as the current mantra goes."

"Are you and Fanny an item?" she asked.

"No. We're old friends, but Fanny will marry the first Gussak who asks her. She much prefers Alex to me, for instance."

"What is a Gussak?"

"A Caucasian, usually. The first white men the Eskimos met were Russian Cossacks, so all strangers became Cossacks, or Gussaks. There's a Black living in Aniak, and I've heard him referred to as a Gussak. Maybe it just means not Eskimo."

"So, I'm a Gussak, huh? Why is Fanny so eager to marry one?"

"It's her ticket out of the village. You can't imagine the luxuries that Gussak wives have; washing machines, TVs, cars, central heating, running hot water. You should consider marrying one yourself."

"Are you or Alex going to marry her?"

"No, and she knows that. She's just keeping all options open. Alex won't give her the time of day. I don't have his iron resolve, so I tend to string her along. She knows I won't marry her, but we play the game and keep in practice. I don't know which way is kinder."

"Well, that explains the sobbing."

"Huh?"

"Most nights I hear Fanny in your room trying to suppress giggles. Then Alex shows up and she spends the night in your room sobbing her heart out. I guess he turned her down."

We listened for a while. It was so quiet that the snapping from our fire sounded like firecrackers, and beyond that there was a breeze rustling branches, and occasional splashes from the river. No snow machines, no smoke on the horizon. We let our fire burn down, and I didn't go for more branches.

"Maybe we should drive up toward Caribou Creek and pick up their trail."

Carolyn nodded and followed me back to the Panther. We couldn't travel fast; there were too many trees, but we wound around the thickets, or cut through where the trees were tall enough. Once in a while we were on bare ground under trees, then climbing over drifts and twisting around rocks. I tried to keep the river between fifty and a hundred yards to our right. We made perhaps a mile in ten minutes, and I shut off the engine to listen.

The silence was profound, in both senses of the word. I had six extra cartridges in my pocket, besides the load in the magnum. I hadn't fired my new pistol yet, so I took the opportunity to make some noise and also check out the gun. I'm no Alex, but I fired three shots in rapid succession, and all of them hit the tree I was aiming for.

"Why three shots?" Carolyn asked.

"Three quick shots are an international distress signal, or at least an inter-Alaska one. They represent the first letter in an S.O.S. but you don't hear that mentioned much any more. In the days of telegraphy, they were recognized by everyone; three dots, three dashes, three dots. A pilot down in the snow would even stomp out that message, but nowadays I think they tend to stomp out HELP."

The .357 magnum can be heard for a mile or more, and I listened for answering shots from Alex. The silence went from profound to oppressive. The afternoon was moving right along, so we fired up the machine and moved along with it. Another half hour brought us to the banks of Caribou Creek, and a moonscape of desolation. The flood had gone up the creek and left a jumble of ice chunks, standing on edge, stacked on top of each other, and water was gushing between them.

"My God, were they killed?"

"Nah, Alex is too smart, K.J. is too tough, and Andy is too old. Between them they would have carried your mother out on their shoulders, machine and all. We saw them round the corner a minute before the water passed us, and that gave them another minute. They were moving at least eighty miles an hour. Let's check upstream a ways." I was whistling in the dark, but whatever had happened, had happened a mile or two upstream. We turned and bumped along the bank.

They had made it a mile, and the tracks were clear. They had climbed up the opposite bank. They had all used the same trail, so I couldn't count the machines, but there were more than one, so I chose to believe that there were four. The carnage from the flood continued on around the next bend. We weren't going to cross that creek, and neither were they. Just for fun, I picked a chunk of ice twice the size of the snowball that Alex had blown off of the runway light. I hit it with two of the three shots, and we listened.

"They're gone." Carolyn appeared devastated.

"Well, yes, gone, but not gone. They beat the flood, but now they're trapped on the other side of the creek. They'll probably go upstream until they can cross, and come back, but I don't think we should wait for them. If they come back looking for us, they'll find our trail and know we're okay. I suggest we make the trail lead them back to Bettles."

"Good. I really need to wash my hair."

I didn't think it was chivalrous to mention that she was going to need a lot more than a shampoo before we got home.

"Before we go, we should leave a message. Let's walk side by side, leaving two sets of tracks, and make a circle back to the machine. That way, if they come here, they'll know we're together."

We took our walk and climbed back on the machine. Carolyn snuggled tight against my back with arms around my waist, but that was because we were bumping and tipping and she needed to hang on.

Bettles was twenty miles away by river, but at least fifty the way we were winding around, and we were doing it mostly at ten miles an hour. Occasionally we came to small lakes, and I crossed them flat out, fast enough to walk on water if there was overflow. Each time we came to a creek we had to follow it upstream before we could cross, sometimes two miles, once almost ten.

We kept coming back to follow the general path of the river. Even though that meant making detours, it was the most direct route to Bettles. I wasn't making any estimates about how far we had come, but there was no doubt that it was getting dark and we were still in the hills. When we came to a lake that the headlight didn't reach across, I circled back into the trees and shut off the machine.

Chapter 16

Hairbreadth missings of happiness look like the
insults of fortune.
Tom Jones—Henry Fielding

Carolyn ran the engine, slowly turning the machine to shine the light through the woods. I followed the light, being scratched by only half of the branches I passed. She had lit half a circle when the light reflected from a pair of pink eyes. I put a bullet between them.

Shooting a rabbit with a .357 isn't recommended, but if I have to I make it a headshot. The head was gone, down to the front shoulders. Carolyn left the light stationary after the shot. I knelt in the woods to skin and gut the rabbit. I was remembering her remark about blood, so I came back to the light with what looked more like a chicken from a meat market than a bloody corpse.

We did it wienie-roast style, although I prefer to call it shish kebab.

I apologized for being an inept local. "Sorry, I don't have any barbeque sauce with me."

"Mother said you inexperienced locals don't know how to travel. That's why she had me carry this." She pulled a saltshaker, no doubt borrowed from Stella, out of a pocket below her knee. "I forgot I had it until it banged against my leg."

"Good girl. Pass the blackberry brandy."

"Sorry, Mother is carrying the brandy. I had pepper and a little jar of mayonnaise, but you made me leave in such a hurry that I didn't repack them."

"A little salt will do just fine. Help yourself to the snow, as long as it isn't yellow."

"Very funny." She salted her drumsticks and passed the shaker. I had the ribs and the front legs, and no complaints whatsoever.

"How far do you think we are from Bettles?"

"Truth? Haven't the foggiest. We've probably come more than halfway. We might be able to make it tonight. We also might spend the night stuck in overflow or at the bottom of a canyon. Better to Siwash it."

"That sounds scary. What's a Siwash?" Carolyn wrinkled her nose.

"The Siwash were a particularly primitive Indian tribe who lived along the Columbia River. They didn't build camps or carry teepees. They slept on the ground wherever they happened to be; in other words, did exactly what I have in mind. The sleeping bag is a double, and a good thick one, so we may survive."

I took the hatchet and started whacking off spruce boughs at the edge of the firelight. Carolyn took a walk out into the woods and came back to stand next to the fire for a while. I kicked a hole in the snow and piled up branches. We tossed our shish kebab skewers into the fire and sat side by side on the sleeping bag.

Firelight reflected and flickered on Carolyn's face and the little ruff of hair under her parka hood. I thought she was the most beautiful woman I had ever seen, but decided not to tell her that right away. Instead, I said, "Time for a story around the campfire. Two of them, actually, unless you'd rather sing a few camp songs first."

"No, you go right ahead with your stories. I'm a captive audience."

"Best kind. Several years ago I was traveling with a buddy from the Seattle area to our college in Iowa. We had hitchhiked to the coast for the Christmas vacation, and were going back to school. Don't bother looking shocked. I did go to college; I just didn't learn anything. Now, on New Year's Eve, never mind which year, we were in Montpelier, Idaho, and we hopped into an empty boxcar that was headed east."

I got up to throw more wood on the fire, and noticed a strip of Northern Lights, pale green, and dancing.

"Come and look. There's a visual to accompany the monologue."

Carolyn jumped up and we walked away from the fire for darkness. She leaned back against me to look up, and I circled her waist with my arms, but it was all companionable and practical. It was warmer that way. I wasn't kidding myself that it was romantic.

"I do love the lights, but they make me feel awfully

small. Go ahead with your story, you were celebrating New Year's in a boxcar."

"The train climbed up into the Rockies, and it was the proverbial slow freight, stopping on sidings and waiting for passenger trains to pass. In the mountains, the temperature dropped, probably to thirty below zero or more, and we were dressed for winter in western Washington State. We just hadn't realized what we were in for."

Another string of light blinked on to our right, and we turned toward it. It was developing into the conga line of flickering pickets that the Eskimos call a spirit dance. I think they're right.

"I had a sleeping bag with me, and my buddy, Ed Guy, had an army blanket. No help at all in the cold. What we did was run around and around that boxcar until we got warm. Then we both jumped into the sleeping bag, wrapped the blanket around that, and rested until we got cold; then up for more running."

"Wow, look over there." Carolyn pointed and we swung left. A red searchlight probed the sky, then dimmed to a streak, and we turned back to the spirit dance.

"We could not have just run all night. We'd have been exhausted, had to stop, and would have frozen. Even taking turns with the bag wouldn't have worked. It took the body heat from both of us to keep warm for half an hour. In the morning, the train stopped in Laramie and we jumped off, but there were two railroad men working in the yard. They stopped and stared at us, and one of them said, 'People usually freeze to death on that run.'"

"End of story one?"

"Yep."

"Is there a moral?"

"Yep. There is nothing swishy about two guys in a sleeping bag, if their lives depend on it."

"I see. I'll try to remember that, and the other story?"

"Look quick, it's blue over there. The other story is also a college story and it happened outside of Anchorage, Alaska, just a few years ago. Boy and girl this time. They were on a field trip, weather turned bad, and they were trapped on a glacier. They had two sleeping bags, and when the rescuers got to them the next day, they were frozen solid, each in their own bag. It wouldn't have been proper, and their classmates might have sniggered, but if they had both been in one bag, with the other bag over it, they probably would have been alive."

"Let me ponder that one and see if I can work out the moral for myself. Wow!"

The spirit dance flared up, as bright as a neon sign, and whipped the dancers back and forth like an angry snake.

"Do you think it's going to get cold tonight, Stew? Even with a campfire?"

"Yes, I predict we'll have an arctic night here in the Arctic. That's why the spirits are dancing so frantically; they're trying to keep warm. On our last night together we had a tarp, a tent of sorts, and it held the heat from the fire. With no tent, not much heat. Snuggle up to the fire to keep warm, and you set the bag on fire. We'll use the machine for a reflector, but, baby, it's gonna get cold outside."

Carolyn really did snuggle against me. "Stew, this is romantic. I wish my husband could see it."

"Your what?"

"Come on, let's get in that bag. I want a really captive audience for this story."

We crawled in, with all of our clothes on, of course. I gave Carolyn an arm for a pillow, but we didn't quite fit side by side. We rolled a quarter turn and made spoons. That seemed to work.

"Okay, I'm your captive. Are you going to tell me a horror story?"

"Well, half of it is horror, but not the part about being married. Mama sent me to a school in Oregon where they have a great music program. I'm a violinist, and pretty darn good, since I'm telling the story. She didn't realize, and still doesn't know that the school's primary focus is forestry. She also doesn't know that I met the most wonderful man and married him two years ago. Have you guessed that he's a forestry major?"

"Nope, never in a million years would I have guessed that. Red over there again."

"I see it, don't keep interrupting me. I'm coming to the horror story. Do you associate the name Whidbey with any geographical features?"

"You mean Whidbey Island, north of Seattle?"

"Yep, that's the one. Named for my great, great, great-grandfather. I don't know how many greats belong in there."

"I'm getting an inkling of where this story is going."

"No fair. Blue over there, try bending your knees a little, we'll fit better. So, yeah, great-great was a lumber baron and made a lot of money, and the family stayed in the business, what little there is left of it, right down to Daddy. Daddy was visiting a logging camp. A cable broke and cut four men right in half, and Daddy was one of them. That's part of the horror story, but only half. Mother went insane, totally bonkers, off the deep end, lunatic city. You get the idea?"

"Yeah, I'm following you. Your left elbow is right in my solar plexus. How about switching to a kidney punch?"

"Is that better? So, we left Washington and moved to San Francisco, and here comes the horror. Mother dived into The Green Army with the intention of wiping the logging industry off the face of the earth. She was so gung-ho that even The Green Army couldn't handle her, so they sent her here as an ambassador, and they hope she'll never come back, only..."

"Don't stop, your elbow is perfect."

"Only, Daddy left us several million dollars. The club wants her to donate, and she just might do it. When I'm twenty-five, I'll have an equal say about the money, but until then, two more years, if you're really nosy. Speaking of noses, would you scratch my head, just above my left ear? I can't get my hands out. Higher; heavenly, thank you. Until then, she could give the money away, if she decided to. My job is to keep her convinced that the money will do more good if we keep it to carry on her good works, and mine when I follow in her footsteps."

"There's going to be hell to pay when she finds out you married a logger."

"A forester. Stew, my bum is nice and warm, but some things on the other side are getting cold, could we roll over the other way?"

"One, two, three, roll."

"Hey, you took my pillow with you."

"Sorry, it doesn't bend that way, and it was going to sleep anyhow. Use your parka hood."

"Okay, but your arm was better. I'll let you know when my bum gets cold."

"Speaking of cold bums, there must be quite a strain on your marriage."

"Don't get nasty. During the school year we live together, and in the summers he's traveling for school anyway, so I understudy Mama. This was a bad year because we came here in March and I had to drop school, but I really couldn't let her come alone. If she gets discouraged and donates money instead of time, well, you see the problem. Bend your knees more."

"The problem that I see is when you finally have to tell her."

"Don't be conjuring up graphic images, but we're being super careful not to get me pregnant. Once I'm twenty-five so she can't just dump the money, we'll lay the marriage on her gently. If your friend Alex can pass for a conservationist, Darren could pass for the Pope."

"Darren?"

"My husband. I'm warm in front, and now my bum is cold, ready to roll?"

"One, two, three."

"Did I mention that mother is thinking with half a loaf? My master plan is to wean her from conservation to grandchildren, and then pull out all the stops. Stew, you do have the loveliest biceps. Keep it right there. I think I'm going to sleep now."

"Shall I check once in a while to see if anything is getting cold?"

"Never mind, I'll let you know. Good night, my hero. Maybe you should marry Fanny."

She did drop off, a gentle purring, and she continued to turn periodically. Her problem was that the suit of many pockets was short on insulation so one thing and then another needed warming. Once she was asleep, she seemed to flow around me and fit just fine in any position.

I napped too. Even ecstasy becomes the norm after a while.

Chapter 17

Be it ever so humble, there's no place like home.
Maid of Milan—John Howard Payne

Morning was cold, but overcast. I slipped out of the bag and built up the fire. Carolyn missed her bed warmer and struggled up to use the fire for a substitute. I rolled the bag, stowed it, and fired up the Panther. We both scooped handfuls of snow to douse the fire, and set out to seek our fortunes.

The lake that had turned us back did appear depressed in the middle. We skirted the edge. In half an hour the hills tapered off and the trees thinned. I recognized the line of hills beyond Bettles and we sailed along at a good clip. The Koyukuk River had been strained. Ice had ridges and valleys in it, but we blasted across, turned upstream beside it, and in a few minutes the lodge appeared.

Carolyn gave me one more squeeze, then bolted up the steps. I was one step behind her, but she turned right toward the stairs and the bathroom. I turned left toward the kitchen and the coffeepot. Fanny understood priorities. She ran to give me a hug, but brought a cup of coffee with her. I hugged with left hand, guzzled with right.

Stella came from her room. "How many?"

"Just two of us now, but the others will be along shortly."

"You got separated?"

"Yeah, when the creek rose, they were on the wrong side so they had to drive around it."

"I thought it was something like that. Who was that who ran upstairs?"

"The lovely Carolyn." Fanny dug her elbow into my ribs.

"Do I need to go comfort her?" Stella asked.

"Nah, she's a strong lady. She'll survive." Stella grabbed two more cups and we moved to the table. Fanny brought the pot with her.

Stella outlined the drama from the other side. "We had company yesterday. The John River stopped flowing and the whole village came to visit. Apparently it was stopped for over an hour."

"Well, it was flowing just fine where we were."

"Do we need to send out a search party, Stew?"

"Are you kidding? They've got four machines, three of the best guides in the Arctic, and Mrs. Whidbey is wearing a grocery store. They'll be along, as soon as they run out of blackberry brandy."

Carolyn floated down the stairs, fresh from the shower, wearing a robe and barefoot. She grabbed her coffee and sat beside me, Fanny was in my lap. It was obvious, from body language, I think, that Carolyn wasn't concerned about keeping covered in present company. Stella gave me a long searching look, eyes narrowed as if she were going snow blind.

"Stew, the shower is vacant. Maybe you should nip upstairs."

"Right, I have a terrible need to wash my hair." I lifted Fanny and set her on my chair. I think they were going to do girl talk, whatever that is.

It may not be macho, but a long, hot shower is a wonderful thing, and clean clothes do make for a clean man. When I got back to the table, Carolyn was wearing blouse and skirt, and those tie-on pumps again. She and Stella were holding hands, like sisters, and Fanny was serving BLTs on big chunks of toasted homemade bread.

I figured out how Stella managed tomatoes. She had a line of green ones in the pantry and served them when they ripened. They do not compare with the ones that ripened on summer vines, but they are a treat in the Arctic. The lettuce wasn't quite as crisp as it had been the week after the mail plane came.

We were still stuffing BLTs down when snow machines buzzed outside the door. It was all one sound when they came, but we heard them shut off engines. One, two, three, four. Stella ran for the door; we followed, carrying our sandwiches.

I very nearly dropped mine. Alex was bent over his machine, but the other three were approaching the steps, arms around each other, Mrs. Whidbey between Andy and K.J. They were doing a dance routine as they came, two steps forward and a hop, and singing loud enough to echo. "Follow the yellow brick road" A hop and a step back. "Follow the yellow brick road."

Madam broke ranks and ran to embrace Carolyn. "Oh, honey, wasn't it wonderful? We found your tracks so we knew you were together and Stewie would take care of my little girl. We camped right there in the circle that you made, and the Northern Lights were fantastic. Alex and K.J. made us a lovely tent. This morning we followed your trail all the way home."

We trooped inside, new arrivals tossing outer layers of clothes. Fanny brought more sandwiches. Mother gave Carolyn one more hug, grabbed a sandwich, and kept talking with her mouth full. "Carrie, my dear, my darling daughter, I thought we were all going to die and I finally realized what's really important. Then we got out of the creek but you were behind us and I was terrified for you. Alex and K.J. kept telling me that Stew would take care of you, but it looked impossible. Then we found your tracks and knew they were a message that you were all right.

"We sang camp songs half the night, K.J. has a lovely bass and Andy is a marvelous tenor. We finished the blackberry brandy, but K.J. had a bottle of medicine too. Alex shot a whole bunch of rabbits, and we stuffed ourselves silly." She paused to wash down that mouthful with coffee and grabbed another bite.

Alex carried his sandwich upstairs, and Fanny followed him. Maybe she was going to wash his back. Mrs. Whidbey turned to me and gave me a hug. I was so shocked that I had to sit. "Stewie, you did take care of my little girl, didn't you? She looks radiant."

"It was my pleasure, Mrs. Whidbey."

"Oh, for goodness sakes, call me Maddy."

K.J. sank down into a chair. He was looking gray around the gills, but he was smiling. Maddy perched beside him but was overcome with emotion and put down her sandwich to squeeze his hand. She grabbed the sandwich again, gnawed off a hunk, and kept talking.

"You know, Carrie dear, I think our work here is done. With Andy and K.J. here to take care of things, we needn't worry. Andy has agreed to be the local ambassador for The Green Army." Another slug of coffee and another bite.

Carolyn wasn't convinced. "Not back to San Francisco, Mama?"

"No, darling, I've been thinking about our lovely home on Vashon Island. The crocuses will be up, the daffodils will need tending. You know the apple trees weren't pruned last fall? It's not right for us to be here when our own back yard is going to wrack and ruin. My, how your dear father loved his apple orchard."

Carolyn gave a little shriek. Her mouth dropped open. She covered it with her hand and ran for the stairs. Maddy (she'll always be Mrs. Whidbey to me) finished her coffee and stood.

"Please excuse me, ladies and gentlemen. I think my daughter needs to tell me about her secret marriage." She turned and ran up the stairs. She had to dodge Fanny, who was coming down with her arms full of dirty clothes, mine and Alex's.

K.J. sagged back in his chair. "Dear lord, I've got to sleep. It's been too many years since I partied all night. Stella, my love, my guardian angel, I'm afraid that some of your beautiful stitchery pulled loose. It was fine on the river, but it wasn't meant for dancing. Would you be a sweetheart and zip me up again?"

He struggled to his feet and limped toward his room. Stella stopped in the kitchen to grab a first-aid kit. She and Andy followed K.J. down the hall, Andy still chewing on a sandwich.

Alex came downstairs, clean, shaved, and combed, which reminded me that I had forgotten the shaving part. He plunked down across the table from me, and grabbed another sandwich. "Man, did you see those nuggets that K.J. is packing?"

"That I did. Did you notice what Mother Nature did to his mine?"

"Never can tell. Maybe the water just came straight up and went straight down."

"Yeah, and maybe the pieces of the box floated back together with all of the nuggets in it. You want to go back up and have a look?"

"Can't. I left passengers in Galena. You should wait a day or two anyhow; let the water freeze again if it will."

"Alex, the river in the canyon is not going to freeze again this year. Next trip will be by boat, but I guess I can run up that way and just see what I can see."

"Man, that one nugget, looks like a peanut, two ounces, at least." There was no doubt where Alex's mind was.

We carted the ladies' luggage downstairs and Alex taxied the Beech up in front of the door. He had six seats in the front of the cabin and a cargo net in back. We stowed the cases.

"Shall we load your Polaris, Maddy?" K.J. asked.

"No, you keep it. There's not much use for snow machines on Vashon Island."

We had a hugging and kissing orgy, with tears, and Carolyn gave me a kiss that only a husband should experience. Alex pointed Carolyn toward the co-pilot's seat. Maddy settled down in a front seat with a copy of Better Homes and Gardens. Alex pulled the door shut, and a moment later the engines cranked and sputtered, then settled down to roars.

We all stepped back to wave. I was still reeling from Carolyn's kiss, but then realized it was Fanny I was hugging.

Chapter 18

When the candles are out, all women are fair.
Conjugal Precepts-—Plutarch

W e gathered around the counter in silent concourse for the weighing of the nuggets. K.J. had four, and together they weighed six ounces, seven penny weight. It's not that Andy and K.J. were mathematical geniuses. Their skill was selective. They spoke in unison: $2,222.50.

Andy solemnly subtracted K.J.'s former grubstake, $403.87, and wrote the balance, $1,818.43 in big black figures. I was doing my own figuring. Half of that, or $909.21 belonged to Alex and me, so my take was $454.60; a hundred and fifty bucks more than I would have earned if I'd spent the last week and a half driving steam points. The difference was probably what I owed Andy for room and board.

"What shall we have for dinner?" Fanny asked Stella.

"How about broiling some moose steaks, and let's fix a couple of packages of frozen asparagus."

Fanny nodded and headed to the kitchen. Stella brought an armload of fabric from her room and spread it out on the far end of the dining table. She was making a quilt. I knew that eventually the pattern would knock your eyes out, but she was in the early stages, so the pattern wasn't yet apparent. Andy and K.J. settled down at the near end of the table to play cribbage. Next to booze, that is the number one pastime in the Arctic. Every sourdough worth his salt has made his own cribbage board. Andy's was a walrus tusk, drilled and scrimshawed. I scrounged through the bookcase.

We were having a typical afternoon in the Arctic. A lot of time is spent waiting for water to thaw, waiting for water to freeze, or just waiting for the wind to stop blowing. A prodigious amount of artwork is produced at such times, typically intricate carving in wood or ivory. Stella's quilt would be a work of art, worthy of a fine art museum, and I gather that doing it entirely by hand is a remarkable feat.

The temperature outside was ten above and would drop below zero during the night. I had volunteered to ride upriver and scout the damage, but I wanted a day or two of freezing first. As I'd told Alex, the running water wasn't going to freeze again, but any puddles that were lying around after the flood would be solid, and the ice on the rivers would cement itself back together.

There are a few people who simply go insane during enforced waits, but the antidote to that is reading. It's not unusual to meet a scruffy, wizened old sourdough who can recite the complete works of Dickens, or maybe the entire

Bible. I spent a winter as caretaker, the only soul at the Red Devil Mine, and the library consisted of Shakespeare's plays. I learned a lot more that winter than I ever did in college.

I found my old friend, the complete works of William Shakespeare, and carried it to the table. It's hard to believe that the Bard lived over three hundred-fifty years ago. He always seems to be writing about today. Like in Troilus and Cressida, the advice to Hercules: "Time hath, my lord, a wallet at his back wherein he puts alms for oblivion..." That always gives me goose bumps because I can see it happening. "Love, friendship, charity, are subjects all to envious and calumniating time... One touch of nature makes the whole world kin, that all with one accord praise newborn gods... and give to dust that is a little gilt, more laud than gilt o'er dusted."

Before I was thirty, I would think about the music idols of my high school years. The new ones are not better, I would say, not nearly as good, but they are new, and that is all that counts. I get a special guilt from that soliloquy because my life is probably half over, maybe much more than half, and I haven't accomplished a damn thing. Emulation does not have a thousand sons that one by one pursue me. I wrestle with the imagery. "Like a noble steed, fallen in first rank of battle, must lie there pavement for the abject rear..." I have the sneaking suspicion that I am the abject rear.

I flipped to Julius Caesar and found the passage that is pertinent. I had been pondering that one as recently as yesterday: "Cowards die many times before their death, the valiant taste of death but once." Well, maybe I don't live up to that, but I try. "Of all the wonders that I have yet heard, it seems to me most strange that men should fear; seeing that death, a necessary end, will come when it will come."

As You Like It describes my encounter with the lovely Carolyn. "No sooner met, but they looked. No sooner looked but they loved... but, oh how bitter a thing it is to look into happiness through another man's eyes."

I didn't want to get maudlin. I flipped to Henry V to get my blood flowing with the battle cry. "And Gentlemen in England now abed will hold their manhood cheap when any speak who fought with us on this St. Crispian's day." I couldn't sit still after that. I had to go out and kick snow berms beside the runway. All those friends and cousins of King Henry are dead, have been for four hundred years, whether or no they died in that battle, but they were cut down with testosterone flowing.

I was thinking that maybe we miss that in our safe modern culture. Maybe men will always feel the need to whang each other with broadswords. I was kicking snow berms, wondering what, if anything, was the point to my life. Should I be looking for a Herculean challenge, or did I just need to grow up?

Dramatists tell us there are three types of conflict: man against man, man against nature, and man against himself. Well, I wasn't fighting other men, and while nature has its moments, it can be handled. My problem must be myself. It would be too demeaning to think that my life had no conflict at all. It would be simpler, and rather satisfying, to have a clear enemy to whang broadswords with.

Dinner was at 6:20, and half the wine was gone before the steaks arrived. Fanny sat down with us and we dug in with gusto. There is nothing like friendly happy chatter to season food. Dinner took two hours instead of the one that had been the custom under the previous regime. We did talk with our mouths full, but we ate slowly and savored the flavors as we went. Dessert was canned peaches and coffee, and roars of laughter while Stella described her meeting Andy.

They were both at a nightclub in Anchorage with other dates, but when their eyes met, they each knew that the end was nigh. They kept excusing themselves to go to the bathroom and meeting in the hallway. By the time their dates got worried and came to check, Andy and Stella were locked in a passionate embrace. Their dates left together, and Andy and Stella have been locked in a metaphorical embrace for forty years.

Even K.J. had a love story. He had left his childhood sweetheart in Seattle, promising to return from the gold fields in a year with untold riches. She promised to wait for him until the end of time. It took him two years to get back. He hitchhiked to Seattle on a tramp steamer with fifty cents in his pocket, and his sweetheart introduced him to her husband and her son.

Fanny and Stella took dishes to the kitchen and continued to chatter while water splashed. Andy and K.J. went back to the cribbage board, and I stepped outside again. The overcast was breaking up and the temperature diving. Stars twinkled like streetlights through the rifts in clouds. Carolyn would be in Anchorage now, or already on a jet for Seattle. A bigger man might have been happy for her and her "most wonderful man in the world" husband. I could feel the solitude in the arctic air. I was still licking my wounds when I crawled into bed.

My solitude was interrupted when Fanny came in to sit on the edge of my bed.

"Hi, Stewie, are you awake?"

"I think I am now. Are you a dream?"

"Well, I wouldn't mind being a fantasy. Want to scoot over a little?"

"Fanny, you know you are the most beautiful girl in the world, the most desirable person I've ever met, and I love you dearly. However, you must know that I will never ever marry you, till death do us come together."

"Yeah, I know that, Stew. I think you're great, and I hope my husband will be just like you, only younger and richer. I seem to be much more attractive, since Carolyn left. It was really disgusting, the way she threw herself at you."

"Nah, she was just giving her mother a hard time. Didn't you get the word that she's a married lady?"

"Worst kind, they have nothing left to lose. Did you boff her on the trail, Stewie?"

"Bite your tongue. I'm a perfect gentleman."

"Well, I suppose that is possible. Whatever happened, thanks for denying it."

Fanny had pulled her sweater off, no bra of course; she didn't need one. She was unzipping her skirt. "Are you going to move over, or do I have to sleep on top of you?"

"Fanny, I simply cannot feel good about taking advantage of you." I wasn't prepared for her burst of derisive laughter.

"Stewie that is the most sexist crack I've ever heard. What kind of masculine superiority makes you think that you are the one taking advantage?"

I didn't have an answer for that so she continued.

"The way I figure it, we have just so many nights on this earth and every one spent alone is wasted. If you're not with the one you love, love the one you're with."

She crawled in and snuggled. "Now, Stewie, isn't this

really much better than sleeping alone? Want me to show you a trick that Alex taught me?"

"I don't know, do I?"

"Yeah, I'm pretty sure you do. He learned it from a girl in Fairbanks named Joanne. Stewie, is Joanne pretty?"

"Fanny, Joanne doesn't hold a candle to you."

Chapter 19

An optimist is a guy who has never had much experience.
Maxims of Archy—Donald Robert Perry Marquis

The temperature had kept right on dropping and, according to Andy's thermometer, had passed fifteen below zero. I was fortified with a dozen pancakes, floated in blueberry syrup. That has to be the best condiment in the world. I have a cousin, Lela Ayers, in Palmer who makes syrup just like Stella's. If I ever settle down, it might be in Palmer, just for the occasional invitations to Lela's house.

The Panther was purring; it doesn't care about temperature. The river was rough, but the Panther didn't mind that either. So long as I held on, we were zipping right along, past the village, toward the pot of gold.

When I came to Waterloo, the scene of Mrs. Whidbey's

dunking, it was a lake covered by clear ice. The riverbank where I had cut the spruce to build the bridge was now naked, and had moved back fifty yards from where it had been. Cold or no, I skirted the edge of the lake. The river was now a broad, straight highway toward the canyon, and it appeared to be frozen over, but I didn't trust it. The valiant may die only once, but there is no hurry. I followed the bank and wound through the trees. Ground was covered with ice, inches thick where it had flooded and frozen, but that ice was sitting on a firm foundation.

The end of the canyon was free of snow and the river was normal size, but when I looked down at the ice, it was clear. I could see bubbles zipping past, two inches below the surface. A gravel bar on the far side reached up into the canyon, so the drill was to cross the river. I turned around and slunk back to Waterloo Lake.

The lake was no longer covered by snow, so the overflow was a thing of the past. The question was how thick was the ice? I left the machine and walked gingerly, several steps out onto the lake. Ice didn't creak. I tested it by bouncing my weight up and down, not jumping, but standing up and squatting. In half a dozen knee bends, the ice was going up and down with me, but elastic, not breaking. I know the ability of ice to carry weight doesn't come from tensile strength. The ice is floating, so if it sags a little, it just displaces more water.

I drove the machine back into the woods to a spot where I had a straight path to the lake. The Panther, it turned out, will go over a hundred miles an hour, flat out with a little run. I felt the ice give when the machine hit it, but if it broke, we were already long gone. The gravel-bar side had the same ice cover reaching back into the trees. I kept the speed up and jumped the creek that had caused the original overflow.

This was the spot where we had first been watched during the extraction of Mrs. Whidbey. The snow, along with any tracks, had been washed away by the flood. I didn't notice any calling cards fortuitously stuck in the trees. I'd been bumping along at a steady pace for several minutes and would have been expected to keep going. Instead, I shut off the machine and listened while it coasted to a stop. I didn't even hear a legitimate echo, so I wasn't being paced. Of course, they might be waiting to cut me off at the pass.

Cliffs at the entrance to the canyon looked a lot higher and steeper than I remembered. There seemed to be two possible approaches. I could ride the machine in and be prepared to make a hasty retreat, or I could leave the machine safely outside and walk in. That way, no matter what happened, if I survived, I'd have a ride home. I chickened out and left the machine.

Something about shutting off the engine underscores where you are. As long as the engine is running, you're connected to humanity. Until it starts again, you're very much alone. I unzipped, and pulled my new pistol out of my belt. Carrying it in a belt is just my habit. Gene Autry and the Lone Ranger wore holsters, but a pistol can drop out of a holster, even if it's strapped or buckled in, and I might not notice. If it's in my belt, I can feel it at all times, and that can be a very good feeling.

I spun the cylinder to check the load and stuck the gun into my parka pocket, but kept my hand on it. That felt even better. The reality was that the canyon was no more dangerous now than it had been originally, probably less, since it had just had a good shaking up. If bushwhackers were ahead of me in the canyon, they may have already found the gold. If they were still waiting for me to show them where it was, I would be ready. The new danger was all in my head, but my imagination was in overdrive. I left the machine on high ground outside the canyon, and walked in, being careful not to make any noise lest a clatter should bring down the walls.

On previous trips, we had stuck to the middle of the river, and the walls looked vertical. Now, I was hugging the wall because the strip of dry gravel was only eight feet wide. The cliff appeared to curve out over me and I was looking up at cracks and shaky-appearing ledges. I was remembering an exercise in some college class, psychology, I think. The scenario was a freeway in California that ran beneath a cliff. Would that be the Pacific Palisades? Anyhow, there were eight lanes of traffic, rushing bumper to bumper, and since it was California, the speed was at least eighty miles per hour.

In the college exercise, a rock the size of a baseball fell off the cliff and hurtled toward the freeway. Since it took the rock six or seven seconds to fall, the cars that were under it when it started were safely past. The car that arrived coincident with the rock was a convertible. The rock hit the driver in the head and killed him. The rock had to hit a six-inch-circle at impossibly converging speeds. It could have hit any hard-topped car, or landed harmlessly on the seat beside the driver. The odds against fatality were astronomical.

I can't remember what the point of that exercise was. Maybe it was just not to make any long-term plans, but I was keeping an eye on the rocks above me.

Inside the canyon, the river was racing with just a tiny skim of ice along the edge. At the first bend, a quarter mile in, there was spray in the air, and ice freezing up the sides of the canyon, not to mention on me. My gravel walk continued around the bend, and into a terrible hissing sound, like maybe the flood was coming down again. This was valiant time. For one thing, it didn't sound like a flood, it sounded like a high-pressure water pipe that has frozen and burst. The river beside me was gushing along, per normal. If the river had stopped flowing, it would have been, "Now I lay me down to sleep..." time. I ventured around the corner.

Two rocks the size of school buses were blocking the canyon, one on each side with a two-foot gap in the center. Water was shooting through the gap like the stream from a fire hose. I plastered my back against the canyon wall, ignored the spray, and sidestepped to the rock on my side. It was fifteen feet tall, but broken and jagged enough for climbing. I scrambled up, mostly to get above the spray.

Upstream from the rocks lay a placid lake, obviously fifteen feet deep, and reaching around the next bend. It was frozen over, except for a crescent fifty feet in diameter by the nozzle. The ice was two feet below me and I could have stepped down onto it, but I didn't. For my money, when you're dealing with real ice, turbulent water, and sudden death under it, three days at twenty below is a minimum. I couldn't see K.J.'s cut bank, and I couldn't be sure if it was gone, or if it was under water. It didn't matter. K.J.'s mine was up there, under at least ten feet of water.

I figuratively tucked my tail between my legs and sneaked back out of the canyon. The spray covered me with a thin layer of ice, so I looked like a glazed doughnut by the time I got back to the Panther.

* * *

"Draw the rocks," K.J. said. He and Andy leaned, one over each shoulder, while I drew a facsimile of Gibraltar on each side of the river and Niagara Falls shooting out between them.

"What do you think?" he asked Andy. I thought we should forget it and come back after breakup, but he wasn't asking me. I wouldn't have minded going up the lake, but in a boat. With the current and eddies in that canyon, the ice might be six inches thick in one spot and one inch thick a foot away. No, thank you.

"Twenty sticks should do it. Need to plant them under the rock, about here." Andy indicated the edge of the waterspout.

"Twenty sticks of what should do what?" I could already tell that I did not like this discussion.

"Dynamite, of course. One little pop, the rock moves, lake drains, and the next day you walk in to pick up the nuggets."

"Just where do I stand while the lake drains? I don't think I want to be on the rock when the dynamite goes off."

"No problem." K.J. at least, wasn't worried. "Andy will cut you a five-minute fuse. You figure it's a quarter mile out of the canyon, so you can walk it in three minutes, easy. You climb up the cliff on the outside of the canyon, and wait for the water to go by."

Andy shared K.J.'s non-concern. "Yep, no problem at all. I've got half a case of dynamite and a new roll of slow-burning fuse. Piece of cake, walk in the park, couldn't be simpler."

I was having the sacrificial lamb reaction, but then I thought about that two ounce nugget…

The cap, the supersensitive firecracker that starts the chain reaction, was packed in bubble wrap and stowed in the toolbox under the cowling. The fuse was coiled, and stuck in my pocket. The box of dynamite was covered by a plastic bag and strapped to the luggage carrier behind. That meant no survival gear, but if anything went wrong this trip, gear wouldn't help me survive.

There is something about sitting on a box of dynamite that makes for smooth, careful driving, but eventually I did come to the canyon. Nothing seemed to have changed; the river was running normally and no snipers were silhouetted anywhere.

The options about leaving the machine were the same as before, but this time I opted to ride it into the canyon, bumping slowly over the gravel. I know that won't work too long because the tracks are on slides that require snow for lubrication, but slowly, for a little while, I seemed to get away with it. The skis didn't like it much. They were screeching and shooting sparks, but heck, that's what the skegs on the bottom of the skis are for.

I've read about a boat called the Maid of the Mist that runs under Niagara Falls. That's how it felt approaching the waterspout. The hiss from the stream of water was overpowering; it filled my head and it hurt. Wherever the floating mist landed, it froze and stayed, so the canyon looked like a limestone cave, or maybe even a cathedral.

Canyon walls on both sides were transformed to glittering white tapestries of pipe organs and stalactites. Ice in places appeared to be several inches thick. Some childhood game came to mind: "heavy, heavy hangs over thy head." I just wanted out of that canyon.

The gravel trail beside the cliff had picked up a coat of ice, and it sloped down toward the river so the machine wanted to slip sideways. At least, the ice stopped the sparks from the skegs. The Panther inched along past the worst of the spray, ice covered but not complaining. Next to the pertinent rock, a few feet of gravel were barely covered with ice, and almost level. I took a tentative step off the machine and didn't slide, so I bravely climbed off, grabbed the skis, and turned the machine around. Leaving the engine running seemed like a good idea.

My instructions were to set the dynamite as close to the waterspout as possible. I took that to mean where the water was swirling around in an eddy behind the spout. The first problem was to lug the case of dynamite down to the edge. Two steps from the machine the slope got steeper. I was sliding, starting a ski run toward the water and no hands to catch anything because I wasn't about to drop the case of dynamite.

I think the activity is called glissading, like skiing without skis. Goodbye, cruel world. Splash. I was standing in two inches of water, the bottom wasn't slippery, and I still had the dynamite in my arms. Some rocks on the bottom were loose, so I used those to make a platform where I could set the case without its floating away. Then it was hands and knees, back up the slope to the machine. My mittens were wet, so if I left them in one place for a moment they froze and stuck. I worked up the slope, one frozen-down hand at a time. Maybe that's the secret to Spiderman's climbing. He climbs steeper walls, but they aren't usually slippery.

I left the detonator cap in its bubble wrap cocoon and slid backward down the slope until my feet were in the water. Next step was to secure the fuse inside the cap. The cap is a copper tube, the diameter of a .22 shell with an inch of empty space on the open end. The fuse fits inside the tube, and you crimp it there with pliers. Old hands use their teeth; I couldn't handle that thought.

Next, I unwrapped the plastic bag from the dynamite case and picked out one stick. I used my knife to cut that stick in half, exposing the cornmeal-with-white-worms inside. Very carefully with the tip of the knife I started a hole into the dry cereal, then shoved the cap-with-fuse into the half stick and put the whole thing back into the case. Gently, of course.

I crawled back toward the machine, uncoiling fuse. I could just reach the machine with one hand when the fuse ended. The knife split the end of the fuse for half an inch and black powder spilled out. I touched the lighter to that and it hissed like a jet engine, spitting a tiny flame that disappeared inside the sheath, way too fast.

I dropped the fuse, crawled onto the Panther, and squeezed the throttle too hard. The track spun and slewed down toward the water. Chop the throttle and go easy. The track worked back up the slope and followed the scratches the skegs were making. Add power gradually, keep the machine pointed uphill, try not to think about how long the fuse has been burning.

When the ice turned to bare rock it was skedaddle time,

let the sparks fly. I was surprised that the dynamite hadn't exploded yet. Outside the canyon, I parked on a shelf that was twenty feet above the river. I shut off the machine, and covered my ears. Time slowed down to normal, then to slow motion, still no explosion. Too late, I realized I should have checked my watch when I lit the fuse.

Wisdom from my youth was that the most dangerous thing, in or around blasting, is a charge that doesn't go off when it's supposed to. You don't know why it didn't explode, and it may yet go off at any time. I marked the time on my watch, but I was thinking I'd wait a week before I went back to see what had happened. Four minutes ticked by with just the peace and solitude of nature. Bright yellow sunshine sparkled on blue mountains, and a gentle river gurgled under thin ice below me. If there had been birds singing it would have been a cliché.

Suddenly the canyon belched fire and smoke like a WW I cannon. Rocks whistled and crackled like bullets when they flew past. I'd been expecting one quick pop, followed by a cascade of water, but the explosion seemed to be going on and on. The flames and smoke tapered off. Rocks stopped flying past, but the crashing in the canyon kept getting louder. I was watching the river, waiting for the surge of released water. Instead, the ice sagged in the middle and caved in. The river had stopped running.

I don't know how fast water runs downhill. Surely not nearly as fast as it had backed up into the canyon. I didn't stick around to find out. For every minute that the river was stopped, the water was backing up at least five feet. By the second minute, I was mashing the throttle and hanging on for dear life. Ice along the edge of the river was bowed and twisted; the Panther was airborne half the time. Ice on Waterloo Lake had sagged down several feet in the center, but this was no time to be making judgments. I raced right across the center and was flying for thirty feet from the ski jump at the end of the lake.

Below the lake, the river ice was bowed and tortured, but it seemed to be holding my weight and I kept the throttle mashed. I flashed past the village and climbed out of the river on the first trail going up, then reefed on the brake. I was in a pack of twenty machines, each carrying two or three fur-clad passengers, and all headed for the lodge.

It was an orderly evacuation. No one else seemed to be panicked, so I calmed down and joined the queue. Machines lined up in front of the lodge beside the runway and fur-clad backs were trooping up the steps. I tried to be inconspicuous and blend in, hoping no one would point a finger and shout that I was the miscreant who had stopped the river.

Chapter 20

If it were done when 'tis done, then 'twere well
it were done quickly.
Macbeth—Shakespeare

Inside, there was a party in progress. The room was packed
with wall-to-wall people and more were streaming in.
Fanny had set two gigantic coffeepots on the table with
extension cords running from the kitchen. One pot was
dispensing into paper cups, the other perking. Stella had a
whole case of Oreo cookies on the table. She was opening
packages and stacking cookies on platters.

I had the impression that the room was knee deep in
running and shouting toddlers, each tiny fist clutching
cookies. The buzz in the room was typical cocktail party
chatter, but ten percent English, ninety percent Inuit. Many
of the new arrivals unzipped parkas and toddlers popped out,

like baby kangaroos from mama's pouch, or is it daddy's pouch? Several women were seated at the table, nursing infants. Breasts are not considered shameful or nasty by the Inuit. I think they rather enjoy them. One particularly well-endowed matron was nursing twins, one at each breast, while she managed to hold a coffee cup and munch cookies.

I lined up at the coffeepot; there was no booze in sight. My cloth parka stood out among the furs, but still no one was pointing accusing fingers. Andy and K.J. were both involved in conversations. They didn't need to ask what had happened, and maybe they were distancing themselves from me, just in case the mood did turn ugly. That seemed unlikely; the party was as convivial as any I've ever attended. No one seemed concerned that the village might wash down the river at any moment.

The line for the bathroom reached halfway down the stairs. I bypassed that and slunk into my room. The natives weren't ignoring me, they all smiled with friendly, open expressions, but no small talk came to mind. I closed my door, peeled off parka and snowsuit, and flopped on the bed.

Perhaps an hour went by before two snow machines pulled up outside. Young men bounded up the steps, so I eased out into the hallway. The line to the bathroom was shorter; maybe twenty people. They smiled and nodded while I squeezed past. The two sentries made their announcement in Inuit, but the meaning was clear, the John River was flowing again, and the party was over.

Toddlers ran to the table for more cookies, and were zipped inside parent's parkas, each tiny fist clutching a maximum load. I watched through the window while the machines departed. Furs were piling onto machines, three and four per, and they must have had an unspecified number of toddlers under their parkas. When mine was the only machine left out front, I turned back to face the music.

Andy had tossed a great mound of paper cups into the fireplace and torched them. K.J. moved to the table. Stella and Fanny lugged the coffeepots to the kitchen and Stella came back with a bottle of bourbon and a bowl of ice.

"How bad is it?" K.J. asked.

"I wouldn't know. I didn't stick around for the flood, but it sounded to me like the entire canyon imploded." I grabbed a glass, chunked in ice, and poured. "I would like the record to show that dynamiting that canyon was not my idea."

"Quite right, quite right. You did set the charge under the impeding rock?"

"Precisely. I braved the swirling maelstrom to set the charge as close to the gap as humanly possible without scuba gear."

Andy joined us and poured a slug for himself. "Temperature should stay at least twenty below through tomorrow. Perhaps the three of us should take a ride up that way in the morning."

With no dynamite to haul, I had the emergency gear back. We didn't bother with shovels, but we each carried a lunch that Fanny had packed. The river was now such a mess that it was often faster, and always safer, to wind through the trees beside it. It was almost noon when we arrived at Waterloo Lake.

The lake was full again, and most of it was once again a pristine ice-skating rink, but we stared in shock. The little creek that had come in from the left and made the overflow was now a full flowing river. Trees and rocks, and great mounds of frozen dirt, were cascading into the lake, forming a delta. Larger splashes sent ripples through the ice like ripples in water. We went around the lake on the right-hand side.

What had been the John River was now an extension of the lake, reaching up toward the canyon, but with no current flowing. It tapered off and quit, leaving patches of ice sitting on dry ground at the end of the canyon. We crossed what had been the river, like Moses on dry ground, and parked on the shelf where I had waited for the blast.

K.J. fished down into his sleeping bag and pulled out a bottle. We solemnly passed it around.

"Want to walk up the canyon and have a look?" Andy asked.

"What, and meet the entire river coming down?" I grabbed the bottle out of K.J.'s hand and took another swig.

K.J. took the bottle back, wiped the mouth with his sleeve, and chugged. "Apparently the river has been flowing the other way for twenty-four hours. Why should it change now?"

"How about just because we tempted fate? You guys go ahead and walk, or ride up the river. I'm going to climb up this cliff and watch from above while you get washed away."

"A capital suggestion." K.J. toasted me with the bottle, but didn't pass it. "We'll wait here for your report."

I grabbed Fanny's lunch out of my basket and zipped it into my snowsuit above the belt. I could feel the can of beer in the sack, so I wouldn't die of dehydration. Come to think of it, that was the least of my worries. I nudged the lunch left so that if I unzipped the parka with my left hand I could grab the gun butt with my right. I wouldn't be fast enough for the O.K. Corral, but not bad for winter. The end of the cliff wasn't so steep as the sides, and the back, or left-hand side, tapered off into trees, so when the climb got tough, I went around.

The top was a plateau with forest. No need to get near the cliff edge, I could hear a freight train roaring downgrade ahead of me. What used to be a small creek had worn a groove into the hilltop, so there had been another gorge almost connected to the river. That was now a raging cataract. I worked closer to the canyon. In effect, the dynamite had blown the side out of the cliff and dumped it into the river. The ridge that was now blocking the canyon was fifteen feet above the water, and with the river running down the new channel, water wasn't going to attack the plug.

The new channel was getting deeper. Rocks the size of basketballs were shooting out of the cataract and cannoning away through the trees and larger rocks were grating underneath and shaking the earth. Someday, the new channel would be as deep as the old one, maybe in a hundred years or so. In the meantime, the canyon had become a permanent lake. K.J.'s nuggets were now under at least twenty feet of water.

I'd never seen a new river being formed before. I guess I always thought it was a gradual process, but this one was fascinating, like watching a construction site. I sat down on a rock, pulled out Fanny's lunch, and played sidewalk superintendent. Water was ripping up full-grown trees and shoving them into piles, then turning when the trees blocked it. Dirt simply disappeared, right down to bedrock, wherever the river decided to go, but overall, it was curving left and following what had been the creek back toward Waterloo Lake.

I finished the lunch. The beer had been inside my snowsuit, so it wasn't frozen, and if I belched it couldn't be heard over the din the cataract was making. I strolled back to report to the real authors of the new scenario.

"Can we get to the mine from the upriver side?" K.J. asked.

"Sure, by boat. That new lake must reach almost to Caribou Creek." I sat sideways on the Panther. We could hear occasional crashes in the trees when the new river took shortcuts. Water does seek its own level, with a vengeance.

"Ready?' K.J. asked.

"Ready for what?"

"We've got to get back immediately and file on the new claims."

"Right. Which new claims?"

"Stew, excuse me, Stan, that old river bottom has to be paved with gold. All we got was a little scum off the top. The river has been a natural sluice for a thousand years. Between me, and you, and your pilot friend Allen, we can claim the whole thing, right down to the lake. I'll stake the claims while you get to town and file them. You'd better pick up a couple of rifles. The minute these claims are filed, miners will come out of the woods trying to jump them. Let's get cracking." K.J. was riding Alex's Panther, and he led off down the slope, like maybe there were a hundred other miners racing to file ahead of us.

I was right behind him. He was absolutely correct. When we cut across the dry riverbed, I could smell the gold in it.

Chapter 21

He is a fool who leaves things close at hand to
follow what is out of reach.
Of Garrulity—Plutarch

KJ and Andy had the Coast and Geodetic Survey
maps spread on the table and were working
with rulers and dividers. Andy was using his pi-
lot's plotter for the vectors. A gold claim is usually 600 feet
by 1500 feet, and they were laying out claims to straddle
the old riverbed. They didn't even notice when an airplane
revved its engine out front.

The young Native man who came in looked familiar,
but I couldn't place him. He was tall for a native, around 5'9,
slender, wearing a wolf-fur parka. The expression "clean-
cut" came to mind. Fanny blazed past me and leapt. The
young man caught her and swung her around. The two of

them were nuzzling and kissing like long-lost lovers, which it turned out, they were.

"Clydie, you really did come back for me." I couldn't tell if Fanny was laughing or crying.

The young man set her down, dropped to one knee and pulled a small jewelry box out of his pocket.

"Fanny, I passed the bar exams and have a job with a law firm in Anchorage. Will you marry me now?" He opened the box to display a ring with a diamond the size of a lima bean. I heard a boo-hoo-hoo sobbing behind me. It was Stella, with tears streaming down her cheeks. She shoved past me to hug and kiss Clyde. Fanny put the ring on and ran to hug and kiss Andy. She actually distracted him from the map. He followed her back and shook hands with Clyde.

"Stew, do you know Clyde?" Fanny asked.

"Yeah, I know him. I'm trying to remember from where."

Clyde extended a hand. "We used to bump into each other when I was at the University of Alaska. I'd sneak into the Rendezvous Club for an underage drink and you bought me a few. That was a while back. I've been at the University of Washington finishing my law degree for the last three years."

"Of course. I wondered where you'd gone." We shook hands. His past peccadilloes were as safe with me as mine were with Fanny. I made a mental note to warn him not to teach Fanny any tricks he'd learned from Joanne.

Clyde and Andy were shaking hands a second time. Fanny and Stella were hugging and crying. K.J. turned back to the maps.

"Come on, Clyde, let's go tell Mama." Fanny ran for her

room and came back zipping her parka.

"Take the Panther that's parked behind Andy's machine." I suggested.

"Thanks. We'll be back in a couple of hours. I rented the 172 in Anchorage, and I have to return it tonight."

Fanny and Clyde skipped out the door, but Fanny called back to Stella. "Shall I send Rose down?"

"Yeah, please do. Get going."

They bounded down the steps, climbed onto my Panther, and raced away toward the village. Stella was still crying. Andy gave her a hug and patted her back, but he was on his way to the table and the maps, so Stella hugged me and sobbed on my shoulder.

"Stella, shouldn't you be happy about Fanny's getting married?"

"I am, Stew. This is the best thing that's happened since Andy married me." She was sobbing quietly, gave me a final hug and ran to her room. I wandered over to check the cartographers' progress. They had laid out nine standard claims, each running 600 feet north and south and 1500 feet east and west, but the claims were offset from each other, so they straddled the old riverbanks and reached from a point above where the new dam had blocked the river all the way down into what was now Waterloo Lake.

K.J. explained. "We'll file each claim in two names, the first one in yours and mine, then mine and Allen's..."

"Alex's"

"Right, then you and Alex, then you and me again. That way, if any one or two of us gets killed, the remaining one or two will still have three or six of the best claims in the world."

"Gotcha, but you'd better let Andy put the names on."

"Right, Andy and I will stake the claims. You get your tail into Anchorage and file them with BLM."

I checked my pocket. I always carry cash, if any, in my left front pocket. Keys, pocketknife, and lighter go in the right front, wallet in the left rear, handkerchief and comb in the right rear. The main point is that the wallet can stay buttoned in. It contains licenses, and if you have any, credit cards. You don't want to be dragging it out every time you buy a bottle in the Rendezvous Club, and you don't want anyone to see you stuffing bills in there. I had forty-seven dollars in my pocket.

"I'm a little short of filing fees, a whole lot short of buying rifles, and I'll be sleeping on the streets."

"How much do you need?" Andy asked.

"Five hundred might do it."

K.J. shook his head. "Not enough. Don't be coming back here with any deer rifles. Buy a couple of .222 Hornets, and enough ammunition for a world war. I kid you not, when those claims are filed, you'll think we've hit the beach at Normandy."

Andy went behind his counter. He came back and handed me twenty one-hundred-dollar bills. He also had a stack of forms with him. The law requires that you attach a claim form in a suitable container to a stake on the northwest corner of each claim, but judging by the stack of forms, Andy was planning to put a form on all four stakes of each claim.

"Don't we need Alex's signature?" I asked.

"No problem. I have it right here.... Stella," Andy called.

Stella came from her room; the crying jag seemed to be over. She took a pen from Andy; glanced at Alex's signature on the blank check he'd left, and commenced signing Alex Price on the forms. Maybe some expert could tell the difference in signatures; I couldn't. We passed pens, signed forms, copied metes and bounds, and eventually we had a stack of thirty-six forms for posting that matched Andy's map. He folded the map and handed it to me. I went upstairs and rolled the last clean clothes that Fanny had washed for me into a bundle with the map in the center. I wondered if Rose would be as accommodating as Fanny had been.

My machine rumbled back from the village and parked. Three people came up the stairs, Clyde carrying a small suitcase. Rose was obviously Fanny's sister, but I couldn't decide, younger or older. Rose and Fanny took the suitcase back to Fanny's lair. Stella had set the table for seven. Clyde declared he'd be delighted to take me into Anchorage with them.

Fanny and Rose came down the hall, Fanny carrying the suitcase. I think that Rose's things had come out of it and Fanny's gone in. She set the suitcase by the door, and we all gathered at the table. The beverage was two large bottles of sparkling grape juice, and the entrée with the strange aroma was Salisbury steaks, like, from a cow. It was a festive occasion, but abbreviated because we were going to fly right after dinner.

Clyde had turned into a brilliant raconteur, not much like the shy Native boy from the Bush that I remembered. He regaled us with tales of Seattle, and promised Fanny that Seattle trips would be frequent. She was too excited to eat, positively glowing. K.J.'s occasional contributions were a broken record. "Don't forget, Stew, two rifles, and get back here fast." Rose was smiling, but remained silent; this was Fanny's night.

Andy had the pertinent information. "Mail plane scheduled day after tomorrow. If you're lucky, you might make that."

Fanny tore her gaze away from Clyde long enough to notice that I was watching her and, for reasons unclear, I was mostly staring at Rose. "What's the matter, Stew? Do you know Rose from Fairbanks?"

I didn't dare answer her. I had no memory of a meeting, but that might only be an indication of how drunk I'd been at the time. The uneasy flickerings I was having were surely because Rose and Fanny looked so much alike. Rose studied me for a pregnant moment with the clearest, most beautiful, intelligent brown eyes I have ever drowned in. Sparks were flying; it was like a physical connection. Finally she shook her head, so I was off the hook.

"I was just wondering which of you is older. Surely at your tender ages, it is all right to ask?" Fanny and Rose giggled at that.

"I am," Fanny said, "by three minutes. We're twins." Rose gave me a smile that indicated I was forgiven for asking. When our eyes met again, my heart skipped a beat, but both girls turned back to fawning over Clyde.

We had another hugging and kissing orgy, but I was left out. Since I was coming right back, I didn't rate hugs from the locals, except for a quick squeeze and a peck from Stella. Rose spent her emotions on Fanny and Clyde. I gallantly crawled into the back seat of the 172, along with Fanny's case and my bundle. Fanny and Clyde buckled themselves in front.

Clyde did a good job of checking the plane while we taxied, and took off with the sure, confident hand of a pro, so I relaxed and watched the darkness gather in the valleys and work its way up the mountains. We landed in Tanana at the confluence of the Tanana and Yukon rivers for a pit stop and gasoline, and were off again. Fanny and Clyde were chattering nonstop. The sun was skimming the hills, almost behind us. I watched the light work its way up the Alaska Range that was rising ahead of us until finally, only the tip of Mt. McKinley was lit. I must have dozed off, because the tip of McKinley had become the oil well flares in Cook Inlet. Fanny and Clyde were still chattering and he had to interrupt her to call Merrill tower for clearance.

The city of Palmer was off to our left, then the black void of Cook Inlet, and the carpet of lights that was Anchorage outlined the water and reached ten miles to the Chugach Mountains and two thousand feet up those. If you just came from Chicago, I suppose Anchorage is no big deal, but if you have just come from Bettles and flown seven hundred miles over bush, Anchorage is a lot of lights.

Clyde parked the plane at Wilbur's Flight Service and dropped the keys through a slot in the door. A pedestrian crossing had a button on a light post. We pushed the button and a thousand cars stopped while we dashed across Fifth Avenue to the Airport Café.

We made the obligatory pit stop and gathered at the brightly lit counter for Peggy's world-famous pies. I picked a section of the counter where we could see Fifth Avenue through the picture windows, and a minute later Clyde came out still combing his hair, and left a vacant chair between us for Fanny. It seemed like a good time to impart some wisdom to Clyde. I was just a little nervousness about how to begin.

"Uh, Clyde, it might not be a good idea to teach Fanny

any tricks you learned from Joanne, at least not for a while."

Clyde chuckled. "Not to worry, Stew. Maybe you've heard Fanny's motto? 'If you're not with the one you love, love the one you're with?' We're not planning an open marriage, not even an open engagement, but you notice we've only been engaged for eight hours? You know the divorce rate is reaching for sixty percent and we want no part of that. See, if I had married Fanny first, and then met Joanne, there might have been a problem, or at least I would have always wondered. After three years in Fairbanks, three in Seattle, and now six months in Anchorage, you can imagine that there isn't much I'm going to wonder about, and I expect the same goes for Fanny. I wouldn't want Fanny to spend her life wondering what it might have been like with a dashing young pilot or a devil-may-care miner. I just feel so lucky that Fanny was still available that I can hardly believe it, and, buddy, life starts now."

Fanny came out of the ladies' room wearing heels, hose, a short skirt, and lipstick. I very nearly fell off my chair. She was gorgeous. She slid onto the vacant slot between us, and the waitress came right over with three coffees and the pie list. The waitress had a nametag that said, "Peggy" but she wasn't the Peggy that the café' was named for. Peggy's pies were famous before this kid was born.

"Hi, where did y'all come in from?" She wasn't psychic. At 1:00 a.m. we were the only customers. She had heard our plane land, recognized our rush for the facilities, and knew in advance that we wanted pie and coffee.

"We came from Bettles. I'll have blueberry." Fanny handed her list to the waitress.

"I've heard of Bettles. That's on the Kuskokwim, right?"

Fanny had attacked her glass of water, so Clyde took over. "Nope, that's Bethel. Bettles is on the Koyukuk. I'll have apple."

The waitress turned to me. Since I didn't have an engagement to celebrate, I went for the next best thing. "Banana Crème á la mode." She nodded and turned to the rack.

"What were you guys discussing so earnestly?" Fanny asked.

"Clyde was just explaining to me why you are the luckiest two people alive and are going to have the solidest marriage that God ever made."

"He got that right." The waitress brought our pies and dealt them out. Fanny dug in. "Are you going to be a lawyer like Perry Mason?" She turned to Clyde, and he had to swallow apple.

"No, more like a stuffy accountant. My specialty is corporate law and taxes, which means how not to pay any."

"Can we afford to have babies pretty soon?"

"Yeah, I think so. You see, Fanny, there are Native corporations all over the state, some of them making lots of money, and all of them needing lawyers. It turns out that a lawyer who is fluent in Inuit and Yup'ik can do very well."

"Very well?" Fanny was curious, but was getting on through the pie.

"You already promised to marry me, so money doesn't matter, right?"

"Don't be silly, Clyde. If we can eat and live under a roof, that's all I care about."

"That's what I figured. When I took this job, they offered me a hundred thousand a year. I said I was thinking of two, so they said, all right, so I said, to start, and they wrote that down. Can we drop you somewhere, Stew? I have a car in the lot."

They had both finished, and I was just getting a good start. This time I did know what to say. "Thanks, you kids go ahead. You've been engaged for eight hours and ten minutes, it's time you were alone. Speaking of alone, the waitress looks lonely. I'll hang out here for a while."

"Okay, Stew. Sorry you can't stick around for the wedding next Sunday." Clyde shook my hand. I stood up for that, and Fanny melted into my arms for a goodbye kiss. I was surprised when the kiss had a probing tongue in it. Maybe she had watched Carolyn, or maybe that's the way married and engaged ladies say goodbye to old friends.

Fanny beamed. "Call us when you come to town, Stew. Mr. and Mrs. Clyde Edwards."

"You bet, get out of here before I start to cry." They walked out the door, holding hands and almost skipping. A moment later a car pulled out of the lot. I couldn't tell what make it was, but it was long, and black, and shiny. I turned back to the crème pie and ice cream. I was thinking that if Clyde got tired of the law he could have a brilliant career as a before-marriage councilor. Natives do have a way of seeing life as it is, instead of the way we've been told it's supposed to be.

The pie filled one void, but left some others that I couldn't quite put a name to. The waitress was lonely and hung around close enough that we could have struck up something, but I wasn't in the mood. Maybe Clyde would say that I wasn't wondering about her. I paid the check, tipped her two dollars, and called a cab.

Chapter 22

Some women'll stay in a man's memory if they once
walked down a street.
Mrs. Bathurst—Rudyard Kipling

The cab dropped me at Fourth Avenue and E Street. Not really optional, that's where bushies go when they come to town. Fourth Avenue is the gathering place, and the mix is the same as the Bush, ninety percent Native, ten percent Gussak, and everyone had come to town to party. The block is lined with bars, all doors open, music blaring from each and mixing on the sidewalk. There seemed to be a thousand people weaving in and out of the bars, many of them carrying beers with them.

The bar on the corner is the Union Club, so I started there. It takes a moment to get used to the smoke and the alcohol fumes, and I had to fight my way through the over-modulated music. Every bar stool was taken, so I stood next to the waitress station and ordered a Budweiser. I don't much care for beer if there's an option; my taste has turned to harder stuff. Fanny packing cans of beer in lunches was a good thing, but at the lodge we swilled down bourbon. This was different. On Fourth Avenue there's no point in ordering anything except beer. Pinky owns the joint, has owned it for thirty years, and is as much a part of Alaska lore as polar bears.

Bartenders were opening beers two-per-second and waitresses were whisking them away on trays. Pinky was directing traffic by remote control, like the coach in a football game. When he noticed me, he came over and shook my hand, but immediately turned back to shoo away a waitress who had leaned, or maybe collapsed, against the bar. I took the beer with me and wandered on down the street. A handshake from Pinky validates citizenship better than one from the governor. Governors change every few years; Pinky doesn't. I dodged the weaving horde, wrestled off a very drunken grandmother who was determined to kiss me, and made it into the Malamute Saloon.

Gustav reigns supreme there. He built the Malamute during WWII, the same time that Pauline opened her Side Street Bar around the corner on D Street. In those days, Fourth Avenue was a dirt, usually muddy, trail with as many dog teams as cars. Anchorage has become a paved city with sidewalks. Most things seem to change, but not the Fourth Avenue bars, so they gave me the feeling of a home base to start from.

A Western band was shaking the rafters, electric guitars, a bass, a drum, and a bearded cowboy singing, Jeremiah Was a Bullfrog. The music was so loud that it depressed my skull. It would be impossible to think in there, but probably no one wants to. A hundred dancers were stomping the floor more or less to the beat, and the beer on the tables was sloshing to the rhythm. I ordered another Budweiser, but I didn't see Gustav around. He was there; I just didn't see him. I carried that beer with me and fought the crowd back past E Street. The next block was the library, appropriately quiet and dark. I tossed the empty bottle into a garbage can and walked the two blocks to the other mainstay of bush Alaskans, the Sheffield House Hotel.

The Federal Building in Anchorage is a massive enclave, disguised as a city park with trees and flowers inside, a very pleasant respite on a cold winter day. The building was open; the Department of the Interior was not. The sign on the door claimed a nine o'clock awakening, and it finally happened at nine-twenty. I was the only customer, facing at least a hundred bureaucrats, but all of them were too busy to notice me.

An overhead sign directed me to The Bureau of Land Management, and a portable sign on a stand pointed to Mineral Resources. The young man behind the counter was industriously studying papers, and I hesitated to interrupt him until I noticed it was the Los Angeles Times crossword puzzle. I spread Andy's map over the newspaper, and that caused the minion to look up.

"Hi, I need to register some gold claims."

"Huh?"

"Mining claims, you know, gold, I want to register them."

"Oh, sure, I, uh, believe there's a form."

"Right," I said, "I need nine of them."

He disappeared into a room behind that looked like a bank vault. I could see him in there conferring with confederates and looking though stacks, but eventually he came back with the forms. I spent ten minutes filling them out while he went back to his puzzle. I set the forms on top of the puzzle and he looked up again. "Just a moment. I need to plot these on our map." He was gone for twenty minutes that time, and came back shaking his head. "You can't file claims that straddle a river; you need to file separately on each side of the river."

"Not in this case. That's a dry riverbed. Your maps just haven't caught up yet." I pointed to Andy's map. "See, we have the same map you do, but when the new maps come out in December, they'll show K.J. Lake here, the John River curving around this way, and Waterloo Lake here." I drew in the new features, showing our claims high and dry, but he was looking skeptical.

"I think we need to wait until the new maps come out."

"Certainly not." He had all seven volumes of Code of Federal Regulations, Title 30, Mineral Resources, on a counter behind him. Those books range from the size of a dictionary to the size of a family Bible. His were pristine, as if maybe they'd never been opened, so I pointed at the books and invoked their authority. "Title Thirty, Book Three, Surface Mining and Reclamation Appeals, Code of Federal Regulations, Chapter two, Subpart D, Changing Terrain, paragraph one-point-five-one-four: 'Claims may be filed in accordance with existing terrain at the time of filing, subject to later verification by survey.' Surely you are familiar with that one?"

"Oh, yeah," he said, and I had him. I was making all of that up, but he didn't know that and he'd never find out. He registered the claims as drawn and handed me a receipt.

"Take this down to the cashier on the third floor, and good luck with your mining." He went back to his puzzle, his work done for the week. The cashier took ninety dollars, and we were the legal claimants of the John River bed. The downside was that the river's being dry and the claims filed were, as of this moment, public record. Now, all we had to do was defend them.

In a rational world, I would have walked into the BLM at 9:00 and been finished by 9:30. In the real world, I just had time to grab some lunch and check out of the hotel. My next problem was that the mail plane for Bettles would leave at noon the next day from Fairbanks and I was still in Anchorage. I had a brilliant idea about how to fix that.

Bush types gather at the Sheffield House for a couple of reasons. One is the twenty-four-hour coffee shop. I wouldn't know how many stars it gets, but it is clean and bright, and the service is terrific. Maybe just as important, there's nothing pretentious about it. For instance, the pillars in the coffee shop appear to be Philippine mahogany, but if you look closely, they're contact paper over cement. You get a classy ambience without having to pay for it.

I seated myself at a table next to the window with a view of the sidewalk and Fifth Avenue, and watched the city folk scurrying past. When the sharp young waitress in the orange miniskirt uniform asked, I ordered a ham steak and coffee.

I did recognize some of the other diners from the villages around Bethel, but none who were close enough friends that I needed to join them. I had my itinerary all worked out. I hadn't forgotten K.J.'s insistence on rifles, but I wanted to buy them at the Frontier Sporting Goods store in Fairbanks.

My plan was to grab some clothes and a suitcase at Penney's, loaf around town admiring skirts, have a good dinner at one of the world-class restaurants on Third Avenue, and wander down the hill to the train station in time to catch the 8:00 p.m. train to Fairbanks. That's a twelve-hour run, so I could knock back a few in the dining car, retire to a Pullman, and wake up in Fairbanks with no chance of oversleeping.

My plan was working great. The choice of restaurants was between the Woodshed, the Chartroom at the Anchorage Westward Hotel, or Elevation 92. I had to flip the coin three times before it sent me to Elevation 92. It's 92 feet above sea level, but with a view through picture windows of the Knik Arm, the Matanuska Valley, and Mt. Denali. They fry oysters just the way God intended with a wonderful Roquefort dressing on the house salad, and a wine cellar that probably exports to France.

Right on schedule at 7:30 I walked the two blocks downhill to the train station, swinging my overnight case that contained clean new clothes. The train coming in from Fairbanks was already whistling for highway crossings in the distance. A mob of people, some tour buses, and several taxicabs were waiting for the train to arrive. My memory told me the train would turn around and head back for Fairbanks in thirty minutes.

It turned out that the Alaska Railroad is no longer the dependable, inexpensive way to travel between the city and your homestead. For starters, the Pullman berths were fully booked. The prospect of sitting up all night, or trying to sleep on a seat turned me off, bar car or no. The coup de grace was the listing of prices. It now costs more to go from Anchorage to Talkeetna than I was expecting to pay for Fairbanks. The next price was Anchorage to Denali Park, and Fairbanks wasn't even listed. Apparently tourists are expected to take three days, make a few stopovers, and procure a second mortgage to make that trip. I went out to the curb and grabbed a cab to the airport. Good old Wien Airline still runs a shuttle from Anchorage to Fairbanks and I was on the next one.

Second Avenue in Fairbanks is analogous to Fourth Avenue in Anchorage. I had my East European cabdriver, Yugoslav, I think, drop me at the corner of Second Avenue and Cushman Street. That was partly because he had nearly killed us three times on the way in from the airport and I didn't want to ride with him after the traffic picked up. He was having trouble with the cassette player that was mounted in the dashboard and it required his full attention; he rarely glanced at the road during the five-mile trip from the airport.

The other reason for that destination is that the carnage starts there. With a few exceptions, specifically the Model Café, the Lathrop Building, and the Lacey Street Theater, bars line the north side of the avenue from Cushman Street to the Lathrop Building and the theater with the Nordale Hotel across the street at the Lacey Street end of the block.

Like the Anchorage bars, smoke and alcohol fumes were

pouring out of the open doors, along with music at a volume that rattled the parking meters. I fought my way through the crowd of fur parkas on the sidewalk, swam upstream into the Silver Dollar bar, and ordered a Budweiser, but something was wrong. For one thing, except for the twenty dollars I had left from my original bankroll, the money in my pocket was shared with K.J. and Andy. I used that money for hotels, cabs, airfare, and meals, but it didn't seem right to launch a drinking campaign with it, and more important, there was a strange new dimension to my attitude.

Some knockout gorgeous women were sitting alone in the bar, and these were not professionals in the sense that Joanne and Brenda worked the bars for a living. These were Native girls looking for a good time. They wanted a few drinks, some dancing, and whatever came later. In fact, I was sitting two stools away from the seat where I had first hit on Fanny, with memorable results.

I was into my second beer, trying to fathom why I hadn't moved over. An Indian gal, who probably had a few drops of Russian blood in her, was sitting three stools away. That kid could have graced any Miss America pageant, and she was giving me a shy-but-come-hither smile each time our eyes met. I suspected that Clyde had put a hex on me. If I moved over, it would be a lovely night to remember, but if I didn't, I was not going to spend the rest of my life wondering what she might have been like.

I stayed glued to my stool, sipped beer, squinted in the smoke, and tried to ignore the western music that was blaring from a jukebox. A young serviceman came in, glanced around and made a beeline for the empty stool I normally would have taken. The barkeep set up two beers, the serviceman paid, and a moment later the couple got up to dance. Now that she was taken, I did wonder what she might have been like.

Running a self-analysis was a new experience. I wondered if I was feeling the first icy fingers of maturity setting in. Clyde had impressed me with his views on monogamy, and I found myself in total agreement, but, damn it, I wasn't the one getting married. He was. I decided that if this was maturity, I wasn't ready for it.

Six stools away sat an equally luscious lass, figure of a willow tree with delightful feminine appendages, face from a cosmetic ad. The hair that fanned halfway down her back was one shade lighter than black, and her dark, almost-Asian eyes were glancing my way. Therein lies the problem with promiscuity. It may be that the primal male urge is to wonder about all women, and the logistics doom it to failure. Still, I was programmed to do my part. I reasoned that when I did get married, this would be one more chick I wouldn't have to wonder about.

"Hi, I'm Stew. I think I know you from a village, but I can't place which one. May I buy you a beer?"

"Hi, Stew. I'm Susanna. You know me from Holy Cross when you were staying with my Auntie Ethel, but I'm flattered that you remember. I was just a kid."

I slid onto the stool beside her and signaled the barkeep. He set two more Budweisers without asking, and I parted with another ten dollars. Chance acquaintances are a problem with Alaska, even though it is a big place. When it was admitted to the union and Texas became the second largest state, the joke was that it would serve Texans right if we divided Alaska in two and made Texas the third largest state.

However, population is another matter. Most states have two or three cities with more population than all of Alaska, and most of our population is in Anchorage. It follows that if you spend a few years in the Interior, it's like one small town and everyone will know who you are.

"Susanna," I said, "you are not the sort of girl that a man can forget. I've been seeing your face in my dreams for years, but I was afraid I had imagined you. Care to dance?" I was laying it on thick, but trust me, it works.

"Sure, but only for a little while. I'm staying with cousins and they're going to pick me up here at midnight because I have an early flight to Holy Cross in the morning."

"Not a problem. Let's seize these few precious moments and live it up while we may." We glided, as much as is possible, to over-modulated western music that blasted out of several speakers, most of them with torn cones. Self-analysis set in again and I noticed that I was almost relieved that we wouldn't be spending the night together, but I still had to think about the new perspective. She felt very good snuggled against me, breasts building a small fire in my chest, and the rest of her awakening the usual response. She laid her head on my shoulder, almost kissing my neck, and my blood warmed up. I wonder if that's love?

"You know, Stew, all of us high school girls were in love with you. I used to dream that we might be dancing together some day. Does that shock you?"

"Flabbergasted maybe, more flattered than shocked. 'Thank heaven for little girls; they grow up in the most delightful way'."

"Did you ever find the gold you were hunting? We thought you were going to dig up the whole Yukon Valley."

"Still looking. Maybe getting close, but then, I always thought that. What brings you to Fairbanks?"

"I'm enrolling in the University of Alaska next fall. Do you live here?"

"Not at the moment, but sometimes."

"Good, then maybe we can dance together all next winter."

"Never can tell, but I'd love it. Our beer is getting warm. Let's finish it and start over." So, we did, that beer and three more, with cheek-to-cheek, and other parts to other parts in between. Her cousins showed up at midnight. If they hadn't, well, best not to think about that. Susanna introduced me around, we shook a lot of hands, vowed to get together, and I got another of those full-body-with-tongue kisses.

We were out on the sidewalk by that time, and it didn't seem right to go back in the bar and start over, although that is exactly what I would have done before Clyde's lecture. Instead, I wandered past the rest of the bars, barely tempted, and arrived at the Nordale Hotel end of the street. It was actually quiet there. Across the street, the theater, and Monty's Department store on the first floor of the Lathrop building, were closed. The building next to the Nordale is vacant, and that's a sad story. I wouldn't tell it, except that it might be true, and there may be a moral to it.

The Ford building is two stories that reach through the block, and may have been a hotel at one time. In recent years, the one occupant was a very old lady who owned the building and rarely came out of it. She had taken it on herself to save all the stray cats in Fairbanks, which turned out to be quite a bunch. Eventually she died. The locals claim that it was a few weeks before anyone noticed and checked. Of course by that time the cats had eaten her. Sorry, not a nice bedtime story. Maybe true, maybe not.

The Nordale had the one-horse-shay ambience, a general odor of mild decay. It was clean, but gave the impression that a century of dust is embedded in the finery. Most of the usual occupants were almost as old as the hotel, so not apt to party all night. I got a room on the second floor, two single beds, one chair and one dresser, with the bath two doors down the hall.

I was almost drunk enough to sleep, but I kept having visitors: Carolyn, Fanny, Susanna, Brenda, a half dozen others, and I was getting that frantic feeling, so many girls, so little time. Then the darnedest thing happened. They all sort of wavered and went out of focus. They ran together, and when they focused again, I was staring into those fathomless brown eyes of Rose. Peace and calm descended, maybe for the first time in my life. I smiled and drifted into dreamless sleep. When I opened my eyes, it was morning.

I wandered next door to the Coffee Cup Café for sausage and eggs. It's the place where the description greasy spoon originated, but I was doing penance. I had spent twenty dollars of the trust fund in the bar. Also, the Frontier Sporting Goods is kitty-corner across Second Avenue. That's an advantage of small towns. I did a project one time in Tacoma, Washington, that required a few items from a plumbing shop, a few from an electrical supply, and a couple of things from a hardware store. We drove twenty miles to collect the parts. In Fairbanks, a two-block walk will cover any specialty. In Bethel, you can buy all of them, plus clothes and groceries, in Swanson's store. In Bettles, Andy likely had most of them in his garage.

The Frontier covers every sport, except maybe surfing, and they had the rifles I wanted. A pair of .30 caliber Remington Model 721s with twenty-six inch barrels and telescopic sites had been watering my mouth all winter. Even more important than the rifles was the selection of ammunition, and I bought ten boxes of Speer H&H magnums. I selected the 110-grain bullets loaded with 63 grains of Dupont 4895 powder.

I was going for muzzle velocity. The same cartridges are available with up to 200 grains of lead, almost twice the size I was buying. The trade-off is speed, and speed translates directly to accuracy because of gravity, because of wind, and because the target may be moving. The 110 grains of lead leave the barrel at 3,575 feet per second, and are still ripping along at 2,770 after two hundred yards, compared to the 200-grain bullets that leave the muzzle at only 2,640 feet per second to begin with.

I think those larger bullets are like the police choice of .45 automatics for side arms. They're related to the male anxiety that bigger is better. I once saw a rifle that was called an elephant gun in a museum. Its bullets were the size of a golf ball, and it was probably as dangerous to the shooter as it was to the shootee. The fact is that the 40-grain bullets from a .222 Hornet are plenty to kill an elephant; you just have to get those forty grains of lead into his brain.

That's why the Eskimos' and Inuits' rifle of choice is the .222 Hornet. It's light and the bullets are cheap. They shoot polar bears and walruses with them, and put the bullets into the brains through the eye sockets. For them, muzzle velocity and accuracy are everything. My choice of the heavier rifles had nothing to do with the larger bullets; it was the extra five hundred feet per second that I wanted.

I checked the bankroll, held out two hundred for the mail plane and twenty bucks for a taxi to the airport. Almost all of the rest was left on the counter at Frontier. They packaged the artillery in an anonymous box suitable for checked luggage, and I hailed another Yugoslav for the suicide run to the airport.

Chapter 23

Her voice was ever soft, gentle, and low, an
excellent thing in women.
King Lear—Shakespeare

R ose had served me an open-faced moose cutlet
sandwich, floating in brown gravy, with two spears
of pickled okra and four green olives on the side.
That, along with her dazzling friendly smile, was to tide me
over until dinner. The green spears, and the green olives with
red pimentos peeking out, made an attractive counterpoint
to the gravy, both in color and in flavor. I wondered why I
couldn't manage things like that on my own. I conceded that
I wasn't smart enough to keep lettuce and tomatoes fresh,
but surely, even I could buy pickles and olives. I just had
never thought of it.

While I was eating, Andy filed the claim receipts and

K.J. unpacked the rifles. He was scowling at them, and at me when I joined him.

"I thought I told you to buy .222 Hornets."

"These are what Hornets become when they grow up."

"Do they shoot straight?"

"Let's find out."

We each loaded a rifle and carried them out onto the front steps. I looked around for a suitable target. On the far side of the runway a birch tree was still clinging to two bird's nests left from the previous season.

"See those two nests above the fourth light?"

"Yep, easy shot for a Hornet."

"Watch the one on the right." I found it in the scope, adjusted for three-hundred-fifty yards, and reduced it to a cloud of dust.

KJ swung his rifle up and blew the other one away. "I guess these will do." He marched back into the lodge.

"Did you stake the claims?" I asked.

"Sure did, including stakes on top the cliffs on each side of that new dam you blew. I took Andy's .30/06 with me, and I saw the guys who've been watching you, but they never got within range. Stew, those are the two guys who jumped Dan and me, I can feel it, I even think I recognized one."

"Dan?"

"Dan McGraw, my ex-partner."

"Not Dan McGrew?"

"Nope, McGraw, and he didn't think references to Robert Service were funny, either."

"So, what's your plan?"

"Not much anyone can do until breakup. After that, if the spring floods don't take out the dam and wash our claims away, this will be a piece of cake. We'll rig a pipeline over the dam to siphon water and clean up Fort Knox. The gold will lure those varmints down for a look, and we'll blow them away like the scavengers they are." He patted his new rifle, so he was converted to the Remington model 721.

"You know, K.J., I've been thinking that maybe we shouldn't wait. Waiting was the bureaucratic nonsense that made Vietnam unwinnable. Our troops waited for the enemy to come to them, so the fight was always on the enemy's terms, and on the home turf. Maybe we should do a little late spring hunting of our own."

"I'm listening."

"Well, we made the trip from Caribou Creek on the west side of the canyon and we didn't cross any tracks. Besides, when I saw them above the canyon, they were on the northeast rim. Perhaps they came from Allakaket; I don't doubt that, but they must be camping in the area, and probably in the hills on the east side of the river. Maybe we should ride up there and look around."

"Maybe we should." K.J. patted his new rifle again, and I wondered if I had just made the worst mistake of my life.

We wandered back to the table and sat, so Rose brought coffees and joined us.

"Good trip, Stew?" Rose asked.

"Tolerable. Fanny and Clyde drove away into the sunset in a golden chariot. Did you know Clyde is rich?"

"I saw the rock he gave Fanny, but I thought they'd be paying it off for years."

"Not that boy. He probably picked it up with pocket change, and you know, I don't think Fanny even cared. I've never seen anyone so happy in my life."

"I'm glad. She deserves it. I'd better get back to the kitchen." She took her cup with her and left. I noticed that we seemed to be in a new dimension, so I asked.

"K.J., how come we're toasting my return with coffee?"

"We think this is a good time to stay sober, at least until we figure out what's going on. Some things here do not compute. That's why Andy is walking around with his .45 on his hip, I have my .22 in my pocket, and Stella took the .30/06 to the bedroom with her."

"Shall I run upstairs and grab my pistol, or are you going to fill me in on the details?" I started to rise, but K.J. plunged ahead.

"We don't have any details, only questions. We had been back less than forty-eight hours when you tried to drown Mrs. W. and already someone was watching you. We wrote that off to the bush telegraph, and it can be fast. Facts and rumors spread up and down a river in a very short time. However, it is a four-hour ride from Allakaket, if that's where these guys came from. When you think about that, they didn't just hear I was back and decide to come, they were expecting me and were already packed."

"Okay, I see your point. So, they've been watching us. We've been putting on a pretty good show; who wouldn't watch?"

"Twenty-four hours a day, seven days a week? Stew, every time one of us goes upriver there they are. Do you think they're watching all the time, or is someone tipping them off when we leave?"

"Yeah, that's creepy, but why the guns all of a sudden?"

"Originally, they were expecting you to show them where the gold was hidden. If you had just dug up the gold like you were supposed to, they would have shot you and finished the job they started two years ago, but you kept dithering around."

"Sorry about that."

"All of that's water under the dam or over the bridge, but we assume these guys are miners when they're not killing people. If they conclude, like we have, that your latest dam is there to stay, then they know those claims we posted are gold mines, so to speak."

"So now you think they're planning to jump the claims?"

"I think that if Clyde hadn't happened along when he did, and you had gone to town on the next mail plane, those claims would already have been filed."

"But, he did, and I did, and they are, so it's too late for them now."

"Stew, there is one fast way to vacate a claim, and that is if the claimants are dead. Does that suggest anything to you?"

"My pistol is upstairs in my dresser. Can it wait until after dinner?"

Dinner was chipped moose and gravy over fresh biscuits with a crisp green-and-red salad on the side because the mail plane had just delivered lettuce, and homemade Roquefort that rivaled Elevation 92 where I had dinner in Anchorage. In fact, this one had more cheese crumbled into it. The centerpiece was a bottle of Beringer merlot. I was glad we hadn't become teetotalers. Andy chewed, checked for gravy on his mustache with his napkin, and sipped before he spoke.

"In my opinion, the bushwhackers have gone until breakup. They won't expect us to visit the site again until water starts to run, so there's no point in them watching. It's probably no fun camping in the woods anyhow. If I were them, I'd be waiting when you start upriver after breakup and arrange a boating accident. Plenty of those, nothing suspicious about them, so no fuss when they take over the claims." He dug into his salad, but had an afterthought. "They won't be in any hurry. We know these guys are not averse to letting you do the work and grabbing the gold later."

K.J. had that deep-in-thought expression. "We could run down to Allakaket and find out who has been missing for a week."

Andy nodded. "Could, probably half the men in the village. You'd have to sort out the moose hunters from the ice fishermen from the claim jumpers, if anyone would talk to you."

Stella blotted her lips and topped off wine glasses all around the table. "What I've been wondering is how the communication works. We haven't noticed any smoke signals, so how are they doing it?"

"Ham radio. Probably two meters." That was a flat statement from Andy.

"Can we listen in?" Stella wondered.

"Oh sure; I've got a couple of VHF receivers that will tune across the ham band. That only leaves a dozen frequencies and a thousand messages to choose from." Andy sampled his wine and approved.

K.J. explained. "There's a lot of traffic on those frequencies, and most of it is in code. For instance, if two schoolteachers are chatting, and one says, 'come see the new baby', that means he has a bottle of booze, and so on. You would have to know the frequency and the code, and maybe even a schedule." He whacked off another chunk of biscuit and tried to sop up even more gravy than was on it.

Rose blotted her lips and sipped wine, very ladylike, and darned attractive. Damn, that woman was pulling me like a magnet. "You must have figured out that they have an accomplice in the village. There are four ham operators, including the schoolteacher. Besides, how do you know the bad guys don't come from Bettles Village?"

That was a conversation stopper. Andy thought about that for several bites and the rest of his wine. Stella reached to pour more.

"You're right, of course. We don't know that. The problem is that every man, woman, and child in the village is a personal friend, so we don't want to think that."

K.J. extended his glass to Stella. "Still, embezzlers are always the most trusted employees, and if your wife is screwing around, it's probably with your best friend. Did I tell you the girl I left behind me married my best friend three months after I left?"

I'd been uncharacteristically quiet for too long. "Tomorrow morning, K.J. and I will take a swing through the mountains and look for snow machine trails. If we find trails, or a camp, we might learn something, and if we find bushwhackers, K.J. is itching to try out his new rifle." That was another conversation stopper. Rose got up to remove plates. Stella followed her into the kitchen and came back with an apple cobbler. Rose was right behind her with the coffeepot. Those stopped conversation again.

It was a typical night before the storm, in other words,

normal. Andy and K.J. set the cribbage board on the near end of the table and hunched over it. Stella brought out her quilt and immersed herself in art. I glanced at the bookcase, but Rose came out of the kitchen looking much more inviting.

"Care to take a walk?" I asked.

"Do you have a gun with you?"

"No, are you kidding?"

"No."

"I'll be right down. Grab your parka." I hustled up the stairs, stuck my new .357 in my belt, put a parka on over it, and was surprised at how eager I was to get back downstairs. Rose was waiting by the door, beaver parka zipped, and wolf ruff framing a face that struck me as a Crumrine painting of Eskimo royalty. Lord, she looked kissable.

We stopped on the steps for a moment. It was relatively warm out, at least fifteen degrees above zero, so we both threw back our hoods. The sky was light, sunset colors in the north, and they were going to stay there all night. The Endicott Mountains were black silhouettes, jagged and forbidding. We could see the runway and the outbuildings clearly. There would be no more dark nights in Bettles until the middle of August.

Days lengthen fast in the Arctic. They go from no sun in December to twenty-four-hour sun in June, so the days get longer by about ten minutes per day. I vowed to time them when I don't have a beautiful woman on my arm. We turned left and strolled along the edge of the airport away from the village.

"So, you think my sister is really going to be happy?"

"Rose, you saw her when she left here, and she escalated all the way to town. She was positively glowing when they left the Airport Café. Besides, Clyde explained a few things to me about their theories on marriage. I'd say they are off to a wonderful start."

"Are you really happy for her, Stew? She loved you, too, you know." Rose stopped and turned to face me.

"Rose, I am ecstatic for her. Sure, I love Fanny, any man would, but we were more like brother and sister."

"Heavily into incest, are you?"

"Don't get technical. Don't you know Fanny's motto?"

Rose laughed, soft, feminine, delightful, took my arm, and we turned to walk some more. "Yes, I know her motto. I don't share it, but it worked for her. By the way, you didn't take advantage of her. She knew your reputation before you picked her up that night in Fairbanks, and that's going some. I mean, since your conquests were on the Yukon and the Kuskokwim, your reputation preceding you to the Koyukuk is a sort of notoriety."

"Do you despise me for that?"

"Despise is a strong word. Let's say I'm leery of you, like I would be if I were walking with a stick of dynamite. You really were good to, and good for, Fanny though, and I appreciate that. Fanny said you have now slept with every girl in the Interior and might be ready to settle down."

"Well, I'm glad to hear that you think I was good for Fanny."

"Oh, you were. She's been talking about you for years, explaining to me all of the attributes we should look for in a husband. I probably know you better than you know yourself."

We came to the end of the runway and continued along a snow machine trail into the spruce trees. I noticed it was the trail Carolyn and I had made the day we came back from the landslide. A quarter moon hung over the trees, making a yellow beacon over the blue and black landscape. The sun was lost in winter mode, but the inconstant moon continued faithfully orbiting from east to west.

I realized that I wanted to go on walking beside Rose forever. Carolyn had been exotic and fun, Rose was real, and I felt relaxed, at home with her. "Tell me about yourself. Who is Rose? What has your life been and what are your aspirations?"

She squeezed my arm, and I could feel her warmth through our parkas. "I'm just a plain, old-fashioned village girl. I finished high school and have been working on a degree in psychology by mail for the last four years. Does that sound crazy?"

"It sounds very smart, and ambitious. When you get the degree, what then?"

"I really don't know. I'm also pretty good at cutting fish, skinning moose, keeping up the home fires in the cabin, and it's not a bad life. A girl could do a lot worse than have my mother's life."

I heard the crackle, the popping hissing sound of a bullet, and felt my parka jerk before we heard the gunshot. I shoved Rose down to the snow and had my pistol out before we hit the trail. The next bullet plowed a furrow through the snow six inches from my nose and sprayed my face with cold drops. I noticed I had automatically covered Rose with my body, maybe one of the less despicable characteristics of masculine genes. The muzzle flash had come from the trail ahead of us and I fired two quick shots at the spot, but under the trees it was too dark for any aiming.

I slithered my left arm under Rose, held her tight against my chest, and rolled us out of the trail into the soft snow beside it while my shots were still echoing. "Stay there," I hissed. I followed my pistol through the woods beside the trail, trying to be fast, silent, and invisible. The shooter might have expected us to run, which would have made us easy shots in the back, but now I figured he had a problem. He wouldn't know if we'd been hit or not, and I hoped he wouldn't expect me to come after him. If he came down the trail to check on us, he'd be a dead man walking, but maybe he knew that, too.

It's hard to move fast in two feet of snow, and I didn't want to be snapping any twigs, so I was trying to dodge the trees but not get too far from the trail. I'd gone maybe halfway to the place where the muzzle had flashed when things started happening. The runway lights came on, and a second later I heard Andy's snowplow fire up and come roaring toward us. I could see his headlights flickering between trees, but they weren't yet lighting the trail.

I dropped down into the snow and crawled to the trail edge, trying to see. A dark blob was centered in the trail, two hundred feet farther, and I thought I saw movement near it. I took a shot at the movement, but there was no chance of aiming with my face in the snow. A snow machine roared to life, headed away from me, and its lights came on. I jumped into the trail and emptied the pistol at those lights. The taillights went out, but the machine disappeared around a bend.

I walked backward down the trail, watching for shadows and cursing myself for not having some extra bullets in my pockets. I got to the hole where I had dumped Rose at the same time K.J. did, and Andy was puffing up the trail behind him, waving his .30/06. I reached down into the snow, found Rose's hand, and pulled her up. She came up spitting and sputtering, and wiping snow off her face.

"Did you get him?" K.J. demanded. He had his new rifle in his hand, ready to hit the beach at Normandy.

"No, I didn't, and he was damned good." I displayed the rip in the shoulder of my parka. "Two shots in the dark, almost a hundred yards, and I felt both of them. I think he was serious."

Andy was leading Rose back down the trail, K.J. and I following, but still walking backward, just in case, and I was glad I had seen K.J. shoot the second nest. Andy boosted Rose up into the snowplow's cab and climbed in after her. K.J. and I stood on the running boards and held onto the mirrors while Andy drove us back to the lodge.

When we walked up the steps, I was expecting Rose to be a bundle of tears, but she wasn't. She was just trying to get the snow out of her ears and her hair. Stella met us at the door and pulled Rose and me into the same embrace. "What in the hell were you kids doing out there?" She noticed the rip in my parka and started unzipping.

"Hey, we were just taking a stroll in the moonlight. Isn't that what young lovers are supposed to do?" Rose shot me a glance that I'm still trying to decipher.

"I guess they aren't planning to wait for breakup," Andy said. He plunked down in his chair, and he looked tired. Neither he nor K.J. had bothered with parkas. They had simply run out the door when they heard shots, so both of them were looking chilly and rubbing their hands. Obviously exertion and exposure to cold had drained them mentally and physically. Rose came out of the kitchen, sans snowy parka, and carrying a tray with coffee cups and the pot. We dropped into our usual chairs, except Stella, who was still rummaging through her basket for thread that matched my parka.

"How did they know you were going to walk down that trail?" K.J. asked.

"They didn't." I'd been giving that a lot of thought while I was wading through the snow. Only one other person knew we were going out, and that was Rose. Going for a walk was my idea, but probably predictable. She had been out of my sight for a few minutes after we made the plan, but it's not like she could pick up an extension phone and call someone. We were two hundred miles from the nearest phone. I don't think either of us planned the left turn or the walk down the trail; they just came naturally.

I had decided that wicked twins who looked beautiful and acted sweet, but were planning to kill you, only happen in novels. If this were a novel, and if I were the hero, I'd certainly fall in love with my nemesis. The thought of my being in love stopped me for a second, but I decided this was real. I'd deal with the love suggestion later. Also, while the shooter clearly had me in mind, he was missing Rose by a foot and, at that range in the dark; that is no way to treat an accomplice. I didn't say any of that, only wondered about it. What I did say was, "He had parked his machine and was walking toward the lodge when we went out. He was still in the trees, or we would have seen him. He just went back to a long straight stretch of trail and waited for us to walk into his shooting gallery."

"Which you obligingly did." K.J. was looking around for the bourbon, but settled for more coffee. "Do you realize that if you hadn't gone out, we'd now all be the victims of a drive-by, or walk-by, shooting?"

I'd been doing some more thinking. I'm a slow learner. "Maybe we shouldn't wait for morning. I might even have hit the guy. I shot his taillights out, so he could be wounded. We have a fresh trail, maybe, at least as far as the river. Let's go see if he's dripping blood."

K.J. nodded and went for his parka. Stella brought mine from her sewing pile, and I had to hunt to find the rip. I picked up my rifle and was waiting by the door for K.J. when Rose came over.

"Thanks for protecting me, Stew. I do see what Fanny saw in you. We should do a lot more walking and talking." She stood on tiptoe to give me a kiss, not much body, and no tongue, but I followed K.J. out the door floating on cloud nine. The Panthers were in the garage. K.J. hit the electric switch to open the door and rode out. I hit the switch to close it again, and followed him, slipping under the door while it came down. He was sitting on his rifle and it was pointed forward.

That told me he was going to lead, so I pointed mine backward, and followed him to the end of the airport and down the trail. The remains of a shattered taillight shone like jewels in our headlights, but there weren't any great splotches of blood. We followed the trail to the river, but it joined a hard-packed highway, tracks made by dozens of travelers. K.J. climbed off his machine and studied the tracks in the headlight.

"He went that way." K.J. waved his rifle toward the village, straddled his machine, and raced in not-so-hot pursuit. No obviously fresh trails veered off before we arrived at the dark, quiet village. "We need Andy," K.J. said. "I'll wait here and watch." He spun his machine into the shadow at the edge of the river, held his rifle across the handlebars and waited. He was right. If we started banging on doors and asking questions in the village at night, we'd be shot, gold or no. Andy could handle the job with immunity. I raced back to the lodge.

"Sorry, Stew. Andy's lying down. Rose tells me he made a hundred-yard-dash down the trail tonight, and he's a little out of shape. I'll go with you, or Rose could."

"Or both of us?" Rose asked.

"Better yet." Stella and Rose both went for parkas. Rose sat behind me, Stella on the back reaching around to hang on and make a sandwich. K.J. was sitting on his machine where I had left him. He got up and walked over to us for a conference.

"We don't want to panic the village because this is our problem, not theirs, but we need to know if a machine went past on the river in the last forty minutes, or if one came back here, and if it did, we'll want to look at the taillight."

Stella and Rose nodded and climbed the bank to the nearest house. I stood there holding my rifle and feeling like an idiot. I mean, what if they walked right into the arms of the shooter? They came out of that house, were in the next one for several minutes, and then proceeded to a third before they came back to report. K.J. and I carried our rifles and walked along the river ice below them. It was almost daylight when Stella slid down the bank.

"Sorry, the first couple of houses hadn't noticed anything because the kids were making noise, and snow machines aren't exactly memorable. Nana was in her outhouse, and she heard a machine. She noticed it because it didn't stop and she thinks it went up the Wild River, but she isn't sure."

"Take the ladies home," K.J. told me. "We're going after him. I'll stay here, just in case he comes back. He still might live here but be too smart to bring his machine home with a shot-out taillight."

Rose and Fanny climbed on behind me and I took them back, but the lodge was in nighttime mode, showing only one light in the dining room. I wondered if we might be walking into a trap. I motioned them to stay on the machine, got my pistol in my hand and started up the steps, but Andy opened the door, carrying his .30/06. The ladies trooped up the steps, I gave them a wave, and roared away to join K.J.

Chapter 24

And durst thou then to beard the lion in his den?
Marmion—Sir Walter Scott

"Which river?" I asked.

"Let's check the tracks." We drove up to the *Y* where the John River comes in from the left, the Wild from straight ahead of us, and left the machines running for the headlights. The sun was up, but not climbing higher. It was scooting along the northeastern horizon so the shadows were long and dark. I took the Wild, K.J. took the John, and we both walked back and forth studying tracks, but it was hopeless. The whole area was packed down, hard as cement, and dozens of tracks looked sharp and fresh. K.J. came stomping over in disgust.

"If I had a coin, I'd flip it."

"Let's try the Wild," I suggested. "We've been driving

up and down the John, and haven't noticed any suspicious tracks leading off after we got away from the village. Maybe they went half a mile up the Wild and turned to parallel the John."

K.J. nodded, tromped back to his machine, and we drove up the Wild River, looking for something, but we didn't know what. Tracks veered off to both sides, most of them one-time passes by single machines. We were concentrating on the left bank, had passed several trails, and were approaching the hills when K.J. locked up his track and slid to a stop. He made a circle and came back with his headlight on a well-traveled set of tracks that led up the bank. A red ruby was sparkling in his light. A machine had climbed the bank at a steep angle, and dislodged a tiny shard from a broken taillight.

We shut off our machines and listened to the profound silence of an arctic night.

"Next plan?" I asked.

"Well, it isn't to go bombing down the trail making a racket that can be heard for five miles, straight into a pair of high-powered rifles."

"Right," I said. "We won't walk up the trail because it might be thirty miles."

KJ nodded. "Whatever happens, it's got to happen here. If we get killed, well, that's the breaks, and it goes with the territory, but if we let them come to the lodge for us, Andy and Stella might be peripheral damage and we can't risk that."

I didn't point out that we could just take down our stakes and go away. By that time, we were envisioning a gold nugget under every rock in the riverbed. Getting killed might be an option; walking away wasn't. "I do have an idea. I need that old sled from Andy's garage. You carrying any rope?"

"Fifty feet of three-eighths hemp and twenty feet of quarter-inch nylon."

"Perfect. I'll be back in a flash."

K.J. started his machine, rode across the river and parked under some spruce to watch the trail, rifle across the handlebars again. I lit a fire under the Panther and flew back to the lodge.

The lodge was dark, a long shadow in front. I parked at the edge of the shadow and waited. The porch light came on and I stood in the light, making myself recognizable, and also a perfect target if the wrong people were inside. It was Stella who stepped out carrying Andy's rifle and gave me a wave. I waved back and drove to the garage. The sled I was after was hanging on the wall. I jerked it down and tied the painter to my trailer hitch. We called that type of sled an akio. Sometimes spelled ahkio or akhio. The confusion is because the design is from Finland, so it's open to translation. It's a fiberglass tub, four inches deep and the size and shape of a stretcher.

A lot of gear can be piled on one. I've read that the Finnish Santa used one in the past, but this one was military surplus. The army uses them for arctic rescue. It has ropes strung down the sides, so it can be carried, or slung under a helicopter, and a bridle on one end for towing. A couple of wooden slats underneath run lengthwise, but they aren't runners, just keels to make the sled more apt to slide forward than sideways.

Several old worn-out sleeping bags were in a box, so

I grabbed an armload of them. Andy's rubber slicker and overalls were hanging on pegs, waiting for summer rain. I took them, too. The akio has laces down the sides so I laced the goodies in, killed the garage lights, and raced back up the river. When I got to the trail, I turned up onto it and K.J. was behind me in a moment, uncoiling his rope. He tied the hemp to the handlebars. I took his nylon and opened the Panther's hood. The throttle is a lever that's pulled up when the thumb piece on the handlebars is depressed. I tied the nylon to the lever, ran it past the sediment bulb to keep the pull straight, and strung it back to the akio. K.J. had his rope strung from each handlebar, like the bridle on a saddle horse.

We stuffed sleeping bags into Andy's raingear and laced the scarecrow onto the Panther with the sleeves tied to the handlebars. K.J.'s bridle turned the handlebars back and forth and the dummy steered and leaned admirably. With the rubber slicker hood up, it looked like the grim reaper, but maybe that was good. The last sleeping bag was spread out on the akio, my rifle on that, and my body on top of the rifle.

K.J. checked out the scarecrow. He was dubious, but not offering any better ideas. "When the shooting starts, you roll left and I'll roll right."

I nodded and pulled the nylon, the engine revved, and the Panther obediently trundled forward. K.J. was right behind me, almost lying down on his machine, and we bumped along the trail making five miles an hour and weaving back and forth until I got the hang of steering with the reins. A little more pull on the nylon, and we were sailing along, maybe ten miles an hour.

I'd never appreciated the springs on a snow machine until I was being dragged over the trail on an akio, nose three inches from the snow, exhaust blowing in my face, and every bump a personal insult. The trail followed the edge of the hills, dipping down for creeks, then rose up, mostly through scrub alder groves. Several times we got glimpses of the John below us, and eventually Waterloo Lake.

To see over the edge of the trail I had to hike up on my elbows. The second time I did it the Panther ran off the side of the trail, but the dummy hung on for dear life, and I got us straightened out without rolling over. The trail did some serious climbing, up onto the ridge our canyon had cut through. Twice, trails branched off down the hill and K.J. stopped to study them. I waited, because the dummy was the decoy for both of us and he needed to be right behind me. Each time, he concluded that those were old trails, and waved me straight ahead.

It was good luck, not good management, that the sun was directly behind us and anyone shooting at us would have it in his eyes. That advantage was more than offset by the sound of our engines that preceded us by a mile. K.J. was lying flat on his seat, his legs no doubt sticking out behind, and he was peering around the edges of his cowling, checking one side, then the other. His view was a heck of a lot better than mine; all I could see was the machine in front of me, and just enough trail past the skis to stay on course.

K.J. hollered and stopped. I glanced back and saw him roll off his machine into the snow on the right, so I dropped the ropes and rolled into the snow on the left. I came up on my elbows, rifle ready to fire. The Panther trundled another ten feet down the trail and stopped. I spotted what K.J. had seen, the tip of a tent under some spruce trees a hundred feet ahead. Our dummy would have been an easy shot from the camp, but he was still sitting up, healthy and unperforated. The bad guys didn't take the bait and shoot the scarecrow, and if K.J. hadn't yelled, I would have ridden right into their camp.

K.J. crawled up the other side of the trail. He was too far away for whispering, but he was speaking softly with enough urgency to carry. "Best we fan out and come in from opposite sides. Go down the hill fifty feet, then across, and we'll converge on the tent in exactly five minutes."

"Check," I said, "but you do realize we're setting ourselves up for the usual scenario where we shoot each other."

"You're not scared, are you, Stew?"

"Me? Heck no, I'm just ready to shoot these guys and go home for coffee."

"Right. Then there's no problem. Pay attention to who you're shooting. If you get buck fever and start getting wild, just lay down and I'll shoot both of them." He didn't wait for an answer, he checked his watch, turned right and made like a gopher up the hill through the snow. I noted the time, flipped my hood up, and tried not to shake any snow off the alder scrub I was crawling under.

The Panther was still idling, I hadn't rigged a way to shut off the engine, but I decided that was good because it would mask any sounds we made crawling through the brush. I didn't worry about the fifty-feet instruction. The hill dropped off pretty steeply after thirty feet and I didn't want to be looking up at any rifles. I turned and followed the scalloped edge, trying to keep a close watch for rifle barrels ahead.

I was thinking that they had two options when they

heard our machines coming. One was to shoot us on the trail, the other was to take cover in the woods and shoot us when we rode into camp. Since they hadn't taken the first option, I was expecting them to be under the spruce trees ahead of me, and if one of those trees had twitched, I would have shot it. K.J. had better be on his own side of the trail.

I kept reminding myself that partners shooting each other is classic. Everyone knows it, but still the most experienced hunters do it, and it accounts for at least eight out of every ten hunting accidents. It happens when two guys follow a moose into a thicket. One guy goes around the thicket to wait for the moose; the partner goes through to flush the moose out. When the brush moves on the far side of the thicket it gets shot, and more often than not, it's the partner. The moose turned off somewhere.

I made it out of the alder into the spruce and still hadn't been shot. I stood up behind a tree and peeked toward the camp. Smoke from a fire was drifting up in front of the tent, a snow machine with a broken taillight was parked beside it, but nothing was moving. I froze and scanned, up into the trees, down the trail as far as I could see, beyond the tent where I was expecting K.J. to appear in two minutes.

If they had heard or seen K.J. coming and were waiting behind trees for him, then I would have seen them, and if they were behind trees waiting for me to step out, he'd see them when he arrived. I stayed put and waited. Four and a half minutes had gone by when I saw a branch move on the far side of the tent. I covered it with the rifle and waited, but it didn't move again. At the stroke of five minutes, the same branch moved again and K.J. came charging out of the woods like a mad bull, including the bellow.

I gave an Indian war whoop and ran to meet him, but at the last second he dropped behind a tree again, so I did the same. We were making another visual sweep from the new perspective, in case we were doing exactly what we were expected to do. The tent did some twitching, and I swung the rifle that way, but it was K.J.'s feet disappearing under the edge, and a moment later the flap opened.

"Better come in, Stew, but you'll have to make your own coffee."

I crouched my way backward, watching the trees behind me and feeling the bullets hit until I could step into the tent, and then the tent looked pretty flimsy until I spotted the body lying on the sleeping bag.

"Is he dead?" I asked.

"Close, very close. Looks to me like someone shot him in the back with a .357 and punctured a lung. He's got a handkerchief stuck in the hole, but he won't last long. Good thing you thought to bring a stretcher with us."

"Where's his partner?"

"Long gone. One body, one snow machine. Are you going to stand there staring, or go get the stretcher?"

I leaned my rifle against the tent pole and ran for the Panther. I had to wrestle the dummy for the handlebars. I won, shoved him aside, and raced back to the tent. K.J. had ripped off the guy's parka and shirt. There was a neat hole in his back. K.J. stuffed his own handkerchief into that and rolled him over. The victim had done a good job of stuffing the hole in his own front, and that one wasn't nearly so neat.

We jerked sleeping bags out of the dummy and wrapped the guy in half a dozen before we laced him onto the akio.

"I'll go ahead and alert the troops. You come fast, but

don't be dumping him out in the snow." K.J. ran back down the trail toward his machine. I sat on my rifle, swung a circle around the tent, and by the time I got back to the trail, K.J. was a cloud of exhaust in the distance.

Chapter 25

It hath been often said that it is not death, but
dying which is so terrible.
Amelia—Henry Fielding

I tried to be fast, but the sled was banging against the sides
of the trail at every turn, threatening to roll over. I read
an article one time about how many people are killed in
accidents while they're rushing someone to a hospital. The
point of the article was that in most cases there was no hurry
about getting to the hospital in the first place. If this guy
died, I wanted it to be from the gunshot, not from trauma on
the trail.

When I eased down the bank onto the river, the sled
caught up, climbed right over the seat, and slammed me in
the kidneys. Damn, that hurt. I counted it as the third time
this guy had tried to kill me. Even on the open river ice, I had

to hold it down because the sled wanted to whip back and forth and that made it slide sideways, in danger of rolling over. It felt like we might die of old age before I got to the runway.

K.J.'s machine was in front of the lodge. I pulled up behind it, killed the engine, and jerked the akio's bridle off the hitch. Andy, Stella, K.J. and Rose bounded down the steps. We all lifted and made it up the steps without spilling our load. Stella had cleared the dining table for the akio. We plunked it down and unwrapped sleeping bags.

Stella felt the pulse in his neck. "He's still alive, thank heaven."

Rose came from the kitchen with a pan full of steaming towels and ran back for another load.

"Mouth-to-mouth," Stella ordered. "We don't have any oxygen." Neither K.J. nor Andy jumped into the breach so I bent over, pinched his nostrils closed, and blew into him. I could see his chest out of the corner of my eye, just a suggestion of rising and falling when he breathed, so I matched his rhythm and tried to blow him up like a balloon on the intake. Out of the corner of the same eye, I could see a lot of activity going on. Stella leaned close to jam a needle into the guy's arm.

"Somebody relieve Stew. He's turning red." She was pouring something into a hanging bottle. K.J. pushed me aside and took over the oxygen detail, just in time; I was getting dizzy. When my eyes focused, there was Rose, pouring the liquid out of a glass jar into the bottle and it seemed to be running down into the guy's arm. Stella was wielding towels and pouring alcohol around the bullet hole. The wound was making a gurgling sound and little droplets of blood and alcohol spurted back out until she shoved gauze into the hole and taped it there. "One more boiled water," she commanded, and Andy dashed for the kitchen.

Stella pushed K.J. aside, felt the guy's neck again, and bent to listen to his breathing. "I think he might make it. Take a break, Rose." Rose stopped pouring. Stella pulled the needle out, bent the tube double and clipped it. She stood there pressing a pad of gauze on the needle track.

"What do we do with him now?" I asked.

"Medevac is on the way." Andy answered. "It's a King Air out of Fairbanks, should be here in thirty minutes."

K.J. turned to Andy. "Do you know him?"

"Vaguely. We were right about Allakaket. He's a handyman, sells a few hides, mostly lives subsistence. I'm glad he's a Gussak, that will make it easier. His name is Jake, something-or-other."

"How about his partner?" I asked. "His partner ran out on him and left him to die. No honor among thieves."

"Nope." K.J. said. "His partner ran out on him to save his life, and when we find him, you owe him a big vote of thanks, Stew."

"Want to slow down and make some sense?" He seemed to be speaking in non sequiturs and I wasn't getting it.

"It would be easier if I had a wee drap of the Balm of Gilead." He looked at Rose. She looked at Stella, who nodded, and Rose went into the kitchen. The chairs had all been shoved aside, but K.J. dragged one to his usual spot, so the rest of us dragged chairs and settled down at the table, facing each other across the body. Rose brought glasses and a bowl of ice. Stella dealt out the glasses one-handed while Rose went back for the bottle, and we all helped ourselves. I noticed that Rose took a spoonful and sipped it more slowly than Mrs. Whidbey had drunk wine.

K.J. slugged a healthy blast and leaned back in his chair. "Okay, Stew, it was like this. If his partner had taken a shot at us, or even stuck around to slow us down, Jake here was dead. His only chance of survival was if we did exactly what we did."

"Yeah, Jake should thank him, but why should I thank him?"

"Well, Stew, you did shoot Jake in the back."

"Hey, that was self-defense."

"Sure, in the inner city. Cops can have a suspect handcuffed on the ground and beaten unconscious, and if they shoot him in the back, it's still self-defense. Out here, it would have been legal to shoot him in the front, but the back gets a little murky."

"It was dark under those trees. All I could see was his taillights."

"Right, and that's your best defense. You might get off with only reckless endangerment." K.J. had emptied his glass and reached for the bottle.

Andy protested. "Hold it down until after the medevac arrives. We don't want those guys testifying that we were a bunch of staggering drunks."

K.J. grunted and shoved the bottle away, but he tilted his glass again for a final drop and then sucked an ice cube. "Any other questions?"

"Just one." I turned to Stella. "How come you were shooting water into his veins?" She left the gauze over the needle track but took a glass, ice, and bourbon before she sat down. "That was just bush medicine, Stew. His heart has got to keep pumping liquid. If it's the wrong liquid, it will just pump faster and the second time around it will be mixed. During WWII wounded soldiers were given transfusions of coconut milk because it's sterile and that's all that really matters."

She took a sip of the bourbon and licked her lips. "You really did a nice job of shooting him, Stew. No veins or arteries, only two broken ribs, and I don't think the lung is even going to collapse."

Andy turned to me. "Don't worry about it if he does die, Stew. You did the right thing. K.J. has some good points, but if Jake dies and there is an inquest, Rose can cry and tell how you saved her life, and so on. A trooper will be out tomorrow. I'm hoping for Lieutenant Hurlburt, in which case it will all end right here. Mostly we want Jake to stay alive so he can answer some questions."

Jake groaned, and flopped his arm out of the stretcher. K.J. decanted a finger of bourbon into his glass and more or less poured it into Jake's mouth, but Jake swallowed.

We heard an airplane land and taxi up outside. Stella threw a sleeping bag over Jake. "Let's go, guys." We picked up the akio, trooped out the door and down the steps. A young medic met us halfway to the plane and clapped an oxygen mask onto Jake. The turbine on the near side was winding down and the big cargo door was open, so we shoved the akio inside. The medic scrambled up the steps. An accomplice appeared, and together they hoisted Jake into a bunk that was attached to the wall.

Our medic stayed with Jake and started prodding and checking. The accomplice came out with the akio and a clipboard in his hands. "I need someone to sign." K.J. took the akio, Andy signed the form, and I'm sure he had just invested another $2,000 in the venture. The clipboard wielder climbed back up and pulled the door after him. The turbine spun, we stepped back, snow flew, and a moment later the King Air soared into the sky and banked toward Fairbanks.

"Now, let's get gloriously drunk," K.J. suggested. We trooped back inside.

Stella scrubbed the table with one of the unused sterile towels, took her glass down to the far end, then went to her bedroom and came back with the quilt and the sewing basket. Andy brought out the cribbage board and he and K.J. filled glasses and got serious. I took a shot of the bourbon, but I wasn't in the mood for drinking. Rose was standing in the kitchen door, indecisively, or maybe expectantly.

"Care to go for a walk?" I asked.

"How about a fire in the fireplace and a quiet morning at home?"

"Wonderful." Andy kept a box of kindling and a few logs beside the fireplace. It took two minutes to get a blaze going, and I shut off the light over the office for maximum effect. Rose and I sat on a throw rug facing the fire, close, but not touching.

"You know, Stew, life can get pretty real sometimes. I understand Fanny a lot better now."

"How so?" I tried Rose's trick of tasting the liquor without drinking it.

"Did you know she almost died when she was sixteen?"

"What happened?"

"Fishing accident. She was out with my father and an uncle, drift netting. They were pulling the net, loaded with salmon, and Fanny fell in. She got tangled in the net and they had a terrible time getting her out. The net was so heavy they couldn't lift it, had to cut the net to pull her up, and she very nearly drowned. After that, she tried to explain to me how precious life is, and how we're wasting it. I understood her words, of course, but I didn't really understand what she meant until last night."

She took a sip and stared into the fire.

"And now you understand?" I prompted.

"Stew, I felt the wind of the bullet that hit your shoulder. It blew right across my forehead, and it sounded so angry, so deadly, I can't describe it." She shook her head and squeezed her eyes shut. I put a tentative arm around her shoulders and she leaned back against me.

"Stew, I'm twenty-two years old, and I've never done anything. When I thought about it at all, I pictured my life running for years into the future, plenty of time to experience anything and everything. Now I know how precious every day is." She wiped her cheek with the back of her hand, and I realized she was crying. I squeezed her tighter and handed her my handkerchief. She blotted and sniffed.

"Do you think I'm crazy, Stew?"

"Crazy is a pretty strong word; let's just say you're a stick of dynamite. Fanny was right about our days. We should be grateful for every one and savor it, but that doesn't mean we shouldn't work on long-term goals. We have to be who we are and enjoy the pleasures that come along. If we get frantic and try to do it all at once, we'll miss out just as much as if we forget how precious these moments are."

"Is this a precious moment, Stew?"

"Rose, for me this moment is priceless. There is no place else I'd rather be, no one else I'd rather be with, and nothing else I'd rather be doing."

"Nothing?"

"Nothing. I'm hugging the most beautiful girl in the world, communicating our deepest thoughts. We may be shot tomorrow, or struck by a meteor tonight, but we may also have those years and years ahead of us. Let's live today to the fullest, but be damned sure we don't have anything to regret if those years and years happen."

She nodded; I was resting my cheek against her hair, so we nodded together.

"Stew, Fanny said you would never marry her. Was that because she was promiscuous?"

"No, most definitely not. It was because Fanny never wanted to marry me. She much preferred Alex, and now we know she was waiting and hoping for Clyde to come back. Fanny frankly enjoyed sex, and that is a wonderful thing, but we're talking physical only here. Real sex is spiritual. She's having that now with Clyde, and in a very important sense she went to Clyde as a virgin."

"Do you know that I'm a virgin, Stew?"

"In the important sense, I never doubted it."

"Would you like to teach me to be a good lover?"

"I can't think of anything I'd like more, if we have those years, and if we were planning marriage."

"Is that a proposal?"

"Not while I'm a murder suspect, don't even own half the clothes I'm wearing, and haven't the least idea who I'll be when I grow up. Meantime, I'm drawn to you like I've never wanted anything before in my life."

"I expected you to be my brother-in-law, so I need to think about this, but I do trust Fanny's judgment. How long do I have to wait, Stew?"

"Maybe not very long. Maybe the murder charge won't happen, maybe there really is gold in them thar hills, and maybe I'm growing up. This conversation is the most adult thing I've ever done."

We both set our glasses on the floor and stood to face each other. I pulled her into an embrace, and we melted together for a moment.

"Don't keep me waiting too long, Stew. Remember, I'm twenty-two years old. That's an old, old maid by Inuit standards."

I took her by the shoulders and held her so we were looking into each other's eyes. "Rose, I tell you true. You are everything I loved about Fanny and infinitely more. Clyde and Fanny taught me a lot about marriage, and I think I'm ready when I can get my life in order. Let's talk about this again when the bullets stop whizzing, and in the meantime, let's spend every spare moment getting acquainted. How do you feel about Shakespeare? There's the complete works in the bookcase."

She gave me a smile that was worth getting married for. "Oh!" she said, "swear not by the moon, the inconstant moon, that monthly changes in her circled orb, lest that thy love prove likewise variable. Do not swear at all; or, if thou wilt, swear by thy gracious self, which is the god of my idolatry."

We held hands walking to the bookcase. I gave her Romeo's line. "This bud of love, by summer's ripening breath, may prove a beauteous flower when next we meet."

She leaned her head against my shoulder. Stella looked up, smiled and nodded her approval. Rose whispered; "How silver-sweet sound lover's tongues by night, like softest music in attending ears."

Chapter 26

Who rides on the trail of a border thief sits
not long at his meat.
The Ballad of East and West—Kipling

A Cessna 180 on wheel-skis pulled up out front, blasting snow. It was a pretty bird, burnished aluminum with the blue-and-gold state troopers' shield on the side. Trooper Lieutenant Hurlburt climbed out of the pilot's seat, adjusted his gun belt, and let his trooper-blue parka drop into place over it. He tromped up the steps, let himself in, surveyed our assembly and entered, closing the door behind him.

Andy met him with a handshake. "Mornin', Gene. Care for coffee?"

"Bathroom." Lieutenant Hurlburt took the stairs two at a time.

Stella poured a cup for him and set it on Andy's right, the

place that had been consecrated as Mrs. Whidbey's. Andy as always, had the head of the table. K.J. was in his usual spot on Andy's left, across the table from the lieutenant's cup. Stella came to sit between K.J. and me. Rose settled down in Carolyn's seat across from Stella, but she had the chair closest to the kitchen.

Lieutenant Hurlburt came down the stairs at half the speed he had ascended, hung his parka over the chair back, hiked up his gun belt, sat and sampled the coffee.

"I believe you know everyone here, lieutenant?" Andy asked.

"Call me Gene." Hurlburt glanced around the table. "Hi, K.J., Stella more beautiful than ever. Mornin', Stew, Fanny, nice to see you sober and off Second Avenue."

I did the honors. "Gene, this is Rose, Fanny's twin sister, and by the way, you won't find Fanny on Second anymore. She's a paragon of virtue, and married, living in Anchorage."

Gene turned to Rose and extended a paw the size and shape of a fielder's glove with muscles. "Please forgive my indiscretion, and I'm delighted to make your acquaintance."

Rose put her delicate hand with the long slender fingers into Gene's vise and smiled at him. "My pleasure. Was Fanny really such a terror?"

"Nah, I just meant to give her a hard time. She spent the occasional night in the drunk tank, but just to keep her from freezing. It was always friendly." He released Rose's hand and turned back to Andy. "I understand there's been a shooting. The victim is in the Fairbanks hospital in intensive care. Want to tell me about it?"

"Self-defense," Andy declared. "The victim was shooting at Rose and Stew with a rifle. Stew had to stop him."

"By shooting him in the back?" Gene asked.

"It was dark." Andy shrugged.

"Show me." Gene finished his coffee and stood.

We rode the machines down the runway and onto the trail, me leading on my Panther, Gene behind me on Alex's, and K.J. following on Andy's Cat. K.J. was carrying his rifle, and Gene seemed to approve. We stopped just before the hole in the snow where I had tried to suffocate Rose.

"We were walking here. It was dark under the trees and we didn't notice the shooter lurking there. His first bullet hit mc here." I showed the rip on my parka's shoulder that Stella had mended. "We hit the dirt, and the next bullet plowed into the snow here." We could see the furrow the bullet had cut and the hole where it disappeared. Gene pulled a clasp knife out of his pocket and dropped to his knees. He must have calculated the ballistics in his head, because he dug eighteen inches behind the spot where the bullet had entered the snow. He slipped off his glove, felt around in the snow, and came up with the lead in his hand. He zipped it into an evidence bag.

"I left Rose here, and went through the woods that way." We walked along the trail to the spot where I had emerged. "I shot him from here, but it was really dark. All I could see was a black blob."

Gene nodded, and we walked the fifty yards to the spot where the taillight shards still sparkled on the snow. "Where's his rifle?" Gene asked.

K.J. stepped in and took over. "It's in his tent, twenty miles into the hills above the John River. I'll take you to it."

"He rode twenty miles with half his lung shot off?" Gene was shaking his head, but we tandemed back to his airplane in silence. He reached in through the plane's door and pulled a .300 Savage rifle out of a scabbard.

K.J. still seemed to be in charge. "I'll take him up, Stew. I want to look around the camp. You stay here and try to comfort Rose."

Gene bobbed a sort of a two-eyed wink with the clear interpretation: "Spare me the theatrics." He laid the Savage on the Panther seat. K.J. took my Panther, again sitting on the rifle with the muzzle pointing forward, and the two of them roared up the runway.

I wandered upstairs and lay down on my bed to play the what-if game. What if I hadn't shot him, what if he had hit me six inches lower, what if, what if. A gentle tap on my door ended the game, and Rose slipped into the room. She sat on the bed beside me, crossed a very sleek pair of knees, but her skirt almost reached them.

"Did he believe you, Stew?"

"I don't know. Maybe I was wrong to shoot Jake. He was trying to get away."

Rose reached for my hand, chaste, natural, comfortable. I got the feeling that the two of us sitting on beds together was going to be the best part of my future, if I had a future.

"You did the right thing, Stew. If you hadn't stopped him then, he would have come back. When a grizzly bear is charging, you don't wait for him to draw blood. You know what he has in mind, and you shoot him as soon as you can and as many times as necessary. Don't fret. Remember, whatever happens, I love you." She stopped and turned to stare at me. "I've never said that to anyone before, Stew. Maybe we're both growing up." She bent to kiss my forehead and slipped out of the room.

Two hours crawled by. I had gone downstairs, just in case lunch was going to be served, when K.J. and Gene stopped out front. I opened the door for them, but Gene had gone to stow his rifle, and another one, presumably Jake's, in the Cessna. K.J. came in and headed straight to the table.

"Any good news?" I asked.

"Yes and no." K.J. waited until Gene had come in and sat before he continued. "The good news is that Jake's rifle was still there, so ballistics can check it against the bullet that was in the snow. The bad news is that there were three, not two, men living in the camp. Three cups, three forks, depressions where three sleeping bags had been laid out, but two of the bags were gone. That may explain how they were able to be everywhere at once. With three guys watching, continuous coverage isn't so unlikely."

Rose brought ham sandwiches, pickles, and potato chips. It's not that the troopers don't know we live on illegal moose, but there's no point in rubbing their noses in it. We chowed down. Gene and K.J. seemed to be in a hurry, so I tried to match them. Gene was still chewing and stood up to finish his coffee.

"Grab your rifle, Stew. As of now, you and K.J. are deputized, and these guys may not play nice." He started for the door. I couldn't answer him; I still had a mouth full of sandwich, but I ran upstairs, got the .357 in my belt and a handful of extra bullets in my pocket. The rifle was leaning behind the door. I grabbed it and a box of shells. By the time I got to the airplane, Gene was strapped into the pilot's seat and K.J. was holding the passenger door for me. I crawled in back; he climbed in, and was still clipping his belt when Gene poured the coal to the engine. No need to taxi back; the lodge is at the halfway point of the runway, and half is more than enough for a bush pilot.

We passed the village, followed the Wild River to the trail, and turned to follow it. The camp was still deserted; Jake's was the only machine. We continued up the trail, K.J. watching on the right side, me on the left, but after we passed the end of K.J. Lake there were no more side trails. I could see down into the canyon, and the lake did reach almost to Caribou Creek. The trail led upstream for five miles, turned to cross the John, and made a beeline south toward Allakaket. They had made a wide detour, precisely so that we wouldn't accidentally cross their tracks.

Five miles from Allakaket we were meeting other trails, and ours melded into the maze, but there were no machines on the north side of the village. Gene plunked us down on the runway, more like the one at Livengood than Bettles Field, but this one had been plowed. It didn't matter, because we were on wheel skis.

The trooper logo on the airplane brought the village cop out to meet us. Gene introduced us to Ivan, and he called us his deputies, so I guess it was official. There was more Russian about Ivan than his name. He had the large, heavy frame, and the square head that came from his cousins across the Bering Straits. In an Inuit village, that made him an important man. Inuit do not value pure bloodlines.

"What brings you guys to God's country?" Ivan asked.

"Gathering evidence. You have a Gussak named Jake living here?"

"Yeah, but he ain't here. He's hunting up river somewhere."

"Not anymore." Gene pulled his revolver and spun the

cylinder to check the load. He stuck it back in his holster, but left the flap unsnapped. I think the point of that was to impart some urgency to Ivan, and it worked. "Jake's under house arrest in the hospital in Fairbanks. Charge is attempted murder at the moment, but it may escalate considerably. We believe he has two armed and dangerous accomplices and they may be here in the village. We need to inspect Jake's living quarters."

Ivan turned to lead the way and we walked through the village, being announced by barking dogs as we went. Some authorities will tell you that Eskimo dogs do not, or cannot bark. That's the malamutes. These dogs were Huskies and barking their heads off. We were passing snug log cabins, most with caches up on poles beside them, and several surrounded by dog kennels. Pooper scoopers haven't been introduced to the Arctic, but in winter the dropping is frozen and most of it covered by snow. That's an advantage of spring floods; most villages flush pretty thoroughly most springs.

I always watch the spring dog races. North American Championship in Fairbanks, Fur Rendezvous in Anchorage, so I recognized some of the teams. A snow machine was next to almost every cabin, because dogs aren't used for transportation anymore. Every dog eats half a salmon a day. Snow machines use gasoline, and you can't catch gasoline in the river, but when you're not using a snow machine, it isn't burning gas. Dogs eat every day whether you use them or not. These dogs were kept for racing, and that's a full-time, year-around job for their owners.

Jake's cabin was a small, unpeeled-spruce-log affair at the end of the village. Ivan banged on the door, got no response, and shoved it open. He led with his pistol and stepped inside. Gene followed, and he had drawn his state-trooper-issued .38. That was brave, but not foolhardy because there were no snow machines out front. K.J. waited one beat and followed them in, but trooper Gene hollered at me.

"Hey, Stew, would you open the shutters? It's dark in here."

The cabin's two glass windows were covered by slap-dash wooden shutters with strips of moose hide for hinges. I unlatched them and let them swing open. Furniture consisted of a homemade table with two chairs, a Yukon stove, and two bunk beds against the far wall.

"Two guys living here." Gene made it a statement, not a question.

Ivan was nodding. "Yep, Jake and Shorty. They were cellmates in Washington's McNeal Island, came here to make a fresh start. I was advised officially, but I didn't spread it around. A man's past is his own business here, so long as he doesn't cause trouble."

"Is there a third partner?" Gene asked.

"Sort of. A couple of months ago, Wassilie came home from the VA Hospital in Seattle, and the three of them have been hunting together this spring."

"Damn." K.J. slapped his forehead. "I remember Wassilie from the hospital. I may have offered him a partnership in the mine. I was desperate at the time."

"Explains a lot," Gene nodded. "Wassilie knew about your buried gold and knew you were coming back for it. The other two knew they hadn't found the gold and decided to try again."

He had his official notebook out, jotting with a pencil stub. Pens do not work well in the arctic, and if he started with a new pencil in the morning, it would be broken in half by noon.

K.J. had sat at the table, but he suddenly jumped up and sprang halfway across the room. "There it is, there's the smoking gun," he shouted. He was pointing at a St. Christopher medal that was hanging from a nail next to the top bunk. Gene walked over and took it down.

"Check the back." K.J. commanded. "D.A.M., Daniel Aloysius McGraw, my partner that they killed."

Gene carried the medal by the edges to preserve fingerprints. We all gathered at the table and Gene held it under the light from the window. There were no initials on it, but there were file marks where a monogram had been removed. "Close enough," he said. "If we can nail them for Dan's murder, we may be able to put them away for life without them shooting you two." He slipped the medal into a plastic baggie and put it in the pocket that probably still held the rifle bullet. He turned to Ivan. "Any ideas about where they are now?"

"I seen Wassilie in the village this morning. Let's go ask our local newspaper." By that, he meant the storekeeper, so we closed the cabin door, left the shutters hanging, and trudged back through the village to the center of the commercial district. That consisted of a log house, twice the size of the others, perched on the riverbank near the airport. A one-lung diesel was put-putting in a shack beside the store to provide lights and power the freezers inside. There used to be a joke about a salesman so good that he could sell refrigerators to Eskimos. That salesman had done a fine job here. The left-hand wall was lined with freezers, displaying everything from frozen goat meat to ice cream. The floor space was taken up by head-high racks stacked with canned goods; Van Camp's pork-and-beans, Campbell's soup, Libby's canned fruits. One entire rack was stacked with Carnation evaporated milk, another with various kinds of canned soda. Racks along the right-hand wall contained clothing, and the whole room was brightly lit by hanging bulbs. The only thing missing from most corner grocery stores was a fresh produce section.

"Kin I he'p you?"

The counter was just inside the door, sagging under the weight of an old mechanical cash register. Behind it sat a caricature of Moses, long white beard, hair to match, plaid shirt, denim overalls, and granny glasses. Ivan took over.

"Mornin', Alf. Seen Shorty or Wassilie today?"

Alf stood up, but barely got taller. "They was in buyin' supplies about an hour ago."

"What did they buy?"

"Just grub and ammunition, usual stuff."

"Did they mention where they were going?" Gene asked.

Alf stopped to consider. I could see him wavering between loyalties. He wasn't about to rat out a fellow villager to the state troopers, but the serious expressions on Gene and Ivan told him there was more than illegal hunting involved. Apparently he came down on the side of law and order.

"They're trappin' beaver upriver. Gettin' quite a few. Jake stayed up at their camp and the other two came in for supplies."

"And they left about an hour ago?" Gene asked.

"Yep." Alf swallowed hard and cleared his conscience. "Funny thing, though. When they left, I stepped outside to have me a smoke, and I seen them turn downriver instead of up. Whatcha want 'em for?"

"Oh, just some routine questions," Ivan lied. "Nothin' to worry about. See ya later." We trooped out and turned toward the runway.

"Downriver an hour, headed for Hughes, maybe?" Gene was asking Ivan, but Ivan had no opinion.

"Might be we could catch them. I've got two fast snowmobiles."

Gene had sucked his lower lip in and was biting it. He let it go to address K.J. and me.

"One of you guys go with Ivan. I'll fly ahead and either cut them off or slow them down. If you see me circling, I'll be over them."

"I'll go," K.J. said. "Rifle's in the plane."

"Machines are behind my office, right over there." Ivan pointed at a cabin three doors down. "We'll stop by the airplane on our way." He and K.J. ran for the office; Gene and I double-timed back to the airplane.

Chapter 27

Theirs not to question why, theirs but to do or die.
Charge of the Light Brigade—Alfred Lord Tennyson

van and K.J. had already crossed the runway and turned downriver. Gene did taxi back to the end of the runway; this was not Bettles Field. Wheel skis, like any compromise, are not quite as good as wheels, and not quite as good as skis. They consist of a normal aircraft ski with a slot cut out and the tire protruding down four inches below it. If you're on a paved runway, you have to be careful not to scrape the tails, and if you're in deep snow, the tire sticking down is an extra drag.

It took us three minutes to taxi back, turn around, take off and head down the river. K.J. and Ivan had already covered five miles, hunkered down behind their windshields and running flat out. The 180 was cruising at 140 knots, but we passed them in slow motion. The river was wandering through the Alatna Flats, but approaching the Isahultila Mountains. There are two ways out of the valley, the winter trail that runs to Tanana, a hundred-twenty miles away on the Yukon, or the Koyukuk River that would pass Hughes in sixty miles.

The first outpost of the mountains is two-thousand-foot Mt. George. The trail passes it on the left, river on the right. Behind Mt. George we could see four-thousand-foot Indian Mountain rising up, thirty miles ahead. Before we reached that, the river and the trail would be in their separate gorges, the only two ways through the mountains. Gene climbed us up to three thousand feet and circled Mt. George. We could see pretty well, the trees not nearly as thick as they were around Bettles, but still it would have been easy to miss a couple of machines on either route.

"Which way?" I asked, unnecessarily; Gene was already pondering that.

"The river," he decided. "They're looking for an airplane ride as soon as possible and Hughes is the closest airport." He peeled us off like a dive-bomber starting its run, and we raced down the river at two thousand feet. He was right. We'd covered another ten miles of river in five minutes, and there were a pair of bright-orange Bombardiers zipping down the center of the river. They were moving fast, but not the hell-bent-for-leather dash that K.J. and Ivan were making.

"They don't expect us yet." Gene said. "They probably think we'll spend a day searching north of Allakaket." We sailed on past them. I watched the machines slide to a stop, a rider jump off, and point a rifle at us.

"They're going to shoot!" I screamed. My view became

the sky and my seat tried to buck me off. Gene had snapped us into a barrel roll. The bullet slammed through the window behind Gene and made a second "pok" exiting the window behind me. My view was Mt. George upside-down, the river, the sky, Mt. George again, and the river again, much, much closer this time. The river made a slight bend. Gene slammed us down onto the ice and scrambled out carrying his .300 Savage. That seemed like a good idea, so I joined him.

"What the hell was the idea of the aerobatics? Was your mother frightened by a roller coaster?" I was panting to keep up. Gene was headed for a gravel bar that came in from the left, and threw himself down on the snow behind it.

"They know they hit us. I want them to think we crashed so they'll come to check."

"You mean you did that on purpose?" I knelt down beside him, and the gravel bar didn't look very high, maybe a foot above the rest of the ice. When we stopped moving, I could hear machines running, but slowly and cautiously. They came into the bend on the far side of the river, almost half a mile away, but from there they must have seen that the plane was right side up. They stopped, and Gene blasted away at them.

They started again, turning around. Gene was using the macho trooper bullets. I found them in the scope, adjusted for a thousand yards, and put a bullet through each cowling. One machine stopped instantly, the other did a maple-leaf spin. It started again, turned sideways, and I could see the driver. I put a bullet where his head had been, but he rolled off the machine before it got there.

Then I couldn't see anymore. My eyes and the scope were covered by flying snow. The next bullet did its hissing crackle bit within a foot of my ear. I kissed the gravel and dug snow off the glass. Gene fired again and was rewarded with a snow shower of his own. I used my shirtsleeve to clear the scope and eased it up onto the gravel. It was blurry, but I could see a rifle lying across the seat of one of the machines. I shot at that and saw a chunk of the seat cushion explode below it. The pocket ripped off my parka, and it was the pocket with the box of rifle shells in it. I scrabbled backward and dug the box out of the snow. It wasn't dented, thank heaven.

"Want to try for the riverbank?" Gene asked.

"I want my momma. You're the cop. Why don't you arrest them? This is reckless endangerment." Gravel spurted up from the spot where I'd been lying, followed half a heartbeat later by the sound of the gunshot.

"Crawl left." Gene suggested. "The gravel gets deeper."

He had a good point, and I didn't much like our present spot. I tried to crawl using my elbows so my fanny didn't stick up. The gravel bar did get deeper, maybe fourteen inches instead of twelve. I heard one of those words troopers are not supposed to use when they're on duty, followed by the crack from a rifle, and looked back to see that Gene's fur cap was gone. He'd had his badge pinned to the cap, so now maybe he was just another civilian. He was an expert crawler, elbows digging, legs wriggling like a snake, and passed me to stop behind the biggest rock in the vicinity, at least the size of a basketball.

He glanced to see if I was alive, and he had a trickle of blood running down between his eyes and dripping off the end of his nose. He snuggled the Savage next to his rock and took his time squeezing off the next shot. Just as he shot, a bullet whanged off his rock. The rock rolled over his rifle, but the gas tank exploded on the left-hand machine. That was impressive, orange and red flames and a "baaroom," just like the movies.

Gene let out more un-trooperly expletives, a whole string of them this time. "They smashed my scope."

"Good, charges are stacking up, assaulting an officer, destroying government property, these guys will be in big trouble when you arrest them."

"Will you knock it off with the horse pucky, Stew? I'm not in the mood for laughing. It makes my head hurt. Duck." A puff of smoke shot out of a rifle at the same instant that a bullet plowed through the snow between us.

The riverbank was thirty feet to our left, with scrub alder brush hanging out over the river, but our gravel bar tapered down to nothing for the last twenty feet. I checked the rip where my parka pocket had been shot off, and it looked pretty bad; kapok showing through. Stella could probably fix it, but I decided to sacrifice it. I wriggled out of it and got a face full of snow in the process.

"Since they broke your pretty gun, how about using it for a decoy?"

"Might as well, so...?"

"So, hang my parka on the gun barrel and wave it over this way. If they both shoot at once I might make it to the bank before they can shoot again."

"Yeah, and you might get your tender young ass shot off."

"Got any better ideas?"

"Normally I would have, but damn it, I've got a headache."

I slithered past Gene, handed him my parka, and kept my nose in the snow to the last vestige of gravel bar. "Okay, go." I think we both shouted at once. Gene waved the parka, it flew away downriver along with the rest of his rifle, but I was already scrabbling up the bank. Bullets don't hurt like a knife cut; it's more of a burning sensation, and Gene had called the shot. I wasn't going to sit in comfort for a while, but my legs still worked, and I worked them fast, crawling into the brush.

Gene fired a couple of shots with his .38, but at that range it was just to make some diversionary noise. I slithered up the bank, following my rifle and plowing snow as I went. There was no need to get any of my remaining body parts above the snow level. My objective was to get past the machines so I could see behind them, and then just two more shots, but I didn't want to get too far from the bank in case they tried to run.

The ploy seemed to be working. I hoped they were thinking I was running away, but the snow puffed up beside me and the scope ripped off my rifle. I did a fast roll away from the bank, got tangled in an alder, left the rifle and had to sneak back for it. It seemed okay, it was just that now it had only the open sight. I needed to get within a hundred yards, so I went back to crawling, ten feet farther from the bank. Gene was keeping up a barrage with his pistol, which might discourage them from leaving the shelter of their machines.

My bank ran into a creek, ten feet wide and four feet deep. I slid down into it, but the ice cracked, and I went down one more foot to stand in a couple of inches of water. The creek had stopped flowing after the ice froze and left only a quarter-inch windowpane on top. Still, it felt good to have solid dirt walls on both sides of me. I stomped down the creek to the river, shattering ice with every step.

The junction of creek and river left a solid dirt bank higher than my head, and I peeked around it. My perspective had changed. I could see a shoepack and half a leg of someone kneeling behind the near machine. I guessed two hundred yards.

I have a physical anomaly, other than the perforated gluteus maximus that was screaming its bloody head off. I'm right-handed, but my left eye is dominant, so if I try to sight a rifle with my right eye, I see two targets and can't hit either one of them. That meant that in this case, if I was going to shoot around the corner, I had to stick my whole head out. Not smart, but I had seen a foot, and I owed them one. I squatted down, got the rifle against my shoulder, popped out and fired. I saw the foot jerk, but I jerked too, all the way around and into the dirt behind me.

The burning sensation was coming from my forehead and when I checked I found my right ear hanging half off and spurting blood. I used the new words that Gene had taught me and tried to hold my ear on. My first thought was to wonder if Rose would still have me with only one ear. I stomped up the creek away from the river, rifle in left hand, holding the ear on with my right. That was not going to work when I went back to crawling through snow.

I unzipped my snowsuit and wriggled out of the top half of it, used my knife to cut the sleeve out of my shirt, and tied the sleeve around my head. Problem was that the ears are in line with the eyes, and I didn't want to cover my eyes. I tried starting low in back, covering the ear and tying the sleeve at my forehead, but it slipped down. I started high in back, covered the ear, and tied the sleeve under my nose. It wasn't nice, but the pressure of the bandage held my ear on and was slowing down the bleeding. I went back to crawling through the snow.

Gene shot three times, fast. I took it to be an S.O.S. and looked up over the snow to see a man sprinting toward my bank. I swung the rifle his way, and he seemed to run in slow motion. Still a long shot, should I go for his head, or use the hunter's rule of shooting the largest part of his body? He was carrying his rifle in his right hand, and took six long, slow motion strides while I decided. I put the bullet in his right shoulder. He dropped the rifle and rolled over in the snow, stopping ten feet from the rifle to stare at the sky. That was too close; he was still dangerous. I knew I should blow his head off, that's just rudimentary survival, but bullets were whipping through the brush on both sides of me, so I dropped down again.

I stopped to reload the rifle and kept crawling. If I could get past the machines, force the final shooter to move around the machine, he would have to make a target for either Gene or me. Gene's .38 wouldn't be much use at that range, but still, if he had a clear shot; I kept crawling.

There seemed to be a buzzing in my ears. I checked my bandage, no change, but damn, that ear did smart. I stuck my finger in the other ear and the buzz went away. When I pulled the finger out, the buzz morphed into snow machines, and the engines were screaming. K.J. and Ivan blasted around the bend, skimming the snow like a ski plane taking off.

I raised my head. The machines were still a thousand yards off when a rifle barrel swung out from behind the far Bombardier and puffed smoke toward them. The machines kept coming, but the rider had rolled off one of them and it was coasting down. I expected to see a body lying in the snow, but it was K.J. and he was kneeling, aiming his rifle.

A man jumped up from behind the Bombardier, flinging his arms high, tossing his rifle away, like he was giving up, but he pitched forward on his face in the snow and stayed there. I saw K.J. aiming again, closer to me this time. The man I'd shot had crawled to his rifle and was raising it. I jerked my rifle up, and would have shot him in the head that time, but his head jerked backward, blood and brains sprayed the snow.

K.J. got up and walked toward his machine. Ivan had continued his charge. He stopped beside the body that was lying next to the Bombardier, but apparently decided it was beyond helping or arresting. Gene was walking up the river toward us. Ivan drove on down, picked Gene up, and came back. I slid down onto the river and trudged toward the carnage. I wasn't walking quite straight; my right leg seemed spongy. I noticed that K.J. had a matching limp, and I hoped he didn't get the idea I was making fun of him.

I was the last to arrive. Gene had checked both bodies and was scribbling in his notebook. He was wearing his cap again, but there was a dent in the badge. He'd wiped the blood off his forehead with his sleeve so he looked like he was wearing war paint. K.J. had been inspecting the body with the ventilated head and walked back to meet me.

"You okay, Stew?" K.J. asked.

"Yeah, I'm fine, leaking blood on both ends, but I may survive."

"You don't deserve to. What in the hell were you thinking when you shot that guy in the shoulder? Have you been watching television?"

"No, I just didn't want to kill him. Maybe the cops would have arrested him and asked him questions."

"Boy, if you want to live to grow up, you had better learn fast. You do not leave a wounded animal in misery, and especially not a man with a rifle. If he'd shot you, that would have been fine; you deserved it, but he was aiming at me. If he'd shot me, it would have been your fault."

I was nodding, but K.J. wasn't through with the lecture.

"That was the mistake that Shorty made." He jerked a thumb toward the nearest corpse. "He thought he'd killed me, but he didn't stop to make sure, and he just paid the price for carelessness." K.J. stomped away in disgust.

Gene put his notebook away. "How you holding up, Stew? I like your new head scarf."

"I feel like a bull that has lost. Ear and tail have been taken for trophies."

"I'm glad to see that stream seeping down your pants is blood. That wasn't my first impression." He was shaking his head. "Damnedest coincidence I ever saw. Four accidental shootings on the Koyukuk in two days, you being the fourth, Stew. Hey, Ivan, want to give me a ride back to the airplane? We've got some bodies to load, ambulatory and otherwise."

Ivan fired up his machine and Gene climbed on behind him, but he had to give me one more parting shot. "Maybe you can share a recovery room with Jake. The two of you can talk over old times."

Ivan gunned the machine and trundled away toward the airplane.

Chapter 28

"All's well that ends well."
—Shakespeare

My ear was stitched back on. Maybe not as neatly as Stella would have done it, but it worked. I had a tendency to limp, due to a sharp shot of pain each time I put weight on my right leg. I thought about K.J., dancing the day after his amputation, so I ignored the pain, and walked straight.

My four fellow passengers on the mail plane were miners. Elementary, my dear Watson. Their luggage was piles of sleeping bags, backpacks, and duffle bags, with a gold pan, a shovel, and a high-powered rifle with scope on each pile. They were obviously two pairs, but each pair was eyeing the other, all of them eyeing me, and nobody was talking.

When we landed at Bettles, I expected K.J. to come out with his rifle and tell them to stay on the plane. He came bounding down the steps and hurried to meet us, but no rifle. He was grabbing these guys, shaking their hands, even hugging a couple of them. "Hey, fellas, this is my partner, Stan. You must have met on the plane. Stan, these are Frenchy and Ole. We were neighbors down at Ophir. This here is Charlie and Matthew. We worked together up on the Kobuk. Come in, guys, come in. I'll show you what we got." I shook hands and mumbled "Stew" to each one. I don't think they got it. It didn't matter. Rose came tearing down the stairs, leapt into my arms, and I swung and kissed her just the way Clyde had greeted Fanny. I vowed that the next time we met I'd have a diamond the size of an orange in my pocket.

The mail plane was a Fairchild F-27 with Doc Hickling at the controls. He had shut down the right engine while we unloaded, but the left continued to spin. The moment the unloading was done he pulled the door shut. We turned our backs, the right engine spun and threw snow, and the mail plane was gone.

Rose was inspecting me with a puzzled frown. "Stew, you look great. K.J. said half your face was shot off."

"Nah, he saw me before they washed away the blood. All I got was this little hemstitching job," I demonstrated the ear, "and a wee hole that I'll show you after we're married."

Her shocked expression would have been funny if it hadn't been tragic. I hastened to reassure her. "Hey, it's all right. Everything works. I just have to sit on a pillow for a few days."

Each of my fellow passengers was carrying a box of

groceries inside and I noticed a crate of lettuce so the salads would be crisp again. Another case of bourbon was in the queue. Rose and I draped arms around each other's waists and turned toward the lodge, but an engine purred, and we turned to watch a red Cessna 207 drift down. Alex parked next to the piles of luggage that still sat by the runway, and climbed out. The two guys with him were Hap Leen and Dummy Sakar. We'd prospected and panned useless gravel side-by-side at Crooked Creek on the Kuskokwim, and I was happy to shake their hands. Alex opened the baggage doors and came over to talk. Hap and Dummy started to offload gear and pile it up in the row that had developed.

"Hi, Stew, hi Fanny. Hap and Dummy came around telling me that I had just filed some gold claims on the John River. Naturally they wanted a piece of the action, and naturally, they still don't believe that I don't know what they're talking about."

"Later." I said. "Rose, this is the legendary Alex. Alex, Fanny's sister Rose, and my soon-to-be wife."

"No kidding?" Alex was staring. Rose extended a shakable hand, but Alex ignored it. "If you're going to be my sister-in-law, don't be shaking my hand. Give me a hug." He grabbed her hand and pulled her in, and the two of them did hug long and friendly. I didn't worry about that. He meant exactly what he said, and from that moment on, he considered Rose his sister. Not only would he never threaten her honor, he would die defending it. "I always knew I'd be the best man at Stew's wedding, but I was afraid we'd be using canes and walkers when we did it. Rose, you are beautiful. I couldn't be happier for both of you." He grabbed each of us, arms around our shoulders, and walked between us up the steps to the lodge.

Hap and Dummy had stacked their gear beside the other piles and followed us in. Andy had a new map spread on the table, and K.J. was still making introductions. I pulled Hap and Dummy into the circle and got them introduced.

K.J. called the meeting to order and we all gathered around the map. He stopped to count heads, and turned back to the map. "Nine of us. Perfect. Stan dammed up the John River here." He was busily sketching with a grease pencil. "Stan and Alan and I claimed the dry riverbed from here to here." More grease pencil.

"Alex and Stew" I interjected, but no one heard me; they were concentrating on the map. " Now, the way I figure it, there's good ground on both sides of the river, especially here," grease pencil again, "because for a few days the river flowed this way, but the richest ground, maybe in the world, is going to be this old riverbed." Nods and murmurs of approval. They were almost rubbing hands in anticipation. "Stan built a good earth dam, but it may not hold forever. Maybe one season, maybe two, or it may go out in the spring flood, in which case we can all look elsewhere." He looked around and all heads were nodding. One of the things that all of us had in common was long experience of looking elsewhere.

"What I propose is that you guys all grab claims on each side of ours, sew up the whole valley, but we all work together on the river to cover it fast." He looked around again, heads still nodding. "Naturally we'll ask ten percent of what you dig on our claims, and what the heck, if the river comes back and covers ours, then we'll work your claims on the same terms."

Heads were still nodding, and hands were being shaken,

which, in the Arctic is the equivalent of a notarized contract. Stella was bringing out glasses and ice. Rose was right behind her with her arms full of bottles, and we proceeded to celebrate our new nine-way partnership.

K.J.'s deal sounded good to me. He might be right about us needing to work fast, and it would take years for the two of us to dig up the riverbed. Mostly I was thinking about the six rifles that were leaning against piles of gear beside the runway. Dummy's rifle was an old timer, a .30/03, and I remember him shooting the heads off squirrels when they were on the menu. Having those rifles on either side of our claims struck me as a wonderful idea.

Stella assigned rooms. Andy brought the snowplow up and tilted the blade flat. We stacked the mining gear onto the blade and he trucked it back to the garage. Rifles and personal gear were lugged upstairs. The bathroom was busy, the dining room was buzzing, new partners were getting acquainted and sharing stories.

At six-thirty, twelve of us sat down to moose steaks, potatoes and gravy, more of that wonderful Bird's Eye frozen broccoli, mounds of fresh biscuits, and salad. I took advantage of the new seating arrangement to move over next to Rose's chair, and Alex slid in beside me. Stella kept the conversation humming while all of the new guests fell in love with her. Rose jumped up now and then to refill the steak platter and bring fresh coffee. We reached to clasp left hands so we could both eat with our right, and that put my hand in her lap, an arrangement I could get used to.

We finished a mountain of blueberry shortcake, and K.J. called the meeting back to order. "Gentlemen," he tapped his glass with his spoon. "We'll plot the new claims this evening and start staking them in the morning. Stan will hitchhike into town with Alan, take the paperwork, and file it?" He made that a question and turned to me.

I stood. "I'll be happy to file the claims, but first, my name is Stew, and this is my elook, Alex. Old K.J. there had a pickaxe stuck in his brain and the names leaked out. Other than that, he seems to be functional. You're going to have to hustle to get the claims staked while the river is still frozen. After that it will be two or three weeks before breakup when we can start to work. Therefore, I'm taking Rose to town with me. We have a wedding to arrange, and we'll be back after breakup. We'll leave with Alex in the morning, and this time, I'll need ten thousand dollars to cover expenses. By the way, Rose, will you marry me?"

She stood for a hug and a kiss, to applause, stomping and whistles. She turned to Stella. "We'll go up tonight to tell Mama. Shall I send Hatty down?"

Stella was crying again, jumped up, and ran around the table to hug both of us together. "Yeah," sniff, sniff. "Please send Hatty down." Boo, hoo, hoo. She ran for her room.

"Who is Hatty?" Alex asked.

"She's the next sister, ten months younger than me. She's the pretty one of the family. Alex, she's going to knock your socks off."

~The End~

About the Author

After a childhood in the big woods outside Seattle, Don Porter absorbed a modicum of education at a junior college in Iowa and went to Alaska in 1954 to seek his fortune and pursue an engineering degree at the University of Alaska in Fairbanks.

He never finished that degree because during his senior year he was licensed by the Federal Communications Commission and became the Chief Engineer of KFAR-AM and KFAR-TV in Fairbanks, part of the Midnight Sun Network that covered the entire state. He spent the next twenty years building stations all over Alaska, literally, from cable in Ketchikan, Point Barrow, Nome, Cordova, and Kodiak to broadcast stations in Anchorage, Fairbanks, Juneau, Sitka. You get the idea. Midnight Sun also blanketed the rural areas with mountaintop repeaters.

Midway through that fiasco, time and troubles forced the engineering staff to fly between sites. The company rented the aircraft; Don flew them. After twenty years in broadcasting, and with a commercial pilot's license and five thousand hours in the air, he gave up electronics to become a bush pilot.

He flew charter based in Bethel on the Yukon-Kuskokwim Delta for the next fifteen years and picked up ratings for multi-engine, instrument, and helicopter. If it has an airfoil and an engine, he has probably flown it. Passengers were state troopers, mothers in labor, dead bodies, wedding parties, whatever. On the Delta, Eskimos outnumber Gussaks about ten to one. He was steeped in, and came to respect, the Eskimo culture.

Between his various jobs he covered the state from Ketchikan to Point Barrow and from Tok to the tip of the Aleutian Chain.

He enrolled in the Professional Career Development Institute and has a very handsome diploma from the Professional Private Investigator Program. The point being to make detective novels authentic. He also grubstaked prospectors. He covered the expenses and supplied the transportation; they toiled in the mud looking for gold. His fifty percent of the profits never paid the gasoline bill.

Back to electronics and two years on Oahu making warranty house calls for Sony. A whirlwind tour of the South Pacific, island hopping and building whatever needed building, including two years on Guam resurrecting KUAM, AM, FM, and TV.

He spent the next fifteen years as Director of Maintenance for the ABC television network throughout Hawaii, living, working, and writing in Honolulu. His wife Deborah is an artist who has calmly painted pictures and made a home wherever they've landed. When word processors made it possible, he started writing books about Alaska.